D0093716

NOISE

Also by Hal Clement

Half Life
Heavy Planet

A TOM DOHERTY ASSOCIATES BOOK
NEW YORK

NOISE
HAL CLEMENT

NOISE

This book is printed on acid-free paper.

A Tor Book
Published by Tom Doherty Associates, LLC
175 Fifth Avenue
New York, NY 10010

www.tor.com

Tor® is a registered trademark of Tom Doherty Associates, LLC.

ISBN 0-765-30857-6

Printed in the United States of America

0 9 8 7 6 5 4 3 2

To Tania Ruiz,
who came up with the coral
when the pumice refused to form

ACKNOWLEDGMENTS

Principal thanks go to the writer's group that, I understand, has been named "Hal's Pals" by Harlan Ellison. They have listened, suggested, criticized, encouraged. The membership has been rather variable over the years, but Sherry Briggs, Mona Wheeler, Greg and Anne Warner, Tania Ruiz, Matt Jarpe, and Wendy Spencer have all had their say in this particular Enterprise (pun inappropriate but intended). I don't keep a log of the meetings and hope I haven't forgotten anyone. If I have, I apologize; I do notice that as the years go by the insulation is getting frayed.

Other fans who have listened at conventions to a chapter here and a chapter there and have added their comments can't be named here because I don't know most of their names, but I am most grateful to them also.

HAL CLEMENT
Milton, Massachusetts
March 2003

NOISE

"You still say these folks don't have a Chamber of Commerce?" Mike Hoani made no effort to hide his skepticism.

"Right. There's no native life that anyone had found the last I knew, but they've plenty of experience with pseudolife design; cities, ships, life-support equipment, are all grown just as they are at home. Their offworld trade is mostly specialized seeds, which don't fill freighter holds very well. They haven't much to offer to tourists; when you've seen one mist-shrouded floating city and a few square kilos of misty ocean with no city, you've pretty well covered the scenery. Most of the people I've met there seem friendly enough to visitors, though you may meet exceptions of course, but a few generations in one-third gee means they can't do much visiting themselves."

"So it's just coincidence we popped into real space just where and just when we could see two eclipses at once?" Mike nodded at the screen. "You don't get a small honorarium for arranging that, after we set down?"

Hi-Vac's navigator didn't answer at once. She, too, was staring at the image. The two partly overlapped stellar disks didn't quite blend with each other; an M5 sun is enough cooler than an M4 to let even the human eye detect its lower surface brightness, especially when the cooler one is closer to the viewer and partially covering its twin. The double planets' images, similarly overlapped, were less informative; they were not quite in the same direction as the suns, and showed only thin crescents, one half erased by its twin's shadow.

"If I'd set it up," the navigator remarked at length, "I'd have composed the picture better. Everything is practically in a straight line. A million kilometers or so *that* way"—her thumb gestured toward the lower left corner of the screen— "would have made it an artistic presentation."

Mike, who was not an artist, made no comment. Intellectually, he knew that there was no disgrace in not being an expert at practically everything, but he was still a touch neurotic about displaying his own ignorance. The navigator, after a moment's silence, went on.

"It wouldn't be much of a problem, of course. There's a huge locus of positions from which you can see both pairs, sun and planets, in eclipse at once, and the periods of both are short enough, goodness knows. The chances of popping into real space and being greeted by a view like this are pretty good."

Mike nodded, somewhat doubtfully. "I suppose so. Which of those crescents is Kainui? And where do we land?"

"I don't know, to both questions. Kainui's just a little bit the larger, but from here I can't tell by eyeball. Muamoku is the only place we can set down, at least usefully, but it'll take time to find it."

"You don't have a chart of some sort? Aren't there guide beacons?"

"You haven't learned much about the place, have you?

No, I don't have a chart. Neither do the people who live there. Both planets are water worlds, though Kaihapa hasn't been settled. Only the polar ice caps and the equatorial permanent rain belt can be distinguished from space, they're not too clear with all the haze, and wouldn't help anyway with the longitude problem. The cities float; they don't stay put. Why are you going there, anyway? I thought anyone would learn something about a world before starting an expensive trip to it."

"Research, and I'm not paying the freight. I care more about the people than their planet. I know several of the alleged reasons why they left Earth; for example, a lot of Polynesians got tired of the way oil-processing pseudolife stations were crowding the Pacific. There was never a war over the matter, just a lot of very expensive legal squabbling. I don't know why they picked Kainui, even though it's all ocean; it's not an ocean you can swim in safely, I've heard, though I don't know why. We know, we think, how many ships went there originally, but we don't know how many arrived safely and succeeded in growing cities. Only one place, Muamoku, seems willing to spend energy on a landing beacon, so it's the only place where ships can set down and expect to be in reach of anyone who can talk, buy, or sell. Whatever other cities there are seem quite willing to let Muamoku act as middleman in any off-planet trading. I'm a historical linguist by training and taste, and I'm looking for information on language evolution. All the original ships—that we know of, at least—left Earth from various Polynesian islands. We know the times they started out. Some people think there'll be only one language by now, but I doubt it. That has to be affected by how much and in what ways the cities have been in contact with each other—trading, war, religious difference, what have you. I'm reasonably fluent in a dozen Polynesian languages, especially Maori and Tahitian, and should be able to figure out at least something of what's happened, and when, and maybe even to whom."

"Brute information, you mean?"

"Normal human curiosity, I'd call it."

"Well, don't go swimming. That's something I do know."

"Why not? Ocean acid, or something?"

"Yes, as it happens, but that's not the main problem. There's continuous seismic activity at the ocean bottom, and if you swim without armor you're lucky to last five minutes without suffering the fate of a dynamited fish. There's enough carbon monoxide in the air to kill you in minutes, enough carbon dust to hinder visual communication seriously, and enough ionized haze to block practically any e-m communication. A lot of my friends think they picked that world because no one else would want it. There must be some reason they don't get rid of the CO—even I can think of pseudolife genera able to do that in a few decades. You're a historian, you say; maybe you can find out while you're poking around."

The navigator stopped talking and began to manipulate controls.

Three-quarters of an hour later, *Hi-Vac* was hovering two thousand kilometers above the surface of the larger planet. As promised, a fairly bright reflecting belt and a roughly circular patch of white ninety degrees from it gave locations for the permanent rain and ice regions. The blurred reflection of the suns was no help; its position on the disk told about where *Hi-Vac* was orbiting but gave no information about anything on Kainui's liquid surface. Mike couldn't tell by eye whether he was looking at water or fog; he might or might not be seeing surface. The ship, under power of course, was slowly circling the planet at about thirty degrees south latitude, so the north polar cap was not visible.

More and more of the night hemisphere was coming into view, and proved, while much darker than the daylit part, to be much brighter than geometry would have suggested.

"Lightning," remarked the navigator without taking her attention from her work.

"Shouldn't it be sort of flickering?" asked Mike.

"When we're closer and can see separate storms."

"When can we communicate? You haven't tried to use radio yet."

"We can't. The lightning hashes up everything electro-magnetic up to near infrared; radio, even FM, is nothing but noise out to half a million kilometers. The permanent haze is charged enough to take care of most shorter waves. Only Muamoku maintains a reasonably high-powered set of laser beams aimed almost vertically, but we have to find those our-selves. I hope the place hasn't drifted too far north or south. Guiding people like us in to where they are is not their highest priority, and if storms knock them off latitude they don't always hurry back. The city isn't very maneuverable, after all, and there aren't many scheduled arrivals from outside. We're lucky having even one city that's willing to do it at all. They— look! RS-455 on the screen! There they are!"

It must have been a battery of lasers, not just one; the luminous spot below was changing color as the ship moved. At first the signal was brilliant blue; then it was green, then yellow. Then it shifted back to green, and the navigator altered course and speed slightly. The yellow returned and became orange, started toward shorter wavelengths again, but was finally brought to deep red by more control work.

"Now we let straight down, but try to see the city before we land on it," was the remark.

"What *do* we land on?" Mike asked naturally.

"Ocean. Don't worry, we'll float."

"Is there tube connection, or do we moor securely enough for that?"

"We don't. You'll need a suit."

"But why—?"

"They'll probably tell you, but you may not believe it. I'm a ship-driver, not a historian, but I'll bet you'll get a different reason for colonizing the place in every city you visit, if you take in any others, ranging from the moral imperative not to displace alien life, through the right to practice human sacrifice freely, to the simple urge to get away from Earth's legal systems. Probably different groups did have different reasons. I'm going by experience on other colony worlds I've seen, by the way; I haven't asked this crowd. I've only been here three or four times. Use a rigid suit until you're used to the pressure, and start getting ready. If you have recording equipment, keep a close eye on it. The people are as honest on Kainui as anywhere else, but silicon is more valuable here than iridium or platinum. They can get all the metals they need from the ocean, but silicon doesn't dissolve to speak of in acid."

"I suppose I ought to watch out for oddball diseases, too," Mike remarked rather bitterly.

"Only if the colonists have produced them in their own bodies or labs. Evolution presumably moved in with the people, but no one's found any native life here, big or little. And you'll need to practice walking in the local gee."

"You said something about that before. Why? I thought you said Kainui was only a little bigger than Earth."

"Fifteen percent larger radius. One-third—*not* one-third

greater—surface gravity. Most of the world's volume is water, I think saltier than Earth's, but still water. Ocean depth is about twenty-nine hundred kilometers."

"So no islands."

"Not real ones. Ice still floats. Don't bother me for a few minutes. Red is the core of this landing signal, and I want a touch of orange. Landing right on the place would make us unpopular. Check your suit carefully; you'll have to get to the city by boat. Outside pressure is high, and if you have leaks they'll let more carbon monoxide in than oxygen out."

The landing was professional; *Hi-Vac* settled into the water three hundred meters from the nearest part of Muamoku, so the city itself, if not its details, could be seen. Its more distant parts were lost in the mist, so Mike couldn't even guess at its size.

I

OVERTURE

Poetically and almost literally, Kainui's mantle is at endless war with its overlying ocean. Perhaps they are simply too intimate; they confront each other directly, with no identifiable intervening crust. The underside of the interface is not quite liquid most of the time; the upper is technically gas, since the ocean at that depth is far above water's critical temperature.

What pass for tectonic plates, from township to county size, are solid enough to crack and tilt and be carried as individual units by mantle convection. Tsunamis are generated constantly, sometimes by abrupt plate shifts—quakes—sometimes by vulcanism, though there is nothing at all like a Terrestrial volcano on the world.

When magma emerges from the mantle to become lava and meets the sea there is of course violence, but Kainui has never experienced a Krakatoa-type steam blast. The weight of twenty-eight hundred kilometers of water, nearly all of it far saltier than any Earth ocean, provides some eighty thousand atmospheres of pressure. A few hundred kelvins rise in temperature has no real effect on either phase or volume.

So when, one day, a tenth of a cubic kilometer of glowing liquid silicate was suddenly exposed to ocean bottom along the line between two spreading plates, the result was merely a linear-source sound wave.

Its front spread out as wave fronts do, trying to become flatter and flatter as it left its source behind. It failed miserably. It passed through layers of differing salinity, temperature, and tonnage of suspended matter. Sometimes locally it turned concave and was focused so narrowly as almost to regain its original pressure. Sometimes it diverged, but its total energy degraded only gradually toward heat.

Nearly an hour later, when parts of it were nearing the ocean surface, that energy had been distributed over much of the planet, but there were still local, focused, high-pressure regions. Now the background pressure was getting low enough to let the water molecules move noticeably *with* the front.

When it actually reached the next real interface, between ocean and atmosphere, the water—long since actually liquid—was able to rise, and a tsunami was born. Most of it was imperceptible to human senses, since it covered a large area and had no coast to overwhelm; but even in the last few kilometers there had been some local refraction. In several places smaller microtsunamis originated, and Mike Hoani was very aware of one of these.

Its bulge was three or four hundred meters across and perhaps twenty above the general sea level, but this was not itself an easily spotted reference. The *Malolo*'s upward acceleration was only barely noticeable to anyone on board, but her tilt was another matter.

Mike had been trying to get his sea legs for two days now, since his first and last real view of a local tsunami. That had been during launch, when either the arm supporting the dock had been swinging downward or Muamoku had been rising. Cities were massive enough to respond rather slowly to changes in ambient pressure. The ship was different.

Ocean swells, on the rare occasions that they were the only disturbances present, Mike could usually handle; if they were too long-waved to see, they were, under Kainui's one-third Earth gravity, too slow to be a problem. The sometimes strangely shaped and always unpredictable microtsunamis, analogous to the streaks of light focused on the bottom of a washbasin when the water is stirred, were quite another matter; he didn't merely lose his footing, he was often thrown from it.

The catamaran's deck was railed in many places and rigged with safety lines in most of the rest, but not continuously or everywhere; the need to dive overboard or climb back was random in both time and place. It was wet, since there was enough wind to break wave tops and provide spray. It was slippery. This time Mike slid.

He was not hurt, being encased in sound armor fifteen centimeters thick except near joints, but he was frightened. Surprising both himself and the witnesses, however, he did the right thing. He swung the helmet hinged between his shoulders forward over his head, latched it, and *then* grasped at a passing line. He managed to catch this and stop his slide before actually going overboard. The deck was still rocking, and without shame he crawled away from its edge before trying to regain his feet.

Even the child at the masthead was watching him, lookout duty ignored for the moment, and the three native faces showed expressions of approval around their breathing masks. Maybe all four, counting Mike himself, were thinking that this Hoani fellow mightn't be too much of a burden after all, but nobody said anything. Especially Mike. He just stood up, carefully.

A mere day later, that particular wave had long gone to warm the surface water and the air above it. Mike's reflexes had improved even in that time, and he had some attention to spare now when the lookout's shrill voice sounded from above. It was hard to distinguish words over the endless thunder, but he followed them fairly well.

"*I'a'uri!* One hand, port bow, half a kilo, past ripe!" The captain's response was a wave, and Keokolo at the tiller simply changed heading. The breathing leaf had not yet been deployed that morning, and steering was straightforward. Mike, guided by the child's words, made out a dark-colored patch of what might have been seaweed in the indicated direction. It seemed more than a hundred meters across. He assumed it was a sample of the pseudolife they had come to harvest, but it meant nothing specific to him until after *Malolo* had been brought to at its edge.

Even then he could make out no real details, except that the weed seemed to be growing on something clear suspended a meter or so under the surface.

At that point both adult crew members expressed approval of 'Ao's judgment. She had descended from the mast without orders and was waiting with just a faint expression of anxiety visible around her mask. The passenger, who had a youngster of his own on Earth, could interpret this; the child had been afraid of being wrong. She relaxed visibly at the captain's words.

Mike Hoani couldn't quite decide whether he should be surprised or not. None of the crew had seemed to be, and it was reasonable that the youngster would be the first to spot the *i'a'uri*, whatever that was, since she spent much of her waking time at the masthead; but like Mike she was on her first sortie. Unlike him, she was barely forty years old and still carried her doll even on duty.

Her ability not only to identify the *i'a'uri* but to give details seemed to say more about Kainuian education than Mike had guessed so far. Apparently her instructors had more or less outgrown the notion that experience is the best teacher even though she had been sent to sea while still a child.

That was a point to be noted; it might possibly fit in with the convergent-evolution language thesis he was hoping to complete while on the planet. Different floating cities had been built by colonists from different Polynesian islands, but generations of trade among them had gradually caused a blending of tongues that was still far from complete.

Nothing much else had seemed surprising, either, during the time they had now been sailing. The weather had been fine; there had seldom been more than a dozen of the world's immensely tall thunderheads in view at any one time, though of course the ubiquitous ionized haze hid such things long before one's line of sight reached the distant horizon. The thermals had not forced *Malolo* to change her basically northward course; they were routine. Even little 'Ao had needed no verbal orders; she obeyed a simple gesture from the captain whenever the ship had driven into the hail column under one of them, darting over to the collecting sheet and standing by to sweep the hailstones either into the drinking and bathing breakers before they melted and absorbed too much carbon dioxide or, if there was too much of the material, overside.

Only one other vessel had been seen during that time. Wanaka, *Malolo*'s captain, had logged—and reported to the others with some amusement, as though they couldn't see for themselves—that it bore the same name as their own craft, but was a single-hulled double-outrigger of about twice their own tonnage flying the flag of Fou Savai'i and, like themselves, the "nothing to trade yet" pennant. Both adults seemed a little surprised that it was sailing at search speed; their own craft at the moment had its *kumu'rau* deployed, since the suns were high and it was rare for any craft to miss an opportunity to top off on oxygen. This of course could not be done at night, and at least some of each day had to be spent searching for metal.

The name went into Mike's mental notebook, too. *Malolo* meant "flying fish" in more than one classical Polynesian language—on a planet that had no native bacteria, much less vertebrates, as far as anyone had been able to find out.

The thing 'Ao had just seen and identified had been visible enough at half a kilometer, of course. The weather was unchanged, with Kaihapa barely visible through the haze, hanging high in the western sky and the suns nearly at the meridian. There was enough wind to move the ship at a reasonable clip, but not enough to break the swells; and by now, with his improving reflexes, the seismic bumps and hollows in the ocean surface were becoming merely a minor background nuisance to the passenger. They caused the top of the mast to swerve and jiggle in a way that made him avoid watching it, but 'Ao typically held on without apparent trouble and with her doll clinging to her shoulder, neither showing any sign of being bothered.

Malolo was now hove to at the edge of twenty thousand or so square meters of rippling jelly floating just under the surface. Wanaka, the vessel's owner and captain, was still aboard to make sure it stayed there. 'Ao, Mike, and Keokolo had flipped their helmets on and gone overboard to harvest.

The first two were connected by a safety line, since the visitor knew practically nothing of Kainui hand language, and vocal communication would have been hopeless below the surface even if helmets had been unnecessary. Noise from the ocean bottom was continuous, and deafening, and often deadly in overpressure. Mike had been told firmly to stay with the child, as though the connecting rope allowed anything else. He watched her carefully. He already knew why she avoided the nearly black leaves, which spread just at the surface and shadowed more than half the slimy stuff underneath, but he had been told practically nothing about the actual mechanics of harvesting. The items they wanted, he did know, were in the sheet of jelly itself, whose upper surface oscillated vertically under the push of the endless random microtsunamis and more regular swells, varying from half a meter to something like two and a half below that of the even more violently rippling water. Sometimes Mike found himself wading unsteadily on jelly, sometimes swimming. The meter-and-a-quarter-tall child always had to swim.

It seemed simple enough. 'Ao's thinly gloved hands groped over the jelly and every few moments found a slit not visible to the man. Reaching a few centimeters into this she would feel around briefly and pull the hand back either empty or grasping a black purselike object ten or twelve centimeters long that reminded Mike of a shark's egg case. This she would deposit in a circular basket being towed behind her, and resume groping. 'Oloa, the doll, clung to her shoulder still, but 'Ao paid no attention to it; she was working.

Keokolo seemed to be doing the same thing, except that the objects he gathered were clear and glassy in appearance, and the container in which he placed them, unlike the girl's, seemed to need no floats. Periodically one of the harvesters would return to *Malolo* and hand the collecting basket up to the captain, who transferred its contents quickly to something Mike couldn't see, since the salt-stained gunwale was more than a meter above him. Wanaka would then return the bucket to the harvester.

It was a long, rather boring, and tiring process. The noise armor was heavy and much less flexible than Mike would have liked, and the harvesters seemed to be taking a completely random course over the *i'a'uri*'s surface; the visitor could not even guess how nearly finished they might be. They stopped and ate for three-quarters of an hour while Kaihapa eclipsed the suns, then resumed work until the latter set. Mike had tried to calculate how many of the items being collected there might be on the vast surface of the pseudoorganism, and suspected *Malolo* might be there for several days; but when he suggested this aloud, the captain shook her now-exposed head negatively.

"No," she said through her breathing mask, rather regretfully he thought. "If we'd come across it sooner we might have been able to get a full load, but as 'Ao said when she spotted it, this one is quite a bit past ripe. Its batteries are nearly full, and there's no way to keep it from sinking out of reach after the leaves are gone. It's a rather old design, though a very efficient collector. Its iron is very pure and its water drinkable. It's too bad to see so much of it get away, though of course having only one cargo item to trade isn't good policy anyway."

Mike figuratively kicked himself for not having figured out that the pseudoorganism's name probably came from a blend of a Samoan word for "fish" and a Tahitian one for "iron," and added several notes to his mental collection.

"D'you think we should split it, or let it die?" asked Keokolo.

"Oh, split it. It's still a useful type, and if it ever can't compete with newer stuff the problem will take care of itself," answered his wife. "We have about a third of what I want, and should get the rest before sunset tomorrow. When we do, you can show 'Ao and Mike how to divide it without depowering one of the halves."

"I already know about that!" the child cut in.

"Your badge doesn't say so, but you can show Keo if you want. We'll be glad to upgrade you."

Mike had a pretty good idea of what they were talking about. 'Ao was not the child of the adult crew members, though they were married and had a daughter in Muamoku. No children of the same Kainui family ever sortied on the same vessel with their parents or usually even at the same time, but children started their practical education early. 'Ao was not quite forty, nearly ten in Mike's years. Family separation was a custom retained from their Terrestrial ancestors, who had placed high importance on the preservation of family lines. 'Ao's parents and small brother were not afloat just now and none, except the brother, was likely to embark until she herself had either come home or been away long enough to justify assuming that she had been lost at sea or adopted by another city.

Mike said nothing; he listened, fitting what he heard into his increasingly detailed mental picture of the colony world's society and, most particularly, its pattern of languages. By ancestry he was himself as pure Maori as Earth could now provide. By training he was a historian and philologist, and he had already found in trade-centered Muamoku, the only Kainuian city that hosted space craft, that he could make sense out of the Babel of mixed and evolved Polynesian languages in that one Kainuian settlement more readily than most of its citizens could adapt to that of another. He had met and talked extensively with many visitors and adoptees there, where he had stayed until embarking on *Malolo* a few days before.

Not all the time after the suns set was spent in talking; food, sleep, and exercise were all essential for the crew as well as their visitor; the three crew members could not all sleep at once; and maintenance of the breathing and food supply apparatus was always needed. Just now *Malolo* had to be kept close to, or at least in sight of, the *i'a'uri*. Once lost, this would be nearly impossible to find again—certainly not before it had finished ripening, released its water and iron back to the ocean, and sunk back to the deeps to collect and purify more. There was no telling when another useful pseudoorganism would be encountered, though the chances were reasonably good that it would be within a few days.

"Chance" was unfortunately the key word.

Mike's mental notes had to be recorded more permanently. The others knew what he was doing, and the adults paid little attention to him beyond the needs of courtesy.

'Ao's curiosity seemed more genuine. She asked many questions and explained his answers carefully to her doll, who probably didn't understand but at least remembered. Mike questioned the child in turn, trying to learn how she had recognized the iron-fish through Kainui's haze. She had some trouble explaining; color was understandable, but she was also trying to describe leaf pattern, which still seemed entirely chaotic to the visitor. They had not, obviously, been close enough at the time of spotting to recognize the detailed shape of the palm-wide two-meter-long ribbons of leaf. Mike still felt sure of that when the child finally sought her hammock, and still very unsure of what had actually guided her.

There were more clouds the next day than before—still all thunderheads—but the wind was lighter. Hoani had made no sense yet out of the planet's meteorology, and wasn't sure the colonists had either. A world with no land whatever, unless an occasional floating mass of pseudobiology or slab of coral from a detached city raft or dock counted, might be expected to have a very simple air circulation pattern. Kainui did, as far as climate was concerned, but weather was different. It seemed to be simply chaotic.

The tsunamis were as variable as usual, but even the visitor was getting accustomed to them; he had only fallen twice during the short time he had spent on deck that morning. It was the small ones that were troublesome; the really big humps of water extended beyond the range of vision and could barely be felt either tilting the ship or accelerating her up and down. Even in the low gravity the Earth native was usually quite unconscious of such small changes. It was when the deck really tilted that his troubles came.

When the *kumu'rau* was deployed he had had to develop a separate set of reflexes, since the scaly-looking strip of tissue, ten meters wide and two hundred long, trailing from *Malolo*'s stern greatly modified the catamaran's response to waves in general; that was today's problem. The "tree-leaf" was deployed when they were not under way by daylight.

On the *i'a'uri* the swimmers were affected only by the very smallest, most local bumps. These changed the depth of the jelly mass as it humped and hollowed, and meant that a collector floating at a set depth was sometimes within reach of the mass and sometimes not. No one had suggested that Mike should try collecting, and the other two seemed not to be bothered by the irregular motion.

The drinking breakers were now full, so Keo was also

collecting iron today. This time they were trusting their guest without a safety line, and 'Ao was working with visibly greater speed. Mike wasn't sure whether he should feel guilty or not. If *Malolo* couldn't get the load Wanaka wanted before their iron mine sank again, perhaps he should; and even he could see the change in the leaves. They were lighter in color and shrinking in length. He had worked out for himself that they must be using radiation from the suns to make something like ATP or azide ion or some other battery molecule, and that the pseudoorganism's hunger for whatever it was must be almost appeased. He himself must therefore be somewhat at fault for delaying the harvest and decreasing the amount of cargo the crew could collect, though he couldn't think of any way just then to frame an apology. He wished he could do something helpful himself.

Hours rolled by, however, with pods of iron still coming aboard, and Mike kept feeling better and better until shortly after the suns reached the meridian. Then the captain gestured 'Ao out of the sea as she arrived with a full bucket, and a few minutes later did the same for Keo.

"That had better do," she said when all helmets had been flipped back. "'Ao, take down the 'not yet' pennant. You've spotted the nucleus?" Both heads nodded; that bit of body language was standard even on the colony world. "All right. Keo, get the gen kit. 'Ao says she knows mitosis; let her show you. If she messes it up, it won't be very important with this one, so don't interrupt her unless things get dangerous. Mike, you may go back with them and watch if you like, but you won't be able to understand much. They'll—or she will—be installing a chromosome unit which will make this machine grow a new nucleus and then divide. Just once."

"They're not built to reproduce indefinitely?"

"This is a small planet." Hoani almost pointed out that it had a third more surface than his own, then saw the point the captain probably had in mind. *Any* planet is small when confronted with the exponential behavior of life. "We can't afford to let anything reproduce uncontrolled. We *could,* no doubt, design a set of predators to hold down the metal-fish population, but it seems more comfortable to do our own planning than to depend on that sort of statistic, which never worked very well on Earth. Escaped Terrestrial microlife we worry about, but so far it seems to be balancing itself off. The varieties that can survive in the ocean here have both prey and predator types, and the cycles phase locally. With large pseudolife forms, phases would be worldwide, and the times when the predators reach a high count but haven't quite run themselves out of food would be very unproductive."

The visitor nodded. His own world had been painfully slow to learn that lesson, and was still far from being back to its calculated half billion equilibrium human population. His own child had been permitted as a result of an agreement with authorities that either both parents or the child would emigrate when the latter reached self-supporting status.

"You didn't seem to hesitate when Keo asked you what to do this time," he remarked, returning to the question of the iron-fish's disposal.

"I did my hesitating earlier. I'd made up my mind when he asked."

"So this thing you're planting won't reproduce itself; it will just cause the *i'a'uri* to divide once."

"Right."

"Even if 'Ao makes a mistake in the installation?"

"Yes. All she could probably do wrong would either prevent it from dividing at all, or kill it—effectively, the same result. It wouldn't be a catastrophe. I'd've suggested that she try the job even if she hadn't asked to. I'm glad she did; some youngsters are afraid to try anything they haven't done before."

"I've known some who went the other way—were too eager to show off and got badly burned mentally and sometimes literally by failure."

"So have I. We'll hope Keo's judgment about helping turns out to be sound. Here they come. Do you want to go with them?"

"Am I likely to do any damage?"

"Not as long as you do nothing but watch. Come to think of it, you could even help. Ask her to explain things to you as she goes along. That should make her stop to think at each step—though I think she would anyway, with Keo looking over her shoulder."

"But how can she explain to me in the sea? I don't—"

"You can't speak Finger, of course. I forgot. Well, it was a good idea while it lasted. Please don't mention that slip to Keo. Husbands are hard enough to keep properly respectful as it is. But you may as well watch 'Ao anyway, if you wish; I expect you'll learn something, and you seem to have normal human curiosity."

Mike nodded and donned his helmet, fastening it under the critical gaze of the captain. The child had already dived overboard; Keo entered the water more carefully, burdened with a rectangular case about forty centimeters in its longest dimension and a little less than half that in the other two. The visitor followed them over the rippling slime, 'Ao leading the way. All were swimming, the yellow tops and white soles of the child's flipperlike foot armor providing an easy guide for the others.

Mike couldn't tell how close to the center of the huge pseudoorganism they got, but their course seemed straight; there was no wandering around to find their target. Once within a dozen meters or so, even he was pretty sure he could recognize it.

A bulge of darker-tinted jelly swelled almost to the ocean surface, the area for several meters around entirely devoid of leaves. The guest couldn't remember having seen the thing before, but realized that it might not have been so distinct during the harvesting. That was something he could ask later, if the development cycle of this particular form of pseudolife ever seemed to be important to anyone but harvesters. He wouldn't be expected to know about that in advance.

Keokolo and the girl squeezed air from their buoyancy controls and settled to the bulge. Mike remained drifting above them. Keo handed over the case he had been carrying, and 'Ao unlatched and swung back one of its narrower sides. No bubbles rose; it had apparently contained water all along—water of about the same density as that around them. This was probably, Mike realized, about the same as the general upper ocean value at this distance from the equatorial endless rain belt, since there had been no major storms in the last couple of days. Rain and hail could dilute the surface layers almost to fresh water density, at least by percentage salinity and osmotic factors, but more than an hour or so after an ordinary storm even surface water was likely to have too high a concentration of nasty ions like nickel or cadmium to be safely drinkable.

Mike suddenly could guess why Wanaka had decided *Malolo* was loaded enough for now, high as she was still riding.

With obvious care, 'Ao was taking something from the case. It was rather fish-shaped, though circular in cross section and lacking fins or tail. At first its skin was smooth; then, as the child ran gloved fingers along a set of reddish stripes— a dozen or more, though Mike couldn't see well enough to count them accurately—a set of dangerous-looking spikes, each two centimeters or more in length, began to extend. They didn't come straight out, but slanted toward what looked like the rear of the organism. The last quarter of its length remained smooth, and 'Ao held it in one hand by this "tail."

With the other she groped around the iron-finder's bulge, exploring a circle about a meter in radius around its top. After a minute or two of this a smaller bulge swelled on the slimy surface and at its top a sphincterlike opening appeared. With far more care than she had displayed up to this point, the child brought the spiny whatever-it-was close to the mouth— or whatever-it-was—and carefully suspended it, still by the tail, so that the outer curve of each of the "forward" spikes would touch the rim of the opening at the same moment if she lowered it much farther.

For the first time, she hesitated and looked at Keo. Even Mike could understand the answer—an encouraging circle-and-three-finger gesture of the gloved right hand. The child's facial expression could of course not be seen, but both men could imagine the firmly compressed lips and fixed gaze as she very slowly eased the thing, which seemed to be a good deal denser than the surrounding water, downward again.

With only millimeters to go, her hand shook slightly, but she didn't jerk it upward; she merely stopped, steadied herself, and resumed the letdown. Keo repeated the approval gesture, and an instant later contact was made.

As far as the visitor could tell, it was simultaneous all around the opening, though he had no idea why this should be important. For several seconds nothing more happened. 'Ao's hand remained steady—unbelievably so, to Mike. Then a ring-shaped film of tissue pouted away from the opening and contracted around the first three or four rows of hooks. 'Ao let go, and almost instantly the spiky "fish" was swallowed and the opening closed. Thirty seconds later the smaller bulge had flattened to match the curvature of the big one, and the child relaxed visibly.

The job was not quite done, it seemed; the two knowledgeable watchers kept on watching, and Mike followed their example.

Nothing really obvious happened for something like a quarter of an hour. Then the top of the big bulge began to sink, along with a meridian stripe now visible on each side of it. Soon even Mike could tell that the bulge was dividing, and guess what was happening. The meridional groove grew deeper and wider, and when its depth had reached ten or fifteen centimeters Keo rested a hand on the child's armored shoulder and waved presumably toward *Malolo*, though Mike was no longer sure of direction. He did not yet keep mental track of the sister world or the suns as a matter of habit.

They began swimming. The dividing bulge vanished behind them and presently the ship could be seen ahead. The Terrestrial wondered, as he had several times in the last day or two, whether the Kainuian sense of direction was simply an incredible memory for details, a habit of keeping aware of the few visible celestial bodies, or something more subtle.

He had no reason to believe that there was any local technology unknown on the older human-inhabited worlds, and ordinary communication equipment worked very poorly indeed on this planet; the ubiquitous thunderheads and charged haze droplets blocked or quickly damped out all electromagnetic transmission of much longer wavelength than visible light, even when frequency modulated. Only Muamoku had lights bright enough to guide a space craft to a specific point on the surface from directly above; none of the other floating cities could, or wanted to, spare the energy. He had not asked Wanaka or Keo why even Muamoku bothered—probably the reasons were economic—and didn't plan to. The miners might not know, and might dislike showing ignorance as much as Mike himself did. He had no wish to make himself unwelcome, at least until his own project was done. Tact, he often pointed out when the subject arose, would have been his middle name if he had had one, and to him tact meant talking as little as possible when he wasn't sure what to say.

They climbed aboard and doffed helmets.

II

DISCORDS

Keo redonned his again almost instantly, joined promptly by the captain and a little less so by Mike. Even he had felt the jar, feeble as it was, as something struck one of the hulls, but having no knowledge of the appropriate response he imitated the rest.

The helmets, unlike the rest of the armor, were extremely transparent; how they were soundproof at the same time was a question Mike had not considered. Even now, it simply flashed through his mind as a suggestion that Kainuian technology might have something to offer after all; right now the fact that he couldn't read the captain's lips because of her breathing mask and was still left out of the conversation by his ignorance of Finger was his principal conscious thought. He could only guess at her orders by the actions of the crew.

"Mike, hold a safety line for 'Ao. I'll take Keo's." That was obvious enough from what she did with the ropes. "'Ao, starboard hull; Keo, port. One quick runover, then repeat with all possible care, covering as much as you can while there's daylight. Start from the stern."

The child seized the end of the light rope the captain was holding out to her, clipped one end to her belt, threw her doll at one of the mast's climbing rungs that it caught firmly, and disappeared overboard. By the time Mike had secured a good grip on his end of the line and decided it was long enough to let her reach both bow and stern of the thirty-meter hull if he stayed amidships, Keokolo had gone also. Mike looked questioningly at the captain.

She hesitated a moment, then removed her helmet. He assumed it was permissible for him to do the same, and heard the endless thunder once more. Wanaka's voice came over it; he had not had to ask any question.

"It could be any of several things," she said. "We're still drifting, so we didn't run into anything small—not that hard; we did *feel* the impact. We'd have seen anything really large on the surface, like floating coral. The most worrisome guess is a tracer, something jammed against the ship deliberately which will emit chemicals a smeller can follow. It's not quite the most likely explanation; usually, such a gadget would attach itself too quietly for us to notice."

"Why would it be done at all?" asked Mike.

"There are people who have a one-sided idea of what trading means. Not many of them, because cargo is always printed when one takes it aboard—"

"Printed?"

"Scented might be a better word. Identified with the growth code of the harvesting ship. I took care of that as each iron pod came aboard. If anyone took some of it without our consent, the fact could be proved."

"Not the water?"

"No. That or oxygen would be shared with anyone in need, however little we had. Of course, if pirates took our iron and used it up themselves, in batteries or growth tanks or what have you, nothing could be proved later. That's why piracy, when it *is* proved, carries the same penalty here as it did on old Earth."

"And why, I'd guess, pirates would also tend to dispose of the crews they'd overcome."

"Not always. 'Ao would be safe; she'd simply be adopted, swapped with other ships a few times so her story wouldn't do anyone much good, and wind up in a city sooner or later. They *might* do the same with Keo and me, depending on their food and oxygen resources; how they'd feel about you is anyone's guess. You're decidedly unique."

Mike, whose body mass and personal strength were twice those of the much taller Keokolo, nodded. He felt no urge to learn *all* about Kainui's customs firsthand, but saw no need to take the worst for granted.

Judging by the motion of her line, 'Ao had finished one examination and gone back aft to start a second. Keo was almost through with his first check; whether he was a slower swimmer or was just being more careful was anyone's guess. Mike noticed that the captain was glancing back and forth between the two cords and suspected that she was thinking along the same lines. Being Mike, however, he didn't comment. He devoted most of his attention to the child's cord, providing her with slack or drawing it in as seemed in order. Hence, he failed to see Keo's attachment jerk tight twice, less than a second apart, until the captain called out to him.

"Call 'Ao aboard! Give short pulls on her line, and keep doing it until you can tell she's coming!" The man obeyed without question or comment; he'd learn the details as quickly as anyone else, he assumed. Keo, who had apparently discovered something, should be aboard before the child.

He wasn't, however. 'Ao surfaced at a set of climbing rungs five meters forward of the stern and ascended them nimbly without using her flippered feet. Mike reminded himself once more that her weight here was less than seven kilograms. She stood dripping for a moment, looking at Wanaka; the latter gestured her toward the spot where Keo's line disappeared over the gunwale, and said something more detailed in Finger.

Moving a little aft so that her safety cord would miss the captain, the child crossed the deck and reentered the sea. Mike adjusted the slack once more.

"Can you tell what Keo's found?" he asked. "I know you can't see or hear him, but is there some sort of code you can send by the ropes?"

Wanaka shook her head negatively. "He's spotted something worth reporting, but wants the little one to see it too so they can tell us better what's going on, I assume. Otherwise he'd simply have come up. If it makes you feel better informed, the longer they stay down will probably mean the worse it is."

Hoani wondered whether this remark said more about the captain's experience or just her personality. She had not, so far, seemed noticeably pessimistic or even cynical, so maybe it was experience. Before he himself could really start worrying, however, both ropes slackened and two heads broke the surface. Mike, without thinking, stepped toward the side of the deck to help his charge aboard and lost his footing as *Malolo* jerked to an unusually sharp tsunami. By the time he was back on his feet, both the others were aboard.

Keo's helmet was off instantly. "If it's a tracer, it's a kind I've never seen," he reported. "It's fish-shaped, and has a hard shell, about twenty centimeters long. It doesn't seem to have penetrated, but is very firmly fastened against us."

"And we can't really be sure about penetration," added the child. "We can't see under it. It has a jelly coating a centimeter thick all over it and reaching out over our hull for five or six centimeters all around. Someone better check the inside for things that shouldn't be there."

"You do it. You know where to look," replied the captain. "If you have to shift any cargo, get Keo or Mike to help. Keo, help me set sail until 'Ao calls you."

"But the suns are almost down!" exclaimed the child.

"We get away from here first, and worry about missing more cargo and bumping into things *much* later," was the answer. "Don't bother to say it—no, we don't really know it's a tracer, but we can't do anything useful about it after dark, and I want to be far from here and have time to be careful when we can see again by something better than lightning or hand lamps. Carry on."

The child disappeared belowdeck, and the others made sail. For once, Mike could help; he had done some sailing on Earth, and had kept his eyes open so far on this trip. In minutes, *Malolo* was under way, as usual in the direction that let them get the most possible speed out of the existing wind. Hoani had heard about the bits of stuff—"coral"; he could only guess what local item or phenomenon had taken over that word, though he knew what materials were grown to build the floating cities—occasionally found loose on Kainui's oceans, but didn't know how visible such objects might be even by daylight. He decided to let the captain's apparent lack of worry be his guide, until it occurred to him that this might merely be a *minor* worry.

Keokolo stayed at the helm, while the others entered the cabin—the air lock allowed the child and the captain to go through together, but Mike's bulk kept anyone from sharing it with him—and removed their breathing masks. Mike settled down to recording his mental notes of the last few hours, while Wanaka updated the ship's log. 'Ao for some reason didn't seem relaxed. She said nothing to her doll and watched the others, particularly the captain, closely. Eventually both adults noticed this.

Even Mike could see that the youngster wanted to say something, but he couldn't guess what it might be. Not until Wanaka looked up from her writing and caught 'Ao's eye did the problem become clear. The man suspected afterward that the captain had known all along what was on the youngster's mind.

It was Wanaka who spoke first.

"Keo says you did a very good job on that split, 'Ao."

The child's expression brightened, but her words were less happy than they might have been. "Why didn't he tell me?"

"Didn't you know anyway?" Both the listeners caught the verbal trap, and 'Ao avoided it neatly.

"I was pretty sure, but there might have been something no one ever told me about that I missed. I was afraid he was going to tell me what was wrong when he comes off watch."

"He may, of course." 'Ao's face fell. "He didn't tell me anything bad, though. As far as I'm concerned you have another spark in your fire." The girl still seemed uneasy.

"Then—will you—can you—"

"Sure. Let's have it. Permission to doff armor. Do the air checks while I'm scribing."

The upper half of the suit of noise protection, complete with helmet, was peeled off and handed to the captain at once. Mike looked away; in spite of many weeks on the planet, he was still a little uncomfortable at the Kainuian body shape. 'Ao had a reasonable height for her age, by his standards, but massed barely twenty kilograms and on this world weighed fewer than seven. To Mike, she looked unhealthily thin, as did the others. Clad in the bulky noise armor Kainuians looked all right, but in the single leotardlike garment worn in places where one could breathe without masks they were almost grotesque to human visitors. Their uniformly dark hair and eyes, contrasting often with extremely pale skins that were becoming increasingly widespread as generations went by under a pair of red dwarf suns, gave many visiting Terrestrials the impression of a group of walking skeletons.

'Ao went to check the indoor part of the oxygen equipment, which photosynthesized the Kainuian air along several chemical paths to produce sodium peroxide, controlled the reaction rate of the latter with water, and pumped enough of the remaining nitrogen into the cabin to keep any leakage moving outward. This equipment, like the "leaf" itself, was pseudolife powered by battery molecules charged in the "leaf." Mike was not in the least surprised to see the child finish by slicing small pieces from each machine to make sure its healing capacity was normal.

Wanaka took the proffered upper garment and opened a small instrument kit taken from a compartment in her work desk. 'Ao crowded close after finishing her check; Mike couldn't decide whether this was to watch better or because of the rule about never getting far from one's armor when at sea. The captain took several styluslike objects from the kit and turned the garment so that she could see the back.

Mike had noticed the twenty-centimeter-diameter pattern on the child's suit between the shoulders, but had not paid it much attention; the other two had similar markings, and he had assumed them to be crew insignia with meanings he might learn later, since his own suit was plain. The pattern details were extremely complex, and reminded him slightly, but only slightly, of Mandelbrot figures.

Wanaka, using one stylus after another for some ten minutes, modified 'Ao's pattern carefully. Mike could see each change as it was made, but would never have been able to spot any difference between original and final designs if he hadn't been watching the process. Also, he almost missed the fact that each tiny modification kept on changing for a while after the artist had gone on to another section. Once again nanotechnology—pseudobiology—must be at work.

Eventually, the captain put her tools back and handed the armor back to the child. 'Ao looked at it gloatingly for a few seconds, then caught the other's eye and hastily slipped back into the garment. The captain nodded toward the hammock—there were also two shelflike bunks, and Mike suspected the arrangements had been modified to allow for his presence—and 'Ao, with apparent reluctance, started to climb into it. Then she paused.

"Is it all right if I use a bunk until Keo comes in?" she asked. Wanaka looked a little surprised, but nodded permission. Mike guessed the reason for the request; the little one lay down on her side so that anyone else in the cabin could see the new pattern. This would not have been practical in the hammock. The adults glanced at each other, but said nothing. The captain, after a few more minutes of writing, also retired; Mike still had much to do with his own records, and also doubted that the hammock would support him even in the local gravity.

Nothing further happened for some hours. *Malolo*'s motion was as usual, and as long as he was seated Mike wasn't bothered by its unpredictability. A bell whose tongue was mounted on a flexible but still airtight section of the wall signified the end of Keo's watch, and the captain woke up and went on deck. Two or three minutes later, presumably after reporting status details to his commander, Keo came in. He took in the situation at a glance, smiled, and gently lifted the sleeping child and her doll into the hammock. The doll piped, "Good night, Keo." The man answered, "Good night, 'Oloa," dropped onto the shelf left vacant by the captain, bade Mike good night as well, and was asleep in moments. Mike, using the bunk from which 'Ao had been removed, followed suit a few minutes later.

It was presumably still night when he woke again. Some hours must have passed, since the other bed was now occupied once more by the captain, but she, too, was sitting up.

"What was that?" she asked. Mike had no answer, and no idea what had awakened him. Before he could say anything, the bell sounded—not the single tone that signified change of watch, but three sharp notes, louder than usual.

"*Ni'ui kanaau!*" Wanaka leaped for the door. It took Mike a moment to work out her meaning, slightly because of the shifted glottal stop, more because of the mixture of Tahitian and Samoan, more still because he had not expected such language from the captain, and perhaps mostly because he himself was probably the only person now on Kainui who had ever actually seen a shark and might be expected to mention its entrails as a curse. He hesitated for a moment, wondering whether he would be any help on deck or would merely be in the way; then curiosity won. He left the child still asleep in the hammock. Whatever had awakened him and the captain had apparently failed to disturb her.

Or the doll, he thought in passing.

On the deck he could see that dawn was in the sky, though

neither sun was yet visible. Kaihapa's foggy disk showed plainly enough, a little less than full, almost imperceptibly lower than before in the west. Whatever Keokolo had to report to his captain must already have been said; she was giving orders, and included her passenger in them the moment she saw him.

"Mike, take the tiller when Keo has us hove to. You can keep us that way well enough. We're both taking lights overboard. We hit something, certainly not very big but we need to know if there are any nicks or scratches. Keo didn't see anything, but we'll check as completely as we can from bow to amidships. Even small scratches can get infected, and with that whatever-it-is sticking to the port hull we need to be really careful. I don't like stopping even at night when we're on the run like this, but—"

"But we may not be running from anything, after all," cut in Keokolo. "In any case, the quicker we make this check the sooner we can use the wind again. I'm ready, Wan." Without waiting for an answer he flipped his helmet into place, latched it, strode forward, and went over the port bow. The captain also sealed herself and took the starboard hull. Mike followed orders, keeping the boom straight aft and watching the sail ripple.

He could tell the approximate positions of the divers by the diffused glow of their hand lights. They moved very slowly indeed, apparently seeking something that might be hard to find. The passenger had some idea of why; the hulls, like the Kainuian cities and most other human artifacts, had been grown rather than manufactured. They were pseudolife, subject to infection by other pseudoorganisms. Like the crew's armor they had four biologically very different protective coatings, each supposedly vulnerable to only a limited variety of microbes, but even a quite small nick or scratch could decrease *Malolo*'s biological protection by a quarter, or a half, or three-quarters, or completely.

Mike could only guess how serious a worry the little bump, which had barely awakened him, might represent.

He made no attempt to keep track of time, but both suns could be seen through the ubiquitous haze and Kaihapa had shrunk to obviously gibbous phase, though of course not moving visibly in the sky, before the two divers regained the deck and flipped back their helmets. Both shook their heads negatively.

"Think we ought to start over, Captain? It's daylight now."

Wanaka considered briefly, then vetoed the suggestion. "No. Get us under way again, but change course thirty degrees back for an hour or so. We can afford the time to tack if we need to. If that thing on the port hull is putting out scent, there should be a good fog of it all around us by now, and if anyone really is following us it'll take 'em a while to pick up the new track. After an hour, we'll—never mind; I'll be back on watch by then. Maybe I'll have a different idea after I've finished sleeping. At least, we have plenty of oxygen; we can afford a few days at search-only speed, with the leaf not out."

Mike ventured a suggestion, rather reluctantly. He was sure the likelihood was that his ignorance would make it a silly one.

"Could we go back for a while and then change course to cross whatever trail we might have left? Would that be more confusing to anyone following?"

Keo nodded approvingly, to Mike's relief. "Could work,

if no one's close enough behind to see us at it." Wanaka also nodded, but disappeared into the cabin with no further words.

Mike could also have used more sleep, but decided not to bother. There was always a chance of seeing something new even with the haze, or hearing it through the continuous thunder, and as a passenger he could sleep at any time—almost. Also, walking around on the ever-heaving deck was still important practice. He wished what rails there were, were just a little higher; even under Kainuian gravity, there might not be time to lock his helmet if he lurched overboard.

Eventually the captain reappeared, accompanied by 'Ao, and took the tiller. Keo started for the cabin, then paused.

"Maybe we should check below. If anything did get to us, it might be easier to see from inside—and if anything is through either hull we'd better know it."

Wanaka merely nodded. The man disappeared through the forward hatch of the starboard hull, the child taking the port without comment. Mike, who had been on the point of retiring himself, decided to remain out for at least a little longer. It would be nice not to have to worry whether he should be worried or not.

There seemed nothing unusual away from the catamaran. Thunderheads still showed their endless lightning as far as could be seen through the haze, the bumps and hollows of microtsunamis and wind-driven swells could still be felt, and occasional waterspouts were visible. The frequency of these had surprised Mike at first. The low gravity made for a high atmospheric scale height, only partly countered by high molecular weight, and the sea-level pressure was more than twice Earth's to begin with; convection currents, whether driven by heat or humidity, tended to be far taller than at home and much more effective at lifting things. And, most decidedly, much more electrically violent.

No vessels could be seen, though this meant little; sails and even running lights would not be visible a third of the way to the distant horizon.

'Ao reappeared and reported the starboard hull apparently tight. There was a little bilgewater, but no more than usual. The captain nodded, and suggested that the child eat and then take the masthead. Mike expected no objection to this, and was quite right. 'Ao didn't mind the motion, and there was always a chance of glory in spotting potential cargo. Even if the captain didn't want to stop for it this time— Mike had no idea how much the little one knew or could infer about their present course—merely sighting a potential mine would be to her credit.

She was out again in a few minutes, and Mike looked away uncomfortably as she hand-over-handed her way up the rungs of the mast with 'Oloa clinging to her shoulder, and settled with seeming comfort into the broad strap that formed *Malolo*'s crow's nest. It was not too hard to look at her just now, the sky offering little distinct background. Later, when the suns neared the meridian, her wiggling and wobbling as the hulls shifted this way and that would become hard on the passenger's stomach, especially as the deck underfoot would be affecting the line of sight from his own end. He wished there were some way of cutting his semicircular canals out of his nerve wiring—temporarily, of course. It would be worse, he reminded himself, if the horizon were visible, but this fact offered little comfort.

He deliberately looked down and began walking around the deck, keeping safely away from the railing where there was one and even more carefully away from the verge where there was neither rail nor grab lines. He seemed to be getting some sort of sea legs at last; he didn't fall or even stumble once, this time. Keo nodded approval at one point, when their glances met.

'Ao occasionally called a "nothing in sight" from her masthead, to show she was still awake, Mike assumed. He sometimes heard fainter voices from above and wondered whether she were talking to the doll or the latter were keeping her alert. Otherwise there was practically no conversation, and the passenger found his mind wandering among evolved Polynesian vocabulary and grammar rules. He wondered whether Wanaka would have used the term she had if 'Ao had been awake. Some cultures were highly critical of bad language, others had no grasp of the concept; the latter usually expressed annoyance more physically, he had noticed. He thought fleetingly of experimenting, but of course decided against it.

His attention was recalled to the real world by a cry from the masthead.

"Keo! Ship, starboard quarter, hove to. Mining, I think. Only one person on deck."

"Banners?" asked the helmsman.

"Can't see yet."

Keo brought *Malolo* into the wind, gestured Mike to the tiller, and leaped to the marked flexible section of the cabin wall. Wanaka emerged in seconds. She took in the situation at once, glanced at her own masthead to recheck which banners were flying, took Keo's place, ordered him to take in some sail, and slowly approached the other vessel—not driving straight at it, but keeping *Malolo*'s bows some degrees to one side so they approached in a slow spiral.

There was still only one person visible on the other deck; 'Ao's probable inference that the rest were mining seemed valid. Wanaka called to the child.

"Can you tell what they're getting?"

"Copper, I'm pretty sure."

Mike had by now spotted a field of leaves not, to him, significantly different from those on the iron-fish, but the captain seemed to accept the youngster's judgment. The Earth native could see several pennons strung down a line from the other craft's masthead, but could read none of them. He memorized as much of what he could see as possible; maybe 'Ao's next explanation would be more comprehensible. Keo guessed some of his problem, and translated the flags.

"They have copper and titanium, enough to trade." He glanced at Wanaka, who nodded without saying anything, and the man ran up a flag Mike had not seen before.

"Requesting permission to approach." This time it was the captain who translated for him.

The figure on the other deck beckoned the newcomers, then turned to the farther gunwale of its own craft and pulled up a collecting bucket familiar to Mike. It gestured at the invisible bearer, and another figure lifted itself into sight from the ocean. Mike couldn't tell whether either was man or woman.

Wanaka glanced up at her own masthead and called 'Ao down, and the three waited while the vessels, now essentially both hove to, drifted closer together. Keo, Mike, and the child stood motionless until *Malolo*'s port hull was less than two meters from the other's single outrigger. Mike had been examining the vessel with interest. It was single-hulled with an outrigger, the breathing cabin only a little larger than their own, and the passenger, still allowing for his own inexperience, guessed that the crew could hardly number more than four or five.

Wanaka must have reached the same conclusion. She said a few words to 'Ao and gestured toward the other vessel. The child promptly sealed her helmet and went overside. She reappeared at the other's hull and was helped up by the one who had originally been on deck.

In the next quarter hour two more swimmers emerged from the sea and doffed helmets. Mike had now realized with no surprise that he was a subject of close interest to all four of the other's crew. He knew he was an impressive sight. An adult of Kainui looked quite ordinary to a Terrestrial when wearing sound armor, and more like a skeleton only when indoors where one could breathe properly. Mike, in armor, was frighteningly bulky.

When the two crews finally mixed, he judged that the others were rather surprised that he could talk at all, and even more so when he proved, after a few minutes of listening, to be more at ease than any of Wanaka's crew with the language of the others.

It was, to his comfort and pleasure, much richer in Maori, though still far from pure. The languages of even the most literate cultures evolve, sometimes even more rapidly than their religions. He added much to his notes during the next few hours.

The others were quite willing to trade. All four were male, and Mike never did feel quite sure which was the captain. Most of the talk, to which he listened carefully, was bargaining. He found that titanium was cheaper than copper, which might have told a planetologist something, and both were far cheaper than iron. The dealing concluded with a polite exchange of foods, since every ship had its own varieties of pseudovegetables, and a formal-sounding query to 'Ao whether she would care to be adopted by the other crew. She declined very politely and no one seemed to take offense.

The other vessel still had cargo space, and was remaining to do some more copper mining when *Malolo* hoisted sail. There had been no suggestion that she stay and share this particular treasure; Mike had already gathered that finders-keepers was an accepted custom. This "fish" seemed far larger than the one he had seen before, and it seemed to him that there must be more than enough metal for both, again allowing for his own ignorance. But maybe copper-fish were less productive. He didn't ask.

Once under way again, Wanaka was visibly relieved, and made no secret of the reason.

"If anyone really was smelling after us, they'll lose interest when they see those others. We'll get that thing off our hull in the morning, but we don't have to worry about it anymore."

"Did you tell the others about that problem?" asked Mike.

Wanaka and Keo both looked surprised. "No. Of course not. It wouldn't have made them any more careful than they would be anyway, or any better able to fight if pirates did come along. With that much wealth already aboard, they probably won't stay much longer anyway, and I expect they'll be looking for a city by this time tomorrow."

This reminded Mike of something he knew, but hadn't really considered carefully. Cities didn't stay put on Kainui. They floated, and it didn't much matter where, except for avoiding the tropical precipitation belt where the ocean was most dilute and things didn't float so high. It was understood that he would eventually be brought back to Muamoku if *Malolo* survived, and he had been told this might take an unpredictably long time, but he hadn't really grasped the fact that Wanaka really didn't care at all where, or very much when, she disposed of her cargo. Presumably she and Keokolo expected to get back to their child eventually, but it was not obvious just how intense an emotion was involved.

Mike might be going to learn a great deal more about Kainui languages, customs, and history than he had expected or really hoped.

He thought more of this now, but was not yet really worried. It was almost another day before he became so.

They hove to at sunset this time, Wanaka being no longer concerned about followers. When daylight returned, Mike was left at the tiller and all three of the crew went overboard, the adults to work on the object clinging to the port hull, and 'Ao to make another and most minute check for impact scratches or nicks. All were out of sight for more than an hour.

Keo appeared first, and paused to tell the passenger what was going on.

"We still don't know whether it's really a scent tracer or something else," he explained, "but we'd better get it off anyway. It's really stuck to the outer paint, and we may have to damage that to get it loose. If we do, some of our infection defense will be gone." Mike nodded; this was something he already understood. The other went on, "We have cleaning organisms of our own which should be able to grow between the outer coat and the stuff that's sticking to it—bugs that are related to the coat itself. It'll take a while for them to work, if they're going to work at all. Maybe they won't; this thing may have been designed to resist anything of that sort. The fact that it sticks so well to our outer layer suggests that it was made up with that paint in mind."

"Wouldn't that mean they knew it was the *Malolo*?"

"Not necessarily. There are only so many things anyone

uses in hull paint, and this thing might have a taste for several of them—maybe for all anyone knows how to make, if its designer was really good. We might wind up merely clearing its way to the inner coats. Not bored, I hope? Keep *Malolo* as she is; we don't want to be left behind if the sails take wind."

"Don't worry. I'm good at staying put."

Keokolo nodded, went to a locker at the base of one of the cabin walls, rummaged around in it for a while, took several articles out, and reclosed it. Then he nodded once more to Mike, closed his helmet, and went overside.

There was another long wait. Then Wanaka came on deck followed a few minutes later by the other two; Keokolo had apparently gone to fetch 'Ao. All flipped their helmets back, and the child headed for the cabin.

"She showed me a couple of really tiny dents near the port bow," the man said. "I guess we did bump a coral or something, but whatever it was doesn't seem to have gone through the outer coat. We might as well get going again."

"Right. I'll take it. You eat and top off your breathers." Wanaka reached for the tiller, then looked at Mike and smiled briefly. "See how close to best speed *you* can bring her."

The sailing lesson for the next hour was also a language one for Hoani; he had known little of proper sailing terminology even in his native tongue. As usual, they didn't care much just which way they were going; Mike had tried in conversation a dozen different words for "map" or "chart" in various parts of the South Pacific and found that they either meant something like "picture" or nothing at all, usually the latter.

'Ao eventually reappeared and climbed to her masthead, but had nothing to report for a long time. It was Keokolo who finally came on deck with a puzzled expression visible around his breathing mask, looked around carefully, made his way to the after hatch of the port hull, and descended through it. He reappeared in seconds.

"Captain! Heave to! Bilges up!"

Wanaka seized the tiller, though Mike had already started to shift it in the right direction, and in moments *Malolo*, her way gone, was rocking as nearly motionless as anything could on the restless water. "'Ao!" called the captain. "Get down and check the starboard bilges. *Hohoro!*"

As the child reached the deck, touching only two rungs on the way down, hail began to drift down around them and she turned toward the water sheet, but the captain shouted again and gestured toward the hatch. "Water's important, but so is staying on top of it! Check that hull first! *Tere! Oi'oi!*" 'Ao obeyed. She was gone longer than Keo had been, but was shrugging as she emerged.

"All right on this side." She seemed calmer, but scurried toward the collecting equipment at top speed. She slipped once on the now hailstone-covered deck and started to snap on her helmet even before trying to stop the skid, but Mike was in a good position and seized her arm before she went overside. He held her until she recovered her footing. Without a glance or word of thanks she resumed her way, and began shoveling hailstones into the drinking breakers. Wanaka gestured Mike to the tiller, and headed for the hatch where Keo had disappeared. Before she reached it, he emerged again, and with the single word "Leaks!" went overside. He was gone for less than a minute. He had his helmet off before actually reaching the deck, and practically bellowed, "Oxygen!"

III

———

SCORE

" 'Ao, take the tiller—no, let it swing and drop the sails. Mike, we need your muscle. Get as much cargo as you can out of the port hull and into the other. Never mind about nice stowing, we can see to that later. Keo, any food, air, and water equipment not in the cabin to the starboard hull, except the *kumu'rau*. At least it's not out; make certain it's secure. I'll cut rigging and unclip the deck as fast as I can. If I'm not done when you've finished the life-stuff, then help me. *Tere!*"

Hoani quickly saw another reason why they had been so quick loading up with iron in spite of its density, and how Wanaka had kept busy between emptying buckets. Each purse of metal dust was now clipped to a balloonlike float whose volume sharply limited the space for actual cargo. None of these items was heavy and he thought he could fill the other hull quickly, but when he tried to carry several purses at once Wanaka cautioned him about the fragility of the floats.

Hence, a lot of cargo was still untouched when the gunwale of the port hull dipped below the surface. Mike thought of closing the hatches to delay flooding, but before he could make the suggestion the captain must have guessed his thought. She shook her head negatively.

There were readable expressions on the four faces as their owners watched the port hull of the *Malolo* be pushed slightly below the surface by the still attached deck, but it was only annoyance. Showing fear or anger in public, even if the public were mate or sibling, was rude on Kainui, and so far neither of the informed adults felt any real fear. Mike wasn't sure whether he should, but decided to be guided by them. The youngest member of the group might have been slightly afraid or even terrified, but was not going to let anyone else know it.

The fact that neither ship nor city could be seen within the haze-limited vision in any direction surprised no one, and of course Mike, the only one who had ever seen land, knew better than to expect that anywhere on this world.

The swell was high, but its wavelength was great, far longer than the catamaran's hulls; almost too long, just now, to let anyone see one crest from the next through the haze. In the water world's gravity, waves moved so slowly that the five-meter rise and fall of the drifting wreck was not noticeable—would, indeed, have been fairly hard to measure.

"Keo. Take over from Mike. Free as much cargo as you can. I'll take the deck clips. 'Ao, salvage any stowed line from the lockers first, then get the sails. Don't waste time with knots. Cut the lines, but be careful of veins and valves. We don't know when or how fast or even whether that hull will go down. Mike, stay with me, and provide any muscle help I seem to need. If I'm under water and can't talk, use your eyes and head."

There was no argument. Keokolo was seven Kainui years older than Wanaka, nearly twenty centimeters taller, fifteen kilograms more massive, and her husband; but her seamanship rating predated his by over two years. This would automatically put her in charge in any outcity emergency even if she had not been the registered owner and commander of the *Malolo*. Also, shifting cargo that was already under water, even cargo packed to float, would call for muscle; she had divided the duties sensibly. Keo nodded, donned helmet, and slid into the sea.

'Ao did the same, swimming to one of the forward lockers of the awash hull and cautiously releasing its latch. Wanaka watched the child for a few seconds, decided she would need no help and was unlikely to panic, and turned back to her own task of freeing the quick-disconnects that attached the deck to the starboard hull. The latter was listing dangerously as its twin dragged it downward; the crew had already been forced from deck to coaming. If its gunwale dipped under, the commander's hope of salvaging any significant part of her cargo would sink with it.

She was not greatly worried about having to drift for a year or two, but she valued both the metal and her self-respect. Also, if they *were* rescued before chancing in sight of a city, the rescuers would be entitled to much of the cargo.

Two minutes' work freed the starboard hull from its dangerous burden. The deck slid off, or the hull went out from under it—none of the workers bothered to decide which; the important point was that the long, slender structure righted itself before going gunwale under, and crew and cargo still had something presumably navigable to ride. Mike followed Wanaka below the surface.

Keo was still engaged with the cargo lashings of the sinking hull; package after bubble-floated package of iron dust was being freed and rising slowly toward the surface. 'Ao had apparently finished the coils of rope in the lockers with commendable speed and was now slashing rigging lines from the mast and yard, obeying the order not to waste time with knots. Also commendably, she was looking around continually, and saw the captain's approach.

"How much ready cord did you get?" Wanaka gestured as she swam toward the child.

"There were ten eighty-meter coils of tow line, and four two-hundred-meter drums of rigging cord," she replied promptly.

"Did you stow them?"

"No. They're floating. I thought I'd better get to the sails in case they got pulled too deep when the hull sank."

"Good. The metal is most important now, though. I'll help Keo with that, and you join us when you get the sails aboard. We'll stay on the starboard hull unless and until the port one actually does sink. Then we'll string and tow everything we've saved—the starboard hull is pretty full. We'll hope the weather stays calm long enough to get things roped together and at least start the growing. Come on."

The weather obliged, though the suns were quite low when the job ended and work had been slow during the eclipse. 'Ao finished her last knot, dived, and swam back to the nearly awash hull to examine the ulcers near its bow.

The captain tapped her as firmly on the shoulder as the water allowed, and signaled sharply. "Keep away from that! You can see what it did to my ship! Do you want the same thing to happen to your suit?"

"But my suit isn't made of the same stuff. Whatever this is shouldn't infect it."

Wanaka's gesture was not a word symbol. She pulled the child toward her, spun the small body to face away from her, and did something to the twenty-centimeter disk between

'Ao's shoulders. Mike noticed that no tools were needed this time. 'Ao tried vainly to pull away, but the captain maintained her hold and finished what she was doing. A moment later the adults were stroking slowly back toward the intact hull while the smaller figure swam furiously ahead of them.

By the time the older ones broke the surface, their charge was aboard, sitting hunched up in the stern looking away from them.

" 'Ao. We still have to string bags. We can't keep all this stuff aboard." Keo spoke, judging that she was more likely to listen to him at the moment; he didn't know the details of the under water exchange, but could guess closely enough.

"String them yourself. You don't want me to help. Wanaka took points off me just for arguing, and I have a right to argue if you don't explain why you—"

"It wasn't for arguing—" the captain interrupted. "It was for ignoring a warning. You stayed right beside that infected spot while you argued. I know your suit is made of something different from the hull—of course it is. The two hulls are made of different materials and have different coatings for the same reason."

"I know. I was going to remind you."

"Did you know that the hull we've just lost had *four* protective layers, all of different composition, and that all have been penetrated? Do you know anything at all about oxygen gangrene?"

'Ao turned sharply. Her tear-stained face could be seen around her mask, along with its expression of surprise. "No! I—well—I—"

Keo, too tactful or too kindhearted to force an apology, answered her. "I'm sorry no one told you that, but you did know water was getting in. Don't worry; you can earn the points back. We'll be a long, long time getting home. Half a year, I wouldn't wonder, maybe a lot longer. There'll be plenty of time for you to do it."

All three looked up at the setting suns. Pahi, the brighter, was above and somewhat to the left of its slightly cooler and fainter twin. There was no overlap just now, but all three knew that Pale was slightly closer to them at the moment. No one really cared yet; such details as eclipse phenomena were important only during the final and most precise stages of a navigation problem. All but the least sea-oriented residents of Kainui, however, tended to keep aware of the general celestial status.

'Ao, without another word, went to the nearest hatch, took a coil of tow line, and began tying together the float-equipped sacks of iron dust and letting them go overboard. Keo finished climbing out of the water and stood as tall as he could, looking around to see whether any of the salvaged material had been missed and not yet moored. Some had, so he, too, plunged back in. Taking a coil of the light line the child had salvaged, he made his way to the farthest of the bags, and began methodically making crochet loops in his cord and tightening them around the prongs with which each float was provided.

Several times he returned to what was left of the *Malolo* to recheck his view from as high as possible, while 'Ao sat where she was and turned cargo into towage. The starboard hull was already too full, and none of the most recently salvaged material could be kept on board. Any ordinary rain-or-hail storm could drop the ocean's surface density enough to let the craft settle dangerously with its present burden; at this latitude—*Malolo* had shifted to an almost southward course after leaving the copper-fish—even the poleward-eastward relatively fresh surface current from the equatorial rain belt had picked up a fair amount of salt and could be diluted significantly by precipitation.

Rising wind interfered with the last part of the operation, but they lost no bags, to the captain's satisfaction. Everything they could find and catch had been secured, and the second stage of their problem could be faced.

Navigation on Kainui was complicated by the world's having no fixed reference points other than the rotation poles, which were too abstract to be found without rather complex celestial observation and much too far from where *Malolo* was now to be useful. Muamoku, the floating city that was their home port and nominal eventual goal, did not remain in one spot, though like the other cities it maintained latitude fairly well. No one really cared; as far as anyone knew, every part of the planet was like every other part except for current patterns, surface salinity, and coverage of floe ice. These varied with latitude, with minor statistical differences in frequency and intensity of storms, and with the percentage of ocean locally filmed over by fresh water or ice. There were no natural icebergs, since there were no islands or continents to build successive snowfalls up into glaciers. Even the surface water was extremely salty in many places and hence hard to freeze, but Kainui and its slightly smaller twin Kaihapa were far enough from the suns to freeze plenty of floe ice in the high latitudes in the winter hemisphere.

There had been attempts in the distant past to harvest ice from the southern cap and supply water that didn't need desalting, but unfamiliar conditions at the polar region seemed to have caused the disappearance of too many of the ships involved.

"All right, 'Ao, what do we do with the sails now that the

mast can't be used?" Wanaka felt that she had been a little severe with her punishment and hoped that the youngster could earn the lost points back quickly. She had no intention, of course, of broadcasting her doubts by canceling or reducing the penalty.

"We use them as sea anchors under water. The wind won't help anymore. Muamoku tries to stay at the south edge of the southern trades, and I don't really know even that much about any other cities. We'll have to rig a sea anchor and sink it far enough for deep flow to keep the surface current from taking us too far south. Then we can start—"

"How do we know the right latitude?"

The visible part of the child's face showed she had spotted the trap. "We don't need to. It doesn't matter as long as we don't get too near the ice. The suns will warn us of that, and I think we can check stars, too, but I expect you'll show me all that."

If either Wanaka or Keo was amused by the skillful return of the ball, neither let it show. The man nodded.

"You have the right idea, little one. You can help us rig the sea anchor if you're not too tired—"

"Of course I'm not!"

"Not tonight—" the captain interrupted. "Almost time for food, drink, air check, and sleep. In the morning we'll bend lines to the sails and get them back in the water, the sooner the better; the wind isn't taking us the way we want to go, and certainly the surface current isn't either. We're drifting—can you tell me which way?—and we're already way south of the city."

"South and some east, I suppose. That's what surface currents should be doing around here."

"How were we sailing before the hull began to sink?"

'Ao blushed visibly around her mask. The catamaran had *not* been traveling downwind, of course, but at an angle to it that would provide maximum speed. The more ocean that could be covered by daylight, the better the chance of spotting cargo. The child thought for a moment before she could remember which tack they had been on, and risked a guess. "Well, pretty near south." Wanaka smiled, slightly relieved.

"Not too bad. About one-sixty. All right, back to work. We can't accomplish very much more tonight, but should do what we can of the obvious procedures before dark."

'Ao splashed her way to the partly submerged cabin. She was still unhappy from the recent chastisement, but had learned not to argue a point when she knew she would, whether right or wrong, lose the argument. She would eat before being ordered to.

The emergency nourishment provided by noise suits was not particularly tasty, and she had been solemnly warned that people in suits outcity sometimes went dangerously long without eating or drinking when their minds were taken up with other matters. A twenty-year-old had that fact firmly impressed on him or her before ever going "outdoors"—leaving the limits of a city even in a small boat. 'Ao had no wish to lose more points on the same day, and showing initiative might even have the opposite effect.

She finished quickly, however, emerged again from the still floating cabin—Mike had wondered why the air lock sill was half a meter above deck level—swam to the formerly starboard hull, and moved cautiously along it to where the salvaged sheets of fabric had been rather hastily stowed.

"D'you know which was the big one?" Keo, who had followed her, asked. The child nodded and began working the appropriate sail out of the pile. The man took her at her word and began threading a length of cord through each grommet as it came into view.

The captain gestured to Mike to accompany her and swam to the cabin.

The passenger had been wondering why the sail could no longer be used in the normal fashion. Now he found out. The cabin had slid off the now detached deck; apparently some more quick-disconnects had been operated. The mast, still stayed, had fallen over, tilting the deck to a vertical plane as it did so. Wanaka ducked under the cabin, gesturing Mike to follow, pointed out to him a D-ring at the under edge of its floor, and made a pulling gesture. Hoani started to comply, but she stopped him, making a complex but meaningless gesture with one hand and, much more informatively, grasping his wrist with the other. Then she pointed to the opposite side of the cabin and swam toward it, motioning him to follow.

There was a similar ring on this side, which she took in her own right hand. Then she pointed back to the other side, extended fingers successively in a one-two-three gesture, and simulated pulling the ring herself.

Mike nodded comprehension, swam back to the first ring, and took hold of it. Wanaka made the gesture of approval he had seen earlier, which had clearly originated on Earth but not in any Polynesian culture, and repeated the one-two-three signal, pulling her ring at "three." Mike did the same. He was not too surprised to see two rubbery sacks rather longer than the cabin floor begin to swell very slowly. The importance of backup had apparently taken a firm hold on Kainui. One could see why.

He had already learned that sailing craft were extremely expensive here, simple as their basic growth ought to be; now he began to see why that was, too.

The expansion of the floats was so slow that he wondered why it had been important to start both of them at once, but he never remembered later to ask. The captain swam to what Mike still thought of as the after end of the cabin, pointed out two more rings much closer to its center line, and they repeated the coordinated pull. Two more floats began to swell.

It took fifteen or twenty minutes for the filling gas bags to lift the cabin clear of the sea. Mike assumed that the gas was not coming from pressure tanks but was being generated by some form of pseudolife. There would be no way to ask until they got out of the water, however. There seemed no immediate prospect of that; all three of the crew, aided by the unskilled passenger when he could be shown what to do, were engaged in what were presumably life-or-death tasks as *Malolo* gradually was transformed from a sailing catamaran into something of dubious drive source, with its former mast divided in two—there were telescoping sockets along it—to form cross members connecting the remaining hull with the cabin, making the latter a highly inefficient-looking outrigger. There were connectors in the right places for this job, too.

Wanaka did not abandon the separated deck, to her passenger's curiosity. This had tipped back to horizontal and floated awash when the mast stays had been cut. It seemed incapable of carrying anything useful; even little 'Ao's weight pushed a side or corner under the surface unless she balanced herself very carefully at its center. She was amusing herself trying this when the captain ordered her rather sharply to get back to work.

The three adults were now all out of the sea on the remaining hull; it was not necessary to use hand language. Mike could interpret tone as well as words. The child complied instantly without even looking indignant. Her doll, once more perched on her shoulder, made no comment either.

Mike, fully appreciating his own ignorance, decided not to ask about the deck just then. Also, he kept quiet on another point: after sunset there had until now been a light at the top of the mast whose purpose seemed obvious, but there was no suggestion of replacing it on, say, the roof of the cabin, though even the fainter sun was now almost below the horizon. He wondered what the chances might be of their being run down by another vessel in the dark.

His reluctance to look ignorant overweighed his slight worry that the others might actually have overlooked that matter. Once the still floating hull had been attached to the sections of mast and the latter in turn to the floating cabin, he entered with the others and settled down to the usual evening activities.

"Usual" was not quite the right word; it was the first time all four of them had been inside at once for more than a few seconds since leaving Muamoku. Also, there was much more than usual to do with the life-support equipment. Mike couldn't help much with this, but watched and listened to explanations, mostly from 'Ao, as the adult crew members toiled. The least pleasant of the explanations made it clear that they would possibly be eating suit-type synthetics until further notice once the parting gifts from the other ship had been used up. The pseudoplants that produced the more palatable substances might or might not survive their recent immersion; they had been on the deck, and Keo had not gotten them out of the water immediately. The realization that the suit synthetics had been most carefully designed to provide all possible human nourishment needs for an indefinite period did not offset the evident fact that taste had not been considered in the listing of those needs.

Or possibly, Hoani told himself, the notions of what tasted good had also diverged in the last few generations from Earth-human-normal. He promptly corrected that term in his mind to Hoani-personal-normal. There is a broad spectrum of "normal" human tastes.

Eventually the most urgent tasks seemed to be done, and everyone ate once more, quite slowly this time. Then the child was firmly gestured toward her hammock, and Keo without orders tumbled onto a bunk. Mike decided it would be tactless to claim the other, even though Wanaka showed no signs of being ready for it. She settled down to paper-work—*Malolo*'s log, mainly. Mike began to put his own copious mental notes of the day into permanent form, up to the minute.

He finished before Wanaka did, but eventually she stopped writing, too, and looked up from her desk.

"A nonstandard day," she remarked with no sign either of annoyance or humor. "You must have a few questions."

"Some," he admitted, "but I'm figuring out quite a bit for myself. If the kid isn't going to spend any more time at a mast-head, maybe you could have her start teaching me Finger."

Wanaka nodded. "Good thought. I doubt that either Keo or I will be able to give you as much attention as we hoped."

"That's all right. She knows enough more than I do to be an appropriate teacher anyway. But I can't help wondering whether she could tell me much about what turns the oxygen I heard Keo mention into a danger. I could only infer from the spoken words after the episode under the hull that she didn't know as much as she should about it, so maybe you should tell me."

The captain smiled wryly. "She can tell you as much as

either of us could. She was dangerously careless, and I had to downgrade her for it. But I may as well give you the picture.

"It's nasty stuff. You probably know that not everyone on Kainui is completely agreed about everything."

"I'm ready to take that for granted. You're human."

"Some people want to get a lot of oxygen into the air and at least get rid of the carbon monoxide. This, to be managed in less than a good many generations, would require pseudolife able to reproduce itself indefinitely—the sort of thing we told you back at the iron-fish that most of us consider unacceptably dangerous. Others remember too clearly the unforeseen side effects of that sort of seeding on a lot of worlds, including the Old one. The result, since there's never been any way to stop people from using knowledge once it's been acquired, is that some folks, and some whole cities, have gone ahead designing and releasing pseudos able to break down water, and others to take the oxygen and react it with CO before the freed hydrogen made a nuisance of itself, interfering with the redox we use in the city and on board here. Usually these things have been grown as symbionts. Unfortunately, while officially designed systems have so far behaved fairly well, some of those designed by hackers—individuals with less interest in social approval than in displaying their own skill—have gotten loose with some pretty sad side effects. No doubt their planners meant well, but having to keep a project more or less under water divides attention, and not knowing what other people were doing in the field—well, you've probably heard the story of a couple of nations having political disagreements back on the Old World. One of them sabotaged the guidance system of a missile being tested by its enemies, and targeted its makers' capital, not knowing that another department of its own government had already sabotaged the warhead. Not an unusual event in complex societies, or even in our quite simple ones."

"So there are oxygen-producers loose on the planet, not all of them putting their product to its best use."

"Exactly. And several types will leave the oxygen free to attack many other sustances than carbon monoxide. For the last couple of centuries cities as well as ships have had to keep a constant watch for such stuff. Nowadays we also have to watch out for people who dream up organisms which will act as predators for such oxygen-producers. These also, of course, have to be unlimited breeders. I've heard an old aphorism about the perils of riding a tiger, and I can see its implications even if I can only guess what a tiger is.

"Anyway, we've picked up a dangerous oxygen-maker. It's lucky it takes so much energy to break up water, and the things that don't dispose of the oxygen properly usually don't get much of it back. I do wish I could promise we could get you back to Muamoku. But we told you about that before we started."

"You did. No blame. I may have been safer crossing nineteen hundred parsecs between the stars, but I doubt it."

"Anything else you're curious about?"

"Lots, but you couldn't cover it in one night. I gathered the kid did something out of line? Part of what went on was in Finger, and most of the rest out of my hearing in the thunder. Don't give me details that you consider none of my business, but I wouldn't want to make any verbal slips that might either bother the kid or undercut discipline."

Wanaka glanced at the hammock and gave a terse account of what had happened. She skipped her own doubts about the punishment, since she was not completely certain that 'Ao was asleep. More to the point, she was quite certain that the doll wasn't.

Mike nodded as she finished. "All right. Remaining worry: just how sure can we be that that gangrene was confined to the hull we've shed?"

"I rather expected you to ask that. If you were wearing a rank badge I'd award you a couple of points. We aren't sure at all. My guess is that when we hit that whatever-it-was a while back—you remember—we picked up the infection. We'll never know just what the object was, but I'd guess either an egg designed to make oxygen seeds or more likely a bit of coral which had been around long enough to pick up practically anything. Viruses grow best on a solid surface, almost always. We pushed off the old hull, and I hope it sinks; but we'll have to check the one we still have carefully and frequently from now on."

"Something just occurred to me. If oxygen-producing pseudos aren't capable of direct reproduction, couldn't *Malolo*'s breathing equipment get infected?"

"It could. We carry several carefully packeted seeds for replacing that gear; and another possible source of our present infection would be a minor mutation of such a seed lost from another ship."

"Or maybe our own? Infecting from *inside* the hull?"

Wanaka raised an eyebrow, but showed no indignation. "That's conceivable, and we'll check. The seeds were, and I think still are, in the cabin, though. Thanks for the idea—I guess."

"And if the other hull goes, too? I was very impressed by your built-in trouble preparations, but there must be a limit to what they can handle."

"There is." The captain offered no more details, and Hoani decided not to press the point. He himself felt that knowing the worst was no more likely to bother him than not knowing anything, but Wanaka was the captain and he, by now, was quite clear about most of the implications of that fact. That was one reason why he had hesitated earlier before asking about 'Ao's offense.

Wanaka went on, "I'm going to sleep. Since we aren't under way, there's no risk of hitting anything, and if anything hits us there's not much to be done about it at night. Sorry, but you'll have to sleep on the deck."

"The one outside? Is that why you kept it?"

"No. The deck—floor—in here. Your breathing gear wouldn't last outside. I'm sorry if you don't sleep well, but we could be sorrier if I don't. *Au ahiahi.*"

Mike did not, in fact, sleep very well. He was pretty sure that the chance of being struck by anything must be considered negligible by the professionals, since they had both retired without setting up a watch, but he frequently found himself awake and listening.

There was as usual plenty to hear, much of it muffled by the cabin walls, but none of it was informative. He could only guess how much of the night he spent awake, but did not feel very capable when the other adults sat up almost simultaneously. It was dawn, though neither sun was actually up. Kaihapa had not shifted visibly, but that was no surprise; it would have implied hundreds of miles of longitudinal drift in a few hours, which would in turn have called for a most impressive sequence of storms.

The captain left the chamber briefly, and returned with a report that somewhat eased Mike's indefinite worries.

"The old hull's either sunk or drifted away. Keo, check

what we have left for infection, then come back and eat, and we'll set up the deep-sail and seed. Mike, how good are you at knots?"

"Hardly up to your standards, I'm afraid. But I have sailed on Earth."

"I know. All right. When Keo gets back we'll wake up 'Ao if she's still asleep, and she can join Keo and me. I'm afraid you have to stand—and I do mean stand—watch on the other hull, Mike."

Hoani realized that the "I'm afraid" part of the sentence was pure courtesy to a guest; he'd actually been given an order. He acknowledged it appropriately.

Keo was fully twenty minutes at his hull check, but finally reappeared to say that everything *seemed* to be clear. Mike, the captain, and the now awake 'Ao all noticed the choice of words, but no one remarked on them. They ate, checked their own and each other's breathing equipment, and went outside. Hoani would have liked to watch what the others were doing, but controlled his curiosity, swam to the hull and climbed onto it, and promptly had his attention taken from the others.

The sea legs he had acquired earlier were now out-of-date. The hull was less than two meters wide, and responded very differently to swells and microtsunamis than the catamaran configuration did. Also, there was much less to hold on to when he stood up. By the time he was actually able to get his attention away from his own feet, the others were all under water. He hoped he could find one of them if he had anything to report.

It was the most boring morning he had spent since leaving Muamoku. It was also the most tiring; standing in the one-third gravity was not burdensome even in noise armor, but the constant change of stance needed as the hull pitched, yawed, and jumped called for equally constant muscle work. He was quite proud of himself when the others surfaced and joined him; he had not fallen overboard even once.

He yielded to temptation and watched the final operation of the others rather than their surroundings. The deck—the original one—had been moored to the stern of the hull the night before; now an additional line was strung between it and the cabin. Keo took the hull end of what had now to be considered a control line, while Wanaka worked her way onto one of the cabin's floats and juggled with a second. Very gradually, Mike saw, a short and feeble wake appeared at the bow ends of hull, floats, and deck. *Something* was pulling the whole assembly, very slowly, aft, or at least keeping it from moving with the southeast-bound surface current.

A few minutes of watching and thinking provided him with a reasonable guess, and encouraged him to ask a question of Keo.

"How deep is the sea anchor, and how can you keep it there?"

The native answered without taking very much of his attention from the tow line.

"Between seventy and eighty meters. We've weighted it with some of the iron, and floated one corner to keep it more or less vertical, and attached the smaller sail to help handle the high corner. It was tricky arranging, and if we lose too much of the speed difference between the deep and surface currents it's unstable. If it goes too far down the whole vertical line of floats will collapse under the pressure and let the stuff sink, and we'll have to set it up all over again. As long as we're being pulled hard enough one way by the surface current and the other by the deeper one, the difference should tend to keep the whole thing up."

"Why the current difference? Though I think I can guess."

"Surface current is diluted water from the equatorial rain belt. It gradually picks up salt as it flows. The deeper one is saltier stuff returning toward the equator. That's a gross over-simplification, by the way."

"I thought it might be. How long will this stage take us?"

"To grow the new hull? Half a year, give or take quite a bit. Depends on temperature and a little bit on ion content of the water. To get to Muamoku afterward? Probably less, unless the captain decides to hunt up more cargo first."

Mike found himself out of questions. Both of Keo's answers needed digesting.

IV

CRESCENDO

The following weeks ought to have been boring for a person who had never needed much more than an hour to get from one place to another on the same planet, but they weren't.

Hoani was a perfectly capable sailor as long as he could see the sails. Wanaka had checked that very early, though she had never left him alone on watch while all the rest were sleeping. The sails, however, were now under water and quite out of sight. Their orientation with the currents they were supposed to be using could be told only from the length of cordage paid out to the various corners, and their depths from the angle at which these lines entered the water. This last was very hard indeed to observe, since they passed through rings on the sides and corners of the deck, which was now floating level with the surface except as waves lifted one corner or another. Two lines, on the nearest deck angles, led to the deepest sail corners, which were held apart by a length of the former mast; not all of this had been used to improvise "outrigger" booms. The peak of the larger sail itself was attached to the center of a shorter such length, whose ends were controlled by lines through rings on the farther corners of the deck. These ends kept separated the longer side of the small sail, while a fifth ring on the deck, midway between the last two, guided the line attached to its apex.

Had anyone described the job earlier to Mike he would have called it impossible. The small sail was maneuvered mainly to raise or lower very slightly the peak of the larger one; all three of its control lines needed very practiced handling. The other two were used to manipulate the slant of the larger triangle, so as to control its depth more coarsely.

Since even the child was able to do all this fairly well, Mike had no excuse to use the i-word; and to forestall any possible other risk of his suffering boredom, Wanaka had decided that 'Ao's physical strength was not up to handling all five lines. The passenger was therefore gradually earning crew status as well as learning Finger.

He made frequent errors. The child was more than ready to provide advice, but occasionally this was wrong and even more often the man failed to get her message promptly and correctly. The other two adults, when available, often had to do incomprehensible and complex things to correct the errors. The captain was quite tolerant about all this, the child considerably less so. She was young enough still to be more conscious of what she already knew than of what she didn't.

There was no such thing as really heaving to, though that was the theoretical aim. *Malolo* was either being borne more or less poleward by surface current—not precisely south; Coriolis force is ordinary inertia, and not confined to Earth— or dragged the other way by the submerged sail. The idea was to match the two effects as closely as possible to maintain latitude. Wind neither helped nor hindered significantly; it had only a little grip even on the cabin.

Besides latitude maintenance some actual maneuvering was necessary. Chance could be counted on to lead them into storms and hail, which were necessary for water, but manipulation was needed to keep them out of waterspouts that could be and had been both chemically and mechanically troublesome even when the ship was whole.

Continuous duty for everyone was not, of course, possible, and at times they had to accept inadequate control of the sea anchor while people slept, or merely rested, or attended to other necessary jobs. These times would obviously be fewer when Mike could handle an unsupervised watch, and he felt guilty at how long it was taking him to interpret reflexively the almost imperceptible shifts of the control lines.

The general asymmetry of the present craft didn't help, either; one hull paralleling a floating cabin was not the same thing as two essentially identical hulls. Hoani had almost, at one point, asked why the cabin wasn't set to lead, or trail behind, the remaining hull, or even to balance on top of it, but hesitated long enough to be saved from looking ignorant by another of Kainui's phenomena.

Early on the second day after the hull-seed had been fertilized and set afloat on its tow line, everyone's attention had been caught by an explosive sound abeam. Mike had watched with a crawling sensation along his spine as a jet of water far more massive and coherent than the usual waterspouts had climbed skyward a few hundred meters away. A wave spread outward from its base as it rose and another as it slowly collapsed. These did not travel rapidly in Kainui's gravity but were quite high enough when they reached the "ship" to lift first one side and then the other well over a meter. If the phenomenon had occurred much closer, or if the system had lacked catamaran stability, even Mike could see that the rest of their trip would have been performed swimming. He suddenly realized that a waterspout would have had the same effect and was thankful for his earlier silence.

This was unfortunate in a way; anything that discourages a student from asking questions can interfere with education.

He rather suspected that if *Malolo* were more completely wrecked the natives would, after appropriate preparation, start to swim, doubtless towing what they needed; but he decided not to ask. Aside from the possibility that the question would be deemed silly, he was a little afraid of the answer.

He did raise his eyebrows at Keo, who was closest. The man had no trouble understanding the implied question.

"Very rare," he remarked. "Only the second one I've ever seen. Strictly a matter of chance. A really broad sound front somewhere below gets focused just right by salinity or temperature lensing, and puts maybe a hundred atmospheres of pressure on one or two square meters just under the surface. That's one reason we make the cities in separate, flexibly linked units, and why some of us feel safer out on sorties. Actually I've never heard of anything as small as a ship's being hit directly by one."

"Who'd have heard?" Wanaka, 'Ao, and 'Oloa spoke together. Keo simply shrugged. He might, of course, have been merely trying to keep Hoani from panicking; if so, he didn't bother to justify himself, but simply went on. "Cities get hit every now and then, of course. That's why we keep *kinai aki* on duty."

Mike was a little startled at the use to which the term "fireman" had been adapted, but reflected that after all Kainui's atmosphere didn't support combustion even if the air in the floating cities did.

"Do cities get really damaged by these things?" he asked.

"Bad air leaks usually, float damage fairly often. I've never heard of a city's actually sinking—or being missed," he added hastily. "People have died from suffocation or poisoning, of course, when too much air got in."

"I guess I'm glad I didn't know about them before. At least we don't have to watch out for such things."

"Why not?" snapped 'Ao. "Just because one happened here doesn't mean another won't. The laws of chance don't have any memory!"

It was Mike's first chance to correct a native. He wished, though, that 'Ao had been an adult. "I know they don't, *tama-iti*," he answered. He regretted the word the instant he uttered it, but felt more need to justify himself than to apologize. "But we haven't been watching for them so far, and I don't see how we'd spot them coming anyway. Is there something you know about that that I don't?"

"No. You're right. I'm sorry. I thought—" 'Ao's voice trailed off.

"You thought you'd caught a grown-up making a mistake, didn't you? I don't blame you for speaking without thinking."

"I do," Wanaka cut in, "but as long as it was just words, complete with apology, we'll write it off as a lesson."

The child's relief showed around her mask, but she said no more just then. Instead, she flipped on her helmet and went to examine the seedling towing aft—southward, away from the sea-anchor system—of the cabin. She checked her safety line very pointedly first; the surface current being opposed by the sails was fairly strong. Mike wasn't sure whether she was more concerned with being swept away—after all, rescue would have been fairly easy—or losing more points.

The growing ship looked like a small but oddly shaped torpedo, and was already over half a meter long. The oddness sprang from what looked like a pair of short wings sprouting from each side. These, even the visitor could see, were actually keels; there were two hulls growing, deck to deck, just barely afloat. He had not yet asked why this was, or what would be done with the spare one; he was hoping to figure at least the first question out for himself as a matter of self-respect. Like 'Ao, he was feeling a need to be right.

He could not, of course, keep his eyes on the child; control lines were his business of the moment. He had never in any language heard the phrase "The buck stops here," but was very familiar with its underlying concept.

As it happened, although he was in charge of the sea anchor when things did go wrong some days later, it was not Mike's fault. At least, no one blamed him aloud, and he could see plenty of excuse for himself. It happened during one of the most violent storms of the journey so far, and his eyes simply couldn't follow the lines he was holding all the way to the deck. He didn't know that anything had gone wrong until the foggily visible deck itself suddenly went out of sight under water.

Everyone was helmeted at the moment. Mike flipped his own back when he did realize what had occurred, but no one could hear him—they might not have in the storm even if their own helmets had been off—and it was a minute or more before Keo saw him bareheaded and realized something must be wrong. By that time the cords were dipping deeply even at the cabin and hull ends, and the wake had vanished. *Malolo* had clearly ceased to buck the surface current.

Keo was at Mike's side, helmet also flipped back, in a few seconds, and seemed to understand the situation. He selected the line connected to the upper corner of the smaller sail, removed it from Hoani's grasp, and pulled on it hard. There was no obvious result; certainly the slope of the remaining lines did not improve. After perhaps half a minute Keo relinquished his hold on the cord and casually dropped it into the sea. Then he took one of the lower-spar ones and, yelling that Mike should follow his example with the one left to him, began hauling it in. By then it was fairly evident even to the passenger that the whole system had dipped too low, bitten too much into the deep current, and would have to be pulled up and realigned. He wondered whether anything had actually torn loose, but saw no sign of cordage, booms, or sails on the surface.

Meter after meter of tow line came in. Mike's stronger arms brought his side along more rapidly, and his corner of the big sail brought up against the deck and was stopped by its guide ring before Keo had finished with his. The native didn't seem bothered by this. When his own line was in he handed it also to Mike, and bellowed as loudly as he could over the thunder and hail, "Hold 'em both. When I wave hard, up and down, start letting them out together. And I mean *together*." Without waiting for an answer, he flipped on his helmet and dived toward the deck half a dozen meters away.

The captain and the child had by this time realized what was happening, but continued with their own duties. Mike realized that there was now no relative current to sweep a swimmer away, and wondered whether Keo had thought about that problem when the sea anchor would be back in place. He would probably not have dared say anything even had it been possible, but couldn't keep the thought entirely out of his mind, since even the most professional of professionals sometimes slips up. There seemed nothing to do, however, but keep tight hold of both lines as he had been ordered, and a close eye on the swimmer.

The latter soon ceased to be possible; Keo dived before he reached the deck, and was gone for several minutes. Mike could feel occasional tugs, first on one of his lines and then on the other, so he didn't worry as badly as he might have; but when the mate appeared well over a hundred meters beyond the deck—the blinding hail had almost ceased for the moment—the relief at seeing him at all greatly outweighed any anxiety over his distance. The latter feeling disappeared completely when it became obvious that the swimmer was still in contact. At least, he was clearly holding on to a cord, and gradually a sail itself became visible between him and the deck. It must be the small one; its backup float line could just be seen at its far corner, and Mike now realized that the two sinkers at the ends of the larger sail's boom were also against the edge of the deck where the control lines he was still holding entered the sea.

Keo now began pulling himself closer hand over hand. He reached the appropriate sail corner quickly enough and seemed to be examining something for a moment; then he let go of everything and began to swim toward where Mike crouched at the rear of the cabin. The two lines Hoani was holding were too far apart at the deck to be reached by one person at the same time, and he appreciated Keokolo's thoughtfulness. His climbing along one of them would have made it very hard to keep the pair paid out equally as his order had implied.

Of course, Keo *might* merely have distrusted Mike's ability to manage both. The latter decided, of course, not to ask about this when the swimmer clambered up beside him.

"A float got popped by something," Keo reported as his

helmet flipped back. He added a short phrase composed entirely of words unfamiliar to the other. "Nothing we can blame on you, Mike. We'll have to make another as soon as possible. Belay your lines where they are. You might as well go inside and charge up your breather while I get something from the cargo line. I wonder if Wanaka will be able to bring herself to dump a unit of iron."

The implication here was obvious enough; the float from one of the cargo units would have to be put to a new use. Mike said nothing as Keo reentered the sea.

Neither did Wanaka, now close enough to have heard the mate and with her helmet off. Her attenion was otherwise occupied. She gestured 'Ao to approach, and issued some instructions in Finger. She pointed first, which helped the man tell that the orders concerned the floating seedling, but his increasing grasp of the gesture language was not yet up to getting all the details. Apparently she was supposed to take care of it somehow, but Mike had no idea of what danger it might be in.

The child entered the water and flippered toward the little torpedo shape while pulling the now slack line that had been towing it. Reaching her goal, she submerged with it, and Hoani lost track of both in the once more rising storm. He returned his attention to the mate while the latter freed an iron unit from the cargo line and brought it back to the cabin. He received, rather to his surprise, a nod of appreciation from the other; he had expected his watchfulness to be taken for granted. The nod was not accompanied by words as thunder still discouraged speech even out of water, but a few gestures got across; Mike obediently belayed both the cords he had been holding, appreciating Keo's failure to check his knots, and accompanied the latter to the air lock.

Keo insisted by a few Finger symbols and some less formal gestures that Mike use it first, but they were both inside the cabin in moments. The captain stayed outside for obvious reasons. 'Ao had not yet reappeared. Keo kept silent, busy detaching the float from the unit he had brought in. This seemed not to be a very demanding task, and Mike ventured to ask what 'Ao had been told to do.

"She's under the cabin, keeping the new ship from the hail and making certain nothing happens to its tow line. The danger isn't really very great, but that's the only ship seed we have. If we lose it, we have a long swim in a direction we'd have to guess."

"I suppose the captain is watching the kid, then."

"Probably not. 'Ao knows what's going on. She's no more immune to mistakes than either of us, but Wanaka has a lot of other things to do. So have we. Could you check our life support while I'm at this? I'll have to go outside again to install this float as soon as it's ready, because right now there's no way to maneuver if a spout crowds us. I won't be able to watch you, but I know the little one has shown you about some of it, at least."

Hoani nodded and complied. The psuedoliving intake stage oxidized carbon monoxide with sodium peroxide from the "leaf," getting enough energy from the process to feed its own intake pump. This kept the inside pressure slightly above Kainui normal even after the carbon dioxide had also been precipitated. There was no reliable way to keep even self-healing machinery completely leakproof, and it was much more than merely desirable that all leakage be outward. Given the length of a typical human generation, it would be a long, long time before the Kainuian human subspecies' tolerance for CO increased usefully.

Keo had left long before Mike finished his assignment.

When he emerged from the cabin at last, the storm was still visible to the west, blocking any view of both Kaihapa and the suns, but was no longer dropping hail on the vessel. Background thunder was still louder than usual, but now caused Mike less trouble because of his improving skill with Finger. 'Ao had returned to the hull leaving the seedling in the water, but the latter's tow line was still slack. Keo, out of sight and presumably under water, had evidently not yet reestablished the sea-anchor system. Wanaka had three control lines in her right hand and two in her left, and seemed to be giving them her full attention. Mike glanced around, noted the usual number of waterspouts within sight, but was pretty sure that none was a menace at the moment. Experience had taught him that Keo's present job would probably take only a few minutes.

He was right. The mate suddenly appeared beside the deck and gestured rather casually, and the captain promptly signaled to Hoani to take over the lines. 'Ao started to take up her usual position beside him, but was gestured back to the hull and set to another task—Mike, his attention focused on the lines, couldn't see just what. He wasn't sure just how happy the sudden increase in trust made him feel. He had flown sailplanes on Earth, and would always vividly remember his first solo landing. However, the watch ended with no further troubles.

The seedling continued to grow, sometimes several centimeters in a single day, more often slowly enough to need careful measurement. The two little hulls were now separated slightly as a developing deck appeared between them and grew. After a few days, Mike risked a question.

"I don't see any sign of a new cabin. We make do with this one, I take it?"

Wanaka nodded. "That would be a whole set of separate seeds. Cabin and air lock unit, air equipment, sails, furnishings. Much more expensive ones, too. And much more trouble getting them to stop growth just at the right stage in each case to let them fit together properly."

"We have them, I suppose."

"Many of them. The most important. The first three I mentioned, plus the *kumu'rau*. We'll have to deploy that pretty soon, by the way, at the rate we've been using oxygen. It'll complicate handling the sea anchor, and probably cost us some latitude one way or the other, and we'll be really vulnerable to waterspouts while it's out, but that's not a choice."

Hoani nodded. He had seen many times, before the journey had become so exciting, the strip of pseudolife that didn't look particularly like either a tree or a leaf but would at least have been green with chlorophyll if either of the suns had produced much green light. It was nearly ten meters wide and more than a hundred and fifty long, and trailed behind *Malolo* during times when the suns were highest and Wanaka had forced herself to admit that oxygen was as important as new cargo and hence to accept the very low sailing speed demanded by its production. Just now it was reeled up out of the sea at the aft end of the cabin. Mike had been wondering how long they could do without it, but had been reluctant to ask. He knew they had left Muamoku with a very large supply of oxygen cartridges, presumably fully charged, but didn't know what "very large" meant in terms of person-hours of breathing.

Except, of course, that there was no way for it to be a definite number. He himself would have been tempted to top the oxygen supply off every day, but now realized that with the "tree-leaf" deployed they were much more vulnerable to waterspouts. The captain had now decided that the risk had to be taken.

Each of the next ten days, for the four hours when the suns were at their highest, the tree-leaf—Mike had decided that *kumu'rau* was probably an evolved blend of Hawaiian and Maori—was paid out. Fortunately it trailed in the opposite direction from the sea-anchor system, and didn't directly interfere with the control lines; but since it was affected by the surface current, its deployment did add problems to handling these.

Mike was not excused from this complication of control duty after the first day, which he spent watching Wanaka and Keo very closely indeed. Thereafter he was on his own, and to his own slowly decreasing surprise made no serious mistakes. His self-confidence, along with his fluency in Finger, was growing, though there was still very little risk of his reaching the dangerous overconfidence level.

It was 'Ao who was now totally relieved from the sea-anchor duty. Her muscular strength was not really up to it, and there was much else to keep her busy now that Mike needed practically no advice. Actually, everyone except Mike was mostly keeping alert for waterspouts while the oxygen-maker was deployed. *Malolo* was little more maneuverable at such times than when the sea-anchor system was out of action. Whenever one of these whirling towers of spray drew close enough to worry Wanaka or Keo when Mike was on the lines, one of them would take over without comment and 'Ao, without orders, would take the growing shiplet out of the sea and lash it quickly but securely onto the remaining hull. Mike wondered what would be done when it grew too big for this procedure.

He trusted the professional skill of his hosts, but knew

there were conditions that even the most competent of seamen couldn't handle; and he was pretty sure that the captain, good as she was at keeping her feelings to herself, was becoming more and more worried about something.

It was not the oxygen. After ten days of using the *kumu'rau* the cartridges were as full as when the sortie had started, and she made no attempt to hide her relief the last time it was reeled in.

Also, the problem was probably not their location. While it was not really practical to take a noon sight by instrument on the twin suns, it was evident that the ship's latitude had changed. They were too far south. While even Hoani could see that *Malolo* had drifted some distance eastward, since the sister planet Kaihapa was clearly nearer the western horizon, longitude mattered very little. The likelihood of having to circumnavigate a parallel of latitude in order to find a given city went without saying in Kainui seamanship. It was not a difficulty of knowing the ship's longitude, which could be worked out celestially with enough effort; the eclipses of the two suns provided time information. However, knowing that of the ship's intended port with no effective long-range communication was entirely another matter. A marine chronometer is useful only if there is a Greenwich, and it stays put.

Trouble did eventually come, of course, but Mike never found out whether it was the one worrying the captain.

Even the procedure difficulties threatened by the growing replacement ship failed to become serious. Well before the seedling was too heavy to ride the remaining hull without sinking it gunwale down, it had become far too bulky for even Keo and the captain together to hoist, regardless of ingenious improvisations of cordage. This seemed to bother no one. When a waterspout threatened, the growing craft was now simply moored as securely as the supply of rope would permit and allowed to float by itself. This, of course, made the duty on the sea-anchor lines too complicated for a beginner, and Mike was sometimes rather glad to see a spout developing nearby. It saved him labor, and he had certainly not yet become overconfident.

On the second of these occasions, however, one of the mooring lines became slack—no one ever found who was to blame, but 'Ao and Mike could share the happy confidence that it wasn't *their* fault. This allowed a minor collision, and one of the growing keels was badly cracked, while a scratch penetrated all four protective coats of the older hull. Now even Mike was informed enough to worry, though the scratched area was repainted using appropriate seeds as soon as the waves permitted.

Wanaka then changed procedure. Fewer but longer tow lines were used, and the embryonic vessel was kept farther from the rest of the system. This was not too difficult when the wind more or less directly opposed the surface current, which it usually did. Otherwise, while the little craft still floated with keels horizontal, the high side of the developing deck sandwiched between them now caught a good deal of air. And made maneuvering very complex indeed.

This Mike could understand. What bewildered him was that at the next approach of a waterspout, 'Ao was ordered to swim to the tow and lash herself to it as solidly as she could— in fact, the captain went with her and supervised the process before rejoining Keo at the lines.

She gestured to Mike, who for the moment was free of duty, and ordered him in the hand language he now understood quite well: "Keep your eyes on her. If she's swept away, tell Keo. Don't waste time reporting to me."

He nodded understanding and returned to the other hull, which offered both a higher viewpoint, since the cabin roof was no place to ride out a waterspout, and was also closer to the object of his attention.

He was just a little undecided. He would have conceded to anyone the importance of discipline in any sort of crew, but couldn't help feeling that he himself should be more able physically to perform a rescue; the captain might technically be a better swimmer, but in the storm-lashed sea it looked as though muscle might be a greater need.

Demand for strength might explain why she should have ordered him to tell Keo first, rather than attempting rescue himself; no doubt there were routine procedures familiar to the sailors that Mike knew nothing about. His intentions wavered while *Malolo* and her attachments rocked and shivered in the turbulence around the spout.

It was quickly over, waterspouts traveling as they do, and no decision had to be made; 'Ao was still in sight and lashed in place when things quieted down. Wanaka immediately swam to the child and helped free her from the lashings, and they returned to the cabin together.

In another two or three minutes it was safe to doff helmets, and Mike looked for signs of her ordeal on the child's face. He was astonished to find none visible around her mask; she seemed as perky as though she had enjoyed the ride.

It seemed very likely indeed that there was something else Mike didn't know. He decided not to inquire what it might be; he was not yet emotionally convinced that almost the only silly questions are the ones not asked.

There was now a good deal of work for all; the spinning of everything in the waterspout had upset the sea-anchor control system—it was lucky that the oxygen leaf had not been deployed—and badly tangled the set of tow lines that had kept the child and her charge part of the system. The seedling, now more of a sapling, had indeed come much closer to the main hull than anyone had wanted; Mike actually remarked aloud to Keo how much better it would have been if they had managed to salvage more cordage from the diseased hull, and the other had merely nodded. This left Hoani wondering whether he had overshot being merely right and become blatantly obvious.

With the sea-anchor controls reestablished and Mike once more handling them, the other two adults—'Ao was in the cabin, to eat and sleep—left Hoani's range of vision and attention, saying something about rearranging the tow system. When they came back more than an hour later, they were still talking but seemed dissatisfied.

In spite of this, the same general procedure was followed with the next unavoidable spout, and the next. There were no collisions on either occasion, but each time the captain and mate spent a while afterward trying to improve arrangements. Even Mike could see that they were getting even farther south. There was simply no quick way of judging the changing speed of the deep current.

Then several days passed with no real incidents. Spouts were seen, of course; a total lack of them in Kainui's grossly unstable atmosphere would have been really noteworthy, but none came near enough to require action. Just possibly the adults became too relaxed; it was 'Ao who shouted the warning about another approaching menace and dived for her hull station without waiting for orders.

Wanaka followed as usual to make sure of child's and doll's lashings, and by the time she got back to Keo and the lines the *Malolo*-sea-anchor system was again out of control.

Mike did not actually see the separation of their tow; he was almost pulled from station and lifelines by an especially violent jerk, had to glance momentarily around to find another grip, and when he looked up again could see nothing but seething water where seedling and child had been.

It took several seconds to convince himself that tow and rider had really disappeared, and more than a minute to make his way across to the cabin where captain and mate had just stopped working because the sea anchor had been disarranged again.

By this time Mike had no trouble getting his message across in Finger, which was fortunate because all helmets had to stay tight. The captain asked only three questions, and of course her facial expression could not be seen as she gestured.

" 'Ao was still lashed to the ship when they disappeared?"

"As far as I know. I didn't see the actual separation. I told you why. She was there only seconds before."

But Wanaka didn't seem to be thinking along whose-fault-was-it lines. She could not, Mike thought, possibly have blamed him for the loss of the tow, but his failure actually to see it go might be another matter.

"And her lashings seemed secure when you last *did* see?"

"Yes, Captain."

" 'Oloa, too?"

"Yes."

The captain's tension disappeared, as far as could be told with her helmet on.

"Perfect," she gestured.

V

QUALITY

The gesture might, of course, have meant merely "Good," or "All right," or "Fine"; there was a fairly broad spectrum of possibilities. Mike's confidence in the exact meaning was not yet very high. However, as he currently understood Finger, it had been very emphatic indeed, and he couldn't see why.

He found himself almost on the point of asking questions, but there was no time. Wanaka was issuing orders. Also, he was feeling more and more as though he should already know some of the answers.

"Keo, surface the sails. Lucky they're already out of drag mode. Mike, help me deploy the leaf; we might as well stock up on oxygen while we're waiting, and it'll keep us closer to the current."

"Waiting? Shouldn't we be looking for the kid—and the ship?" he added. He certainly didn't know *those* answers.

"No. They'll have to find us, which means we'll have to stay as nearly right here as possible. Lucky the storm's passing. Surface current will be about the only variable they'll have to allow for."

"They?" The word had seemed reasonable when child and ship had been the subject; now it sounded odd. However, Wanaka's hands were too busy with the roll of leaf-equivalent to allow her to answer, and her face was not visible at the moment. She might have made a slip of the finger, no doubt; the gloves of the sound armor were not heavily padded, but were hard-shelled, exquisitely jointed to permit any finger movement, and depended on impedance mismatch rather than padding to keep dangerous noises out. They permitted Finger communication easily. Mike felt a distinct suspicion that she had deliberately given him meaningful information, possibly to see whether he'd wind up more or less confused than before.

Of course, the plural might still have included the ship, but that made two questions rather than one. He glanced at where Keo had been, but the mate was already in the sea carrying out his orders. Hoani felt like a student who had just been handed a surprise quiz with the question in an unfamiliar language. He didn't even have time to think; helping pay out the long ribbon of pseudolife without harming it took too much of his attention. So did the the constant reminder that the storm had not completely passed, that there were plenty of ordinary waterspouts in sight, and that the hull was no steadier than usual.

When helmets could once more be removed, he had another surprise: Wanaka was taking what looked like position sights on the suns and Kaihapa. The instrument she used had no real optical parts; it was basically a simple cross staff, the arms modified with double sights to allow aiming it at both suns at once, with a tray of viscous fluid serving as a horizontal reference. Mike did manage to solve that one after a few seconds; he had, he remembered, used the trick himself when

no horizon was visible, measuring the sun's angular separation from its reflection in a horizontal surface. He could even
see why no lenses were being used here. It was not just that
silicon was virtually unobtainable from Kainui's highly acidic
ocean—carbon-based optics could have been grown, presumably—but because the hazy, ripply atmosphere made really
precise sighting on celestial objects impossible anyway. Magnifying optics would have done nothing for accuracy.

What he didn't see clearly was why such observations
were worth making at all. True, the captain had said something about "waiting" for 'Ao, so it was obviously important
to try to stay put in some sense or other; but if they were
yielding to the current anyway . . .

Maybe it would be more profitable to go back to just who
"they" might be—Wanaka had certainly used the plural gesture. Most likely "they" were 'Ao and the growing ship; but
that, as he had already noticed, posed two major questions. It
was just believable that the child could swim back—if she
knew the right direction. The storm was not a frontal disturbance; Mike had seen no such phenomenon yet on Kainui. It
was simply a local convective instability resulting partly from
temperature and partly from humidity. Its winds were mostly
short, random gusts and the child shouldn't be far out of
sight. Mike had no idea, however, how 'Ao could possibly
know the direction.

If "they" did mean child and ship, it was even harder for
him to see how the latter could be propelled, even granting
that the direction was known. Though the vessel was only
part-grown, the thought of a ten-year-old swimmer towing it
any distance was hard to accept, not to say utterly ridiculous
even granting her background. So was the idea of her separating the growing sections, assembling them properly—includ-

ing attaching the deck, stepping the mast, and setting sail—and sailing.

Hoani was now, however, firmly determined not to ask; if he *were* being tested, he was not going to give up without trying. It didn't occur to him that the captain must know him pretty well by now and might be doing a little research of her own.

The rest of that day, and most of the next, were as close to completely idle time as he had experienced since *Malolo* had left her home dock. For the first time, Wanaka and Keo left Mike alone on the hull, essentially in charge of everything, while they caught up on sleep. The closest to a general instruction he received was a "Keep your eyes open"—from Keo, not the captain. Hoani had gestured agreement, and was left alone with mist, the suns, Kainui's twin planet, and the usual microtsunamis, waterspouts, and thunder. He had not even been told what to do about the leaf-strip if another storm were to find them.

Common sense suggested that it should be reeled in. Or did it? It had drag, Wanaka had mentioned the need for them to stay in position with respect to the ocean, and hail *shouldn't* do much damage to the band of tissue. Besides all that, it would probably be impossible to reel it all in between the time the need was evident and the arrival of spout or storm.

Mike thought about it all for a while, smiled suddenly behind his mask, got to his feet with the usual difficulty, and began scanning the surrounding sea carefully for one partly grown replica of the *Malolo*. No, not yet a replica—probably. He couldn't be sure about that, but at least he could watch without asking silly questions.

Some hours passed. Astronomy distracted his attention

for a while as the suns disappeared behind Kaihapa while in mutual eclipse, but his attention was eventually rewarded.

Malolo junior—he wondered fleetingly, whether his suggestion would really be followed—had come quite near before he spotted it; he had allowed for its being much less than full size, but had no way to guess at its state of assembly. It was hard to see how that could possibly have changed since he had last seen it, and he was somewhat relieved to see that it hadn't.

The growing hulls still floated in contact, on their sides, with the still very small deck sandwiched between them. Part of this was catching wind, obviously; the other part, submerged, must be playing the part of a keel. 'Ao was in the water at the near end, apparently pushing the pair of hulls to one side in order to alter its heading. They were almost exactly upwind from Mike, but not so nearly up current. The man was impressed to see how precisely the "ship" moved toward him when the child stopped her efforts. He watched entranced while it drifted to the end of the hull where he was standing. He almost failed to catch the line 'Ao tossed him, and almost as absently moored the immature vessel while the child, paying him no other attention, swam to the cabin, pulled herself out of the sea, and disappeared into the air lock.

Mike, once more alone, stayed where he was; perhaps he should have called the others when the little ship first appeared, but he had simply not thought of it. Reporting 'Ao's return was now obviously superfluous, and anyone could see that having no one at all on watch was a bad idea.

Bad even with an apparently empty ocean, as a micro-tsunami immediately reminded him.

No one emerged from the cabin for some time. He spent the interval making sure the little ship was secure, and in brooding. He was mystified, and wanted in the worst way to ask questions, but could not get rid of the feeling that Wanaka had already provided at least part of an answer; and he was almost neurotic about making a fool of himself. Ship and child had arrived safely, which seemed to confirm the implication of Wanaka's "they," but still left unanswered several questions Mike didn't quite want to ask because he feared he should know the answers already—she had, after all, been right about the return.

The most mysterious of all, and incidentally the most reasonable excuse for simply starting to ask questions regardless of personal face, was of course: *How had 'Ao found her way back?*

What could the sighting on the suns have had to do with it? There had been no way to get results to the child on a planet where the loudest sound of a bullhorn would be drowned out by thunder in a few hundred meters, the brightest portable signal light stopped by haze in a kilometer or two, and constant lightning and ionized haze made essentially all electromagnetic communication equipment useless. Hoani had no confidence in the concept of telepathy, and was quite sure that if it really occurred and the people of Kainui had reduced it to engineering practice, either their culture would be very different from what he had seen so far or the range of the phenomenon was disappointingly short.

Best to wait for more orders. One could hope that Wanaka, with the responsibilities of a captain, wouldn't merely give him a detail-free command like, "Start it growing again," just to see how much Mike had figured out for himself. He *could* answer that one with some confidence, of course, since he was quite sure the little ship was still growing—but maybe it wasn't! How could he be sure?

Stop it, Mike Hoani. She can't expect you to know *everything.*

Or would she?

With nothing, as far as he knew, left to watch for, Mike immersed himself more and more deeply in his brooding. Speculations that centered more and more, as the minutes went by, around that word "they."

And around the natural near-total absence of silicon in a highly acid ocean. And the long-obvious fact that the doll contained some sort of data-handling gear. And the fact that a good quiz answer might, after all, consist in asking a straightforward question.

Which, of course, might still make him look silly.

Equally of course, the principal set of generally silly questions consisted of those not asked. The only specific exceptions he could think of at the moment were "Are you crazy?" and "Can I trust you?" Maybe he'd get the first for an answer. It would be nice to be able to show he wasn't, and maybe nicer to have someone else appear silly.

Mike made up his mind at last, and brought his attention back to *Malolo*'s surroundings. He could only guess how long he had been musing, but began to wonder why no one had emerged from the cabin. Was 'Ao in real trouble from hunger or possibly oxygen lack? That seemed unlikely. While almost certainly concerned about such matters, judging by her haste in getting to the cabin, she had been active and well coordinated when she arrived.

No doubt she was reporting in detail to the captain. Mike would like to have heard the details of that report, but had, after all, been ordered to stay on watch.

So he watched. No ships. No patches of metal-reducing pseudolife, as least any that he could recognize. Nothing to run into, presumably; *Malolo* was essentially motionless with respect to the surrounding water. No waterspouts with constant bearing; keeping sure of that took more of his attention, now that he had really decided to ask a question, than anything else.

Occasional spells of doubt about the wisdom of asking that particular question at all, or whether to do it inside the cabin or out, or which of the group it would be best to have listening when he asked it, did occur; but he held firm to the basic decision and settled the corollary details one by one.

Outside. With everyone present. With all helmets off, especially the child's; Mike was pretty good now at reading expressions around breathing masks, he felt sure. So what were they all doing? When would they come out for whatever needed to be done next?

He had completely forgotten again that the child had probably had little food or sleep for at least a day and a half, until he began to feel sleepy himself, and that raised a new if minor question. Just when would he be relieved? Should he use the signal bell? Wanaka would never have forgotten such a matter. Never. She was, after all, a rated ship's master. For some reason, even Mike was unable really to worry about such a slip on her part.

He was, however, very tired and almost hungry enough to nibble on his suit's emergency food before anyone appeared from the cabin. Then it was only the adults, reasonably enough, so he couldn't ask his question right away.

The little catamaran was inspected thoughtfully, with no comments that Mike could catch—it was moored now to the cabin, and he was still on the old hull. Then time was spent resetting the submerged sails, with both Wanaka and Keokolo in the water. Then another sight was taken, this time by Keo, on the suns and on the twin planet, which even without instruments was now visibly lower in the western sky. So much for any possibility that the other sighting had somehow been transmitted to 'Ao.

Then Mike was dismissed with the unneeded advice to eat, sleep, and check breathing gear while Wanaka took over the control lines and Keo began reeling in the "leaf."

Inside the cabin there was nothing surprising. 'Ao was asleep, not in her hammock as expected but on one of the cots. Her back was turned toward anyone in the room, and it was obvious even to Mike that the pattern between her shoulders was more complex. Since she was deeply asleep, he decided not to congratulate her just yet. Very briefly he considered asking his question of the others anyway, but thought better of it. After all, he wanted to check *everyone's* reaction, whether or not he got an answer. All he could think of now to worry about was whether, with routine pretty well restored, he would have to wait for another emergency before everyone would be on deck again.

He didn't. The half-grown ship called for nonstandard activity, he found almost immediately on being roused himself. He was told that it *was* still growing, and that the process would cease only when the first coat of protective paint was applied. This would have to be done quickly enough so that one hull wouldn't outgrow the other too much, though actually this would probably happen to some very slight extent. Even though the process was not actually a painting job but merely a planting of very sticky seeds along each keel, the growth of the "paint" was never perfectly uniform.

This was all interesting, but to Mike the good point was that everyone would be outside the cabin for a lot of the time even before the growing was ended. It was less than a day, in fact, before the chance came to ask his planned question.

He was back on the control lines, with 'Ao beside him still giving occasional advice in Finger. The weather was calm enough to allow helmets to be open. The only problem at first was that both captain and mate were on the old hull, too distant for a question asked in a normal voice to be audible above the thunder, even allowing for the usual effect of the thunder on a "normal" voice.

Then for some reason the officers both went to the growing ship, not yet noticeably larger than when 'Ao had brought it back. It was still moored to the cabin, but had been brought between that structure and the old hull to render it more accessible, so Wanaka and Keo were only a couple of meters away.

For just a moment Mike's determination wavered, but he managed to keep control of himself. He got the question out.

"'Oloa, how did you know which way to tell 'Ao to steer?"

Only the child looked startled. She glanced at her elders, obviously wanting advice. The captain gave a very slight nod.

"Tell him, 'Oloa." It was 'Ao who spoke, not Wanaka.

"I have an inertial system," piped the doll. Mike's mind raced.

"Of course, you can't guide us to Muamoko." He made it a statement, not a question.

"Of course. I don't know where it is."

"You couldn't estimate?" The doll was silent.

"I don't think she knows that word," said 'Ao. "I'm just guessing at it myself."

"Too many variables, anyway," the captain interjected. Mike nodded thoughtfully.

"Silicon?" he asked. Wanaka smiled visibly around her mask.

"Yes. Imported. 'Ao's parents are quite wealthy, and are very fond of her. 'Oloa cost more than *Malolo* did. They very much want to get 'Ao back, properly educated, of course."

"Did I get those points just for waiting?" 'Ao asked.

"More for knowing when to stop waiting, and most for the general recovery," was the answer. "You'll have to wait longer before I can post them all, though. I promise that's the first thing I'll do when we have the cabin installed on—what should we call the new ship?"

"*Humuhumunukunukuapua'a*?" suggested the child.

"It won't be very small when it finishes growing, remember."

"Well—it has to be some kind of fish. That's the rule, since there aren't any real ones on Kainui."

"How about *Mata'italiga*?" suggested Mike again. He was beginning to get a grasp of some of the more abstract customs. The hammerhead shark was a variety whose name might not have survived very well in the Kainuian language mixture, and therefore be less an everyday name since Samoan seemed to form a rather small fraction of the evolved tongues.

"*Kumu*," suggested the captain.

"*Pilikia*," was Keo's rather cynical suggestion.

"We have trouble enough," retorted the child and the captain, almost together.

"I know. Sorry. I'll settle for Mike's suggestion."

'Ao approved immediately, perhaps out of courtesy, and the other suggestions were dropped, partly because a converging spout and thunderstorm made maneuvering necessary and upset the sea-anchor arrangement once more. 'Ao scurried back to *Mata* with an armful of oxygen canisters to replace the ones she had used while away, and lashed them and herself in place. Very seldom does only one thing happen at a time.

But practically nothing hectic occurred for several days— at least, nothing out of the ordinary, though no one had reason to be bored, especially when at the sea-anchor controls.

Mata'italiga grew visibly. The captain checked over the seeds that would provide its protective coatings and stop its own growth. She, Keo, 'Ao, and even Mike held several discussions over the best order for applying them, all realizing that any given selection could be wrong. Mike became very fluent in Finger, and while no formal declaration about it was yet made, effectively reached the status of able-bodied seaman. Even 'Ao came to trust him at the sea-anchor lines.

Mata's growth would have to be stopped at a rather precise size, in order to install the old cabin properly. They were, Wanaka and Keo judged, within two or three weeks of this point when temptation reared its head.

And the captain yielded.

Wanaka was a highly skilled sailor and a more than competent trader; she had contributed significantly to the general wealth of the city of Muamoku in recent years. For reasonable decisions, one needed reliable data, and she knew this perfectly well. She became less sure of herself when data seemed less than reliable, but usually made decisions anyway, as she did this time—quite aware that doing so might be expensive or fatal. She knew, in other words, that life was sometimes a gamble, and accepted the fact. She also accepted the fact that failure to decide was itself a decision, and therefore a gamble.

The decision this time was clear enough, considering both

the available and unavailable facts. What was left of *Malolo* drifted into contact with a patch of weedy jelly rather similar to the iron source that had given Mike his first experience with Kainuian metal recovery. It was not quite a collision; the mine, or fish, whose species no one on board could recognize offhand, was riding the poleward surface current, while the ship was holding against this as well as could be managed with the sea anchors. The current itself was not very strong, however, by this time. They were much farther south than Wanaka liked; their "navigation" had been far from perfect.

The pseudoorganism was much larger, apparently, than the iron and copper sources Mike had seen before. Like those creatures, this one's body was a huge and gelatinous expanse floating a meter or so below the surface of the sea, covered even more completely with the energy-drinking "leaves" than the iron-fish had been. Its total size could not be made out from any one spot. Leaf shape and color were markedly different from the others.

Wanaka didn't consider this at first, however; the immediately meaningful fact was that the sea anchor, or at least its control lines, had been trapped in the jelly. *Malolo*'s remaining pieces as well as the growing *Mata* had essentially become part of the drifting organism.

Specifically, they were drifting with it, away from the equator as if they weren't already farther than anyone wanted. No sun-sighting was needed to know that; 'Oloa confirmed the fact when asked. The doll was being consulted much more frequently now; Mike suspected that he had not been told about its nature and uses earlier because he had had no need to know, and might have said something unwise when mixing with the crew of another ship. Neither Wanaka nor Keo had confirmed or denied this suspicion because, being Mike, he hadn't asked.

The drift of the organism was not rapid, and would presumably become less so as the low-salinity current weakened and grew saltier with changing latitude. They would not, Hoani supposed, be carried too far from the latitude where they had met this fish; he guessed they could separate themselves from the thing in a day or two at the most, perhaps much less.

Like Wanaka, he had reached a conclusion with inadequate data. Unlike her, he didn't know it.

Just how long it would have taken to get untangled from the pseudoorganism he never found out. Wanaka issued no orders on the subject. She questioned Keo intensively—excessively, Mike felt—about his certainty that he had never seen or heard of this particular species of fish. She even asked 'Ao. She sent the mate overboard, and even went herself, to collect leaves and leaf stems and bits of the thing's tissue, and to look for pods of water and metal. She spent time in the cabin consulting a voluminous reference work, one of the few items of written material aboard, apparently without result.

There were plenty of water pods to be found, but no metal.

And that was the lack of data that guided Wanaka's decision.

Well, Mike thought quietly, it *was* her profession.

"We don't need to worry about drifting away from this thing," the captain remarked slowly, after much fruitless trying to identify it. "Mike, you stay on the ship in case anything does happen. Keo, 'Ao, and I will examine every bit of it we can reach, for however long it may take us, to find out just what besides water it gives. For a start, though, you and Keo deploy the leaf; you'll have to pull it out, of course, since there's no relative current now to drag on it. 'Ao, check the food; we won't be in motion, and we may have to do something about getting new sea water into the growth tanks."

Mike ventured a question, not seeing how this one could be silly.

"How long do you think we'll stay with this thing?"

What he could see of her face looked determined. "We have no idea yet about how big it is, but we're not leaving until we've either checked every square meter of it or found out what metal, or metals, it traps. It's got to be something really rare, or we'd know already."

"It couldn't be something designed just to desalt water?" The question popped out before he meant it to, but Mike decided that it couldn't be regarded as silly, either. She evidently didn't; she paused before answering.

"I doubt it. The drinkable water is usually incidental to reducing metal ions, and I don't see much use in building a creature *only* for water and turning it loose at sea. Even for a city, there's usually enough hail from storms to keep people in drink and baths. That's one reason cities don't usually let themselves drift too far north or south of the temperate storm belt. I suppose you could think of some excuse for a simple desalter, but this one is big enough for a city, it seems to me, and surely wouldn't be floating free. Anyway," she admitted frankly, "just the possibility of rare metals is enough to keep me right here. We're staying 'til we're sure, one way or the other. I hope you're not too bored after the first few weeks."

Hoani was a little startled at the suggested time, but tried not to show it. He had the sense not to say it, but still hoped they'd encounter another ship now and then; his own project could always use more language data.

He wondered how Wanaka and Keo would react to another ship's appearing. The captain was clearly feeling possessive about this creature, just as the crew they had met earlier had seemed to feel about their copper mine. Wanaka had left this to them without argument, presumably as a matter of custom. If this creature were as potentially valuable as she seemed to hope, custom might not be enough for others—or conceivably, he suddenly thought, for her. He remembered the captain's mentioning people "with a one-sided notion of trading." This was a remarkably gentle description of piracy, after all.

And certainly there would be no question of escaping from anyone on *Malolo*'s remains even if they could be disentangled from the jelly.

Of course, if they were given time, *Mata* would be grown and assembled, and a new, smooth set of hulls might outsail—

No, it wouldn't. Ships didn't grow barnacles on Kainui.

He wondered briefly whether traveling away from the equator would make any change in their chance of meeting other vessels, but couldn't bring himself to ask this question. He should know enough to answer it himself. He probably did; but some of the things he thought he knew suggested one answer, and some the other.

Anyway, he told himself, knowing chances didn't mean much. They were only chances. Wanaka certainly knew them, and had not, apparently, let them influence her decision.

Mike did briefly wonder whether the crew might have some sort of weapons no one had mentioned. After all, he had been left to solve the 'Oloa problem pretty much by himself, and weapons would likely be another item they wouldn't want him to mention at the wrong moment. On that one, though, he couldn't even decide which way even to *hope*.

In the meantime, there were other things to do. Fifty meters in from the edge of the unknown patch of pseudolife, there was much less effect from the tsunamis and other surface disturbances. He asked the captain about the fresh water supply and, with her permission, took advantage of the absence of the crew overboard to doff noise armor and enjoy a bath.

The others had, after all, done the same from time to time. He was pretty sure of this, though he had always been in the cabin when it happened. He tried, in his mind, to connect this privacy attitude with Earthly Polynesian customs, and wasn't sure he'd made any sense of it.

At least, it gave him something to think about besides the current shortage of language data.

Mata grew, and grew, and grew. Wanaka ceased examining the whatever-it-was, though the others did not, and spent most of her time making measurements. The seeds for the protective coating that would stop the growth were ready. Hoani had been told how they were to be used, but didn't expect to be allowed to help with the operation. He was right about this, but they did let him watch.

The seeds were far smaller than the one that had carried *Mata*'s specifications or the one that had controlled the division of the iron-fish. In shape and size, they were coinlike disks about Mike's index finger joint across, and apparently very sticky, and of four different colors—black, bright red, pale green, and deep yellow. Keo and the captain worked together applying them along the still deck-to-deck hulls, about five meters apart, being careful to work from bow to stern and to apply a given pair of seeds at the same moment on each side. They made no effort to plant a given color at the same moment; Mike guessed that the colors represented different protective coatings, and that it must make no difference in which order these were applied.

The seeds lost their coloring almost at once, and seemed to spread out and become too thin and/or transparent to stay visible. Whether they were simply changing shape or taking nutrition from the water and actually growing Hoani couldn't judge at first.

However, the moment the "planting" was done, captain and mate separated the hulls from the deck sandwiched between them, lifted the latter into position, fastened it with obvious haste, and then began briskly splashing sea water on the sides of the hulls that had been mostly above the surface. Mike decided the stuff must be growing.

The next step was to work the cabin up onto the new deck and into position, deflate its floats, and fasten its numerous quick-disconnects along the hulls.

'Ao had been responsible for the newly grown mast and boom while this had been going on. She had lashed them along Mata's port hull, but stayed with them just in case. Now all four lifted the mast onto the deck, finally got it upright, and stepped and stayed it.

Mike had supposed that the original sails would be recovered and used, and was wondering how they would be retrieved from under the jelly. It turned out, however, that a budlike growth he had not really noticed before, about half a cubic meter in volume and now trailing in the water below the deck attached to the latter by a meter-long stem, contained a new set.

Keo examined this object carefully and reported that it was not quite ripe. The intense activity tapered off. Water had been resupplied from the mysterious growth. Equipment and supplies that had been crowding the cabin were relocated to their former positions on the new deck. The "leaf," now in its proper place aft of the cabin, was again deployed; there was now room for more charged oxygen cartridges, and at this latitude the leaf was getting less effective; the suns weren't rising as high in the north.

Mike Hoani resumed his lonely watch, on a thankfully much more stable deck, and the other three went back to their researches with the apparently lonely water pods.

And the suns made their noontime passages lower and lower across the northern sky.

VI

AMPLITUDE

It was not too surprising, Mike told himself later with all the clarity of hindsight, that it was he who found the metal. The background knowledge of the other three had operated against them, though his own lack of Kainuian experience had not really helped at first. It was only after two or three baths when, on his own responsibility, he decided to replace the water he had used that it happened. The other adults were asleep. Leaving Hoani on watch alone had become routine since they had in effect moored the ship to the putative metal source, though he was not at the moment alone. 'Ao was at her masthead. Wanaka pointed out afterward that he should not have gone overboard without having someone else on deck who would not have had to call for help if he got into trouble in the sea, but under the circumstances was quite gentle about it.

It was Hoani's own slight clumsiness caused partly by his lack of experience and perhaps by a little fatigue that caused the discovery.

The water pods in this pseudoorganism were large, more

than three times the volume of those furnished by the iron-fish that had provided his first mining experience at sea. He had collected perhaps a dozen of them, returning each one by one to the ship, and accepting the help of the child in getting them aboard and then into the breakers. 'Ao had descended to the deck when he went overboard. He was beginning to wonder how many more would be needed, so his attention might have been slightly distracted. Also, he was getting a little tired. The pods weren't very heavy, especially in the local gravity, but the sound armor was somewhat clumsy even for the natives.

In spite of the very low weight he started using both hands to extract and lift each pod from its gelatinous receptacle. Since the pods had only one handle, a simple loop of rope-like tissue, his other hand had to reach into the space underneath the water-filled sack to support it.

And there was another, much smaller pod there. Not attached, but there. In the *same* pocket as the water. How had the others missed it?

Obvious enough. One handle had been enough for them; they had not felt underneath, and the reddish jelly was much less transparent than that of the iron-fish.

'Ao was at the rail waiting. With his helmet sealed and his hands full, there was no way for him to say anything; but when she saw the tiny—less than ten centimeters long—container, the child, who had taken her full share of the metal search effort since its beginning, made up for his silence both with her own voice and the signal bell. Wanaka and Keo were beside her on the spot in moments, still adjusting face masks.

Mike climbed aboard without attracting, or distracting, their attention, and looked at his discovery over 'Ao's head.

It was little different in shape from the iron, copper, and

titanium pods he had seen before. It was soft to the touch, so the contents were probably in powder form like the others. The color was black, which might have been due either to the fineness of the powder or the composition of the envelope. The captain was weighing it thoughtfully in her hands, tossing it from one to the other, but this could hardly be helpful in guessing at density; there would certainly be space between the tiny grains, and there was no telling from outside what fraction of the whole volume this might represent.

Wanaka finally looked up from the object and caught Mike's eye. "How did you find this?"

He told her. She and the mate exchanged glances, but no words, which were superfluous. She simply nodded her head toward the others and gestured to the rail. Both flipped on their helmets and disappeared overboard.

One fear, that they might have been wasting days by not looking under the water pods, was quickly dispelled, to be replaced gradually by another. In the first half hour of search, neither the child nor the mate found any more metal.

Wanaka seemed to be on the point of sending Mike into the sea with them, but visibly changed her mind. Instead, she ordered him to stand watch and joined the searchers herself. It was she, some fifteen minutes later, who found the second pod, under a water sack just as the first had been.

By sunset, six more had been located. Since no one had tried to keep track of the area covered or of the number of water pods checked, there was no reliable way to guess at the amount of metal that might be available; it was not even certain whether or not any of the water sources had been counted more than once.

The search was better organized the next morning. Instead of simply groping under each water container and leaving it where it was, the finder removed it from its pit. There was no way to take it all aboard, since the breakers had been filled the day before, and the thought of setting drinkable water adrift would never have occurred to a Kainuian; but since the water itself was fresh, and at this distance from the tropical storm belt the surrounding ocean was quite salty enough even at the surface to let the pods float, they had a compromise. Two hundred meters of line were used, with a pod attached every two meters, to form a ring of water-filled floats; and each new pod thereafter was released inside the ring. By the end of the day, some statistics were available: out of twenty-seven hundred water sites investigated, forty-one had also contained metal. The next day produced a nearly identical ratio.

No one yet could guess what the metal might be.

It was rare, obviously. This did not, unfortunately, mean that it was valuable. While the pseudoorganism might have been deliberately designed, in which case the stuff *should* be worth keeping, pseudolife was little more immune to natural mutations than any other kind. For a little while Wanaka had been thinking, or perhaps dreaming, of something like silicon, but this was ruled out very quickly. Even in powder form, with presumably nothing but water between the grains, the stuff was much too dense. She thought of platinum and its relatives, though these were useful only in small quantities as chemical catalysts on Kainui, but the creature now calming the sea around them differed greatly from any of the royal-metal trappers to be found either in the reference book or anyone's memory. For one thing, having water and metal in the same pit seemed to be unique.

Mining boats simply could not carry large amounts of

sophisticated analytical equipment like X ray or neutron diffraction cameras or NMR machines. This was a matter of economics, not size. Very rarely a skipper with enough capital might decide to specialize, ship one such device and ignore the commonly traded materials, but Wanaka had never regarded this as a hopeful technique.

She also lacked any reliable way to decide how far from the equator she should ride this possible Golconda. They were already well south of the latitudes maintained by most cities in this hemisphere. Temperatures were dropping, though not yet far enough to affect either safety or comfort. They were riding with the current and pretty well shielded by the organism itself, so there seemed no risk of a serious collision. The winds were weakening; in a few more degrees of latitude they would be in a belt of calms, she knew. This might make it difficult to get back to a city, Keo pointed out.

The captain shook her head negatively. There *were* cities all over the south temperate zone, though not, of course, in the ice floe regions near the poles; and in any case there would be some chance of meeting other ships. If the metal were worth trading, of course . . .

The crudest of tests—exposing a small sample of the material to the quite acidic sea water—eliminated the alkali and alkaline-earth metals at once, and made items like zinc and even tin unlikely; density had already ruled out most of the latter anyway.

Wanaka was becoming irritated. "Mike, you're a linguist, aren't you?"

"If anything, more of a historian, Captain."

"Not a chemist." There was no question mark.

"Well, Captain, I learned what you might call—"

"*Not* a chemist."

"No, Captain. I could figure an equilibrium constant if you gave me the electrode potentials involved, but—"

"Would that help with this problem?"

"It might, but you—"

"But I don't have a handbook with the potentials."

"I don't suppose so, Captain. I have no equipment to measure them, either."

"Then we'd both have saved breath if you'd stopped at 'No' a few sentences ago."

"Yes, Captain. Sorry."

"*I'm* sorry, Mike. I'm getting bothered by all this. I know what I should do, but can't make myself do it. I'm setting a very bad example to 'Ao, too, and I suppose I'm letting you in for more risks than you bargained for."

Mike grinned behind his mask, and gestured quickly, "I'm not bothered. There's nothing that's happened yet that hasn't been interesting." He was not exactly lying, but tact seldom is. Not exactly. "I'll be able to write an adventure story as well as a thesis."

"And you haven't done anything that was a bad example to me," 'Ao shrilled, "except that time when—"

"You asked for that," Wanaka cut in firmly, "and you've earned back more points than you lost then anyway, which was zero. I'm not apologizing for anything. We're staying with this creature as long as we possibly can, and that could be pretty long, considering the water situation."

"Then we'd better keep on collecting this stuff, whatever it is," pointed out Keo, "and treat it a little more carefully than we have been. The little screen says it's not very radioactive if at all, but it could be as poisonous as osmium or nickel, say."

So they collected carefully, without the help of Mike or of 'Ao, who as a growing child should not be exposed to chemical risks if at all possible. She made no objection, and both of them as the days passed grew a little casual about marine discipline, especially in the matter of conserving fresh water.

Storms and waterspouts were becoming a little less frequent as their distance from the equator increased; the surface water was saltier as well as cooler, and had a lower vapor pressure. Extremely well-focused sound waves should not, of course, be affected by this factor; but Keo, who had made such a point of their rarity, began to wonder if they might not be favored by it. Twice in the space of a few days they occurred within sight of the ship, once a couple of hundred meters beyond the edge of the metal-maker and once actually within it too close for comfort to the ship, tearing a two-square-meter patch of the jelly loose and hurling it far into the air. The only one to react visibly was 'Ao, who looked down at the mate from her crow's nest in rather critical fashion the second time.

The stock of metal grew very slowly, of course, but it did grow, and eventually Wanaka developed a new worry. Did they now have too much of the stuff to be safe? At Muamoku's latitude, if they decided to go there, the ocean would be decidedly less salty and *Mata* would float correspondingly lower. Sadly, there was no way of calculating "correspondingly," since there was no precise measurement of *Mata*'s depth-versus-displacement function on hand.

And would it be a good idea to bring the material back to the city at all? The captain found herself developing a touch of Mike's fear of looking silly, with much better reason for it than he usually had. Spending weeks or seasons collecting something completely useless, however excusable by the circumstances, would certainly make her colleagues and competitors smile behind their masks, and in a city there'd be no masks to hide the smiles.

Maybe it would be better to get away from this creature and simply cruise around, remaining in deep-south latitudes, of course, but not going as far as the ice, or even the calms, hoping to find another ship rather than a city, and trade off some of this stuff before going home.

She could tell, with perfect truth, why it *might* be of unheard of value. The opposite possibility would be obvious to any competent trader, so there would be no need to mention it aloud, and practically any skipper would be willing to take at least some of her stock on chance, she was sure.

So she finally ordered the loading to stop. Plimsoll marks didn't grow automatically on hulls, and the paint certainly provided none; there was no more magic in nanotechnology or pseudobiology than in "real" life. She and Keo spent some time trying to calibrate *Mata*'s still unmeasured displacement. Their guesses were based mainly on the assumption that it wouldn't differ much from *Malolo*'s. Memory provided some highly imprecise estimates of those.

It also took a day or so for her really to make up her mind to abandon the vast supply of fresh water now floating in its pods beside her ship. She did not actually let it go, finally; she moored it to the remains of *Malolo*, still anchored to the nameless organism by her sea-anchor equipment.

She couldn't quite decide whether to hope that someone would find it, or not. She wasted no actual time on the question since she had no real faith in the efficacy of hope.

Mike suspected a little of this, though much less of it came up in conversation. He was mainly going by the length of time it was taking the captain to announce decisions.

She hesitated only once more. 'Oloa, on request, reported that their latitude was forty-three degrees south, which agreed with the rudely measured apparent height of the noonday suns. Wanaka decided to wait until it was just forty-five before leaving the scene. She offered no explanation, though even Keo raised an eyebrow. 'Ao showed no reaction; Mike wondered whether she was afraid of losing more points, or was genuinely indifferent. He himself would have preferred, by now, to get on with whatever might be going to happen next.

He was therefore somewhere between relieved and delighted when 'Ao, who was again spending most of her time at *Mata*'s masthead, called out, "City! A hand south of east!"

What they all saw was certainly city-sized, looming indistinctly through a kilometer or so of haze. Even to the Earth native, however, and at this distance through the haze, there was something about it that did not suggest human design. It was not very dark in color, rather a light gray, with an occasional brief sparkle that might have meant fabricated metal. Unusually for him, he expressed the doubt aloud.

"Are you sure, 'Ao?" he asked. "I've only seen Muamoku, I know, and I suppose cities differ from each other, but still—" He doubted this on-the-spot conclusion even as it left his lips. Cities on Kainui all had the same environment and faced the same engineering design constraints. They should be pretty similar. He did not end his sentence, and closed with "Are you sure?" again.

"What else could it be?" the child responded indignantly. "There's nothing else in the world anywhere near that big."

"You mean that high out of water," Keo corrected.

"Of course I do. Metal-fish are *bigger*," granted the child. Even Mike could feel her effort to make the lack of precision seem unimportant. "But I couldn't have seen a metal-fish or anything *except* a city that far anyway."

"Of course you couldn't," the captain interjected soothingly, "but how about Mike's question? Are you really sure that's a city? We're heading within a few degrees of it; keep your eyes bright and let us know when you spot anything strange."

Everyone noticed the "when," but only Mike wondered whether the captain, too, thought there was something odd in the sighting or whether mere wish might be involved. He felt pretty sure by now that Wanaka was in no real hurry to reach a city. She was not actually an indecisive person—no one in her position could be—but, at the moment, would have been very pleased with any source of data that might make decisions less nebulous.

"Don't spend all your time looking at that hump. Check for ships in the neighborhood," she added to 'Ao after a few minutes. Hoani conceded her a point; there had always been scores of full-sized ships and smaller vessels busy, and visible if close enough, within a few kilometers of Muamoku. He had seldom known just what they were about, but they had been there. Of course, *Mata* was too far yet to let 'Ao spot such an entourage, but he, too, followed Wanaka's order as well as he could from deck level.

The captain's next command, only a few minutes later, fully restored Mike's normal tendency to keep his question count low. It was called to the masthead, but not to 'Ao.

"'Oloa! Look as closely as the haze will let you for the next few minutes, and see whether you can figure how much of that thing's motion is due to wind alone. A city's floats wouldn't reach very deep. You know what the shallow currents are from this metal-maker's drift. Is there any sign that the big thing is being influenced by deep currents as well as wind?"

The doll's tiny voice was inaudible over the background noise, of course, but 'Ao reported that it had acknowledged the command and was presumably obeying.

The object was farther away, and much larger in size, than anyone had guessed at first. One side of its water line was now almost on *Mata*'s course as she was borne along by the metal source; the other, Keo and Wanaka judged as their viewing angle changed and gave them a better idea of its size, must extend at least two kilometers to the left of it. It was certainly not following surface currents, though the wind should be having some influence on anything that size; its peak seemed three hundred meters or more above the sea, though estimation was difficult. As it neared, the general gray tone showing through the haze became patchier. The spots reflecting the sparkles of sunlight remained too small to show any details, but did grow brighter.

"Hadn't we better get out of this mess so we can maneuver, before it's too close?" suggested Keo. Wanaka shook her head slowly.

"Anyone spotted any boats?" she asked, loudly enough to be heard aloft. No one had. 'Ao, however, saw *something*.

"There are floating things. Not boats. Some of them are almost black. Some of them might be ice floes—but remember I've never actually seen one of those. Just pictures. These are sort of humped up out of the water, and I thought ice floes were pretty flat. If they're mostly ice, they must go too deep to get over this creature we're on; but if they're shallow-draft enough to float over it, maybe we'd better get clear. We're not actually aground on it, but it sometimes humps up enough to push on the keels, and it'll drag on them if we're sailing. I can feel that from up here."

Wanaka took the advice, to the child's delight. "Right, 'Ao. Quarter sail, Keo; if we do hit anything, we don't want to hit it hard. Head us to starboard of the big lump. 'Ao, keep us clear of any small ones. There shouldn't be much ice until we're farther south, of course, but you're right. Some of those bits could be floes, and we certainly don't want to hit the higher stuff."

A thought struck Hoani, and after a moment he decided it offered an excuse for a question. "You said something, a long time ago, about people who assembled bergs—big ice masses—and rode them into city latitudes to sell for water."

"So I did. But this is a hundred times as big as anything of that sort I ever heard of. Besides, all that was long ago, early in history. Of course, someone may be playing with some improved technique. That may be why it doesn't all look like ice."

"And why I thought it was a city."

"A bigger berg would lose a lot smaller percentage to melting in a given time," Mike remarked.

"So it would. On the other hand, a piece of ice that size would lose most of itself to melting before any city could use much of it up. I don't see why anyone would make one that big. 'Ao, take a look at that thing and see if you can spot any people on it."

"Can't, *tautai*. There's too much of this smaller stuff floating around us, and I have to watch that. We're starting to move, so I won't be able to look out for anything else. Mike has good eyes, though."

For the first time since reaching adulthood, *Mata* was

moving under her own sail, drifting slowly over the jelly, dragging on it sometimes, but finally reaching not very open sea. Nothing, as far as anyone could tell, was under her keels but water for nearly three thousand vertical kilometers.

The huge drifter was less than a kilometer away by now.

" 'Oloa, do you think it's mostly wind or mostly current?" Wanaka called to the masthead. The doll's owner answered.

"She's not sure, since she doesn't know how deep it goes, but there must be a good deal of deep current. She says to tell you, 'Three unknowns at least, only one equation.' I don't know what she means, but those were the words."

"I do. Thanks," shouted Wanaka.

Mike knew, too, and assumed that Keokolo did.

Keo, at the tiller, guided them close enough to one of the small floating objects to give everyone a good look. For a minute or two they examined it silently.

It was about three meters across and extended something over half that distance above the surface. If it had much vertical symmetry, which seemed doubtful, it must be nearly spherical. There was indeed ice covering much of the thing, but under, or inside, that ice was some much darker material. Keo hove to, a few meters from whatever it was, without waiting for orders. Its motion was almost entirely current controlled, apparently, like their own at this point.

"Shall I take a real look, Captain?" asked the mate.

Wanaka shook her head negatively. "Mike," she said slowly, "take a safety line and see what you can make of it."

The order made sense. The thing was unfamiliar to the natives; Hoani was as likely as they to make some sense out of it—perhaps more likely. If he got into trouble, Wanaka and Keokolo were much better qualified to help him than he would be to help them. He flipped his helmet forward, latched it, and went overboard. Two or three strokes, even with his limited—by Kainui standards—swimming skills, brought him against the object. He could not, of course, remove his helmet, but the others were close enough to read his fingers. He reported after only a minute or two of examination.

"The light stuff is ice, all right. It should be melting; I suppose it is. It feels a lot colder than the water. What there is above the water line is mostly dark stuff glued together by ice, but just below the surface and as far down as I can see there's more ice and less of the dark stuff. It's mostly orange and red in color. Just a minute. It's either bobbing up and down a lot, or staying put as the waves pass; there's no telling which." The others had seen this already, and given up much hope of Mike's being able to make a detailed examination, but Wanaka made a brief, encouraging gesture.

Mike turned back to the floe for a moment, then faced *Mata* again with a golf ball-sized fragment that showed no ice coating at all resting on his palm, and held it up for the others to see. "Shall I bring this aboard, or could it be something that shouldn't touch the hull?"

"Bring it. Just don't pound on anything with it," replied the captain. Keo gently pulled Mike back by his safety line, allowing him to give full attention to keeping the specimen from striking the hull. Hoani reached up, handed it to Wanaka, and climbed aboard. Examination was interrupted briefly by a call from the masthead.

"Keo! Maneuver! There's another one closing in." The mate sprang to the tiller, and started to work *Mata* over to a less crowded area. The motions of the floes had a random component; they were high enough to be affected by wind, but no two were more than vaguely alike in shape. The captain stopped him almost at once. "Heave to again. There's no dodging everything. Look." She gestured around.

Every two or three meters there floated a dark, apparently ice-free fragment of the red-brown material. The hulls had already struck a number of the pieces, apparently with no damage; the impacts had not been hard enough to attract attention, though Hoani suspected there'd better be another close paint check before long. He lay down on the deck, reached overside, and picked up a much larger ice-free piece. This one crumbled into almost invisibly small particles in his grip.

The fragments that fell back into the water sank at once, to his surprise. He thought about this for a moment while getting back on his feet. The others had not, apparently, seen; the adults were still examining the first specimen, and 'Ao on her masthead wasn't close enough.

The captain looked up, first at the mate and then at Hoani.

" 'Amu," she said firmly, "but I've never seen any just like this. Have you, Keo?"

To Mike, the word was a general Samoan one for *coral*, but must, he was sure, carry a different meaning here; this ocean was far too acidic for anything made of calcium carbonate, and silica wasn't an option.

"The big pieces float higher than ice," he pointed out vocally. The others looked at him quizzically. He lay down once more, reached overboard, and repeated his previous attempt to pick up one of the dark floating fragments. The result was the same, including the behavior of the crumbled bits. Wanaka nodded thoughtfully.

"Full of air cells whose walls break very easily. I wonder why they last as long as they do? That whole piece pulverized under finger pressure, but some of them have hit the hulls time after time without collapsing; and that big chunk you took this one from . . . I don't understand. Does this remind you of anything you've seen on Earth—or anywhere else?"

Mike had to admit it didn't.

"Air cells would account for the low overall density," he admitted slowly, "and the actual cell walls must be a lot denser; but why are they so fragile under one treatment but hold together, as they'd pretty well have to, under storms, waves, hail, and other ways this world of yours can beat things up?"

Since he had merely restated Wanaka's implicit question, he got no answer.

'Ao called their attention to another bit of data.

"Look! The big piece is turning over!"

It was, though not very rapidly. The side toward *Mata* was rising, revealing a new ice-coral mixture. Mike wondered briefly whether his removal of a few grams from the near side had upset some remarkably delicate equilibrium, but decided as the turning went on that this couldn't be the answer. The lump did not stop rolling until it had made something like a third of an overturn. Not an exact half, they all could see, though it was now evident that its overall shape was very nearly a sphere.

The masthead made another report. "There's a little more ice showing in what's just come up." There was a brief pause, then, " 'Oloa says we all should see that the ice is denser than the other stuff, and says I should be able to tell her why the big lump turned over. I can't, right now. How long do I have before I lose points?"

"At least an hour after one of us figures it out," Wanaka answered promptly. Then she added, "And if that takes more than ten minutes, you don't lose any." The doll's voice could just be made out in a momentary pause in the thunder, but its words were indistinguishable to Mike. If they carried any meaning to the captain, she did not relay it.

It was evident that there was no use trying to dodge all the flotsam. If it were going to do any damage, it had probably already done it. Keo, at the captain's orders, got under way again, though very slowly indeed—they were still avoiding the larger collections of ice and coral. The city, which it probably wasn't, still floated with its near side about half a kilometer away, and a trader would no more forgo a closer look than would a scientist.

The fine bits of coral were everywhere; there was no avoiding them. The larger chunks of ice-coral mixture, many up to ten meters across, were no problem. Twice, as they passed close to one of these, it turned itself leisurely over; the roughly spherical shape was starting to seem reasonable to the adults, but well over 'Ao's allotted hour had passed before any of them actually worked out the cause. As usual, it was embarrassingly simple. Keo, for good reason, saw the answer first.

He was still at the helm, and had been watching a particularly large chunk for many minutes, since their course lay quite close to it. It slowly dawned on him, as they neared, that it was not now turning over but was, very slowly indeed, *rising*. There was more of it out of the water than had been the case five or six minutes before. Then as *Mata* reached the nearest point to it on her course, the turnover started with unusual speed. This time, again, the near side was rising, and without waiting for orders the mate steered even closer. Wanaka seemed about to say something, but apparently decided to trust the helmsman.

He used voice, and his tone held satisfaction.

"I get it. I see what 'Oloa meant. The ice is denser, and of course the part under water melts faster. The body rises, and its center of gravity rises faster because it's the part under water that's losing weight. When the center of gravity gets higher than the center of buoyancy, it has to turn over. Anyone who's ever planned a boat knows that. Since the things aren't perfectly round, and probably don't have the same density all through, they don't always tip in the same direction or by the same amount."

The others nodded slowly, and Wanaka called the information up to the masthead. 'Ao, while long since relieved from the worry about losing points, was audibly annoyed at not having worked the answer out for herself. She had, after all, been taught the relevant physics, like anyone who would be expected to spend her entire adult life between floating cities and boats.

They had reduced their distance from the "city" to a few hundred meters when the child restored her own self-respect.

She called a question down from her perch. It was carefully not worded as a warning or even a question, of course, but it deflected the thoughts of all three adults onto an interesting line.

"I wonder how often this big thing turns over . . . and which way is next." Wanaka and Keo reacted, but not verbally.

The basic wind was still fairly strong at this latitude, but its direction was inconvenient. Keokolo had to tack several times. He also made skillful use of the more or less random gusts around two local storms, in a maneuver that Mike thought of as slingshotting; but it was over an hour before they were out of the thickest part of the flotsam. Even then, three of the crew felt a little uneasy whenever they looked back at the huge drifter; their line of sight was still uncomfortably upward. That was unusual on Kainui.

Wanaka looked straight back, without any upward component to her line of sight, and a frustrated expression showed around her mask.

"Well, it can't be a city, but there's a lot more there than ice. I wonder what it would be worth?"

"We could wait until it does roll. Then there'd be plenty of time before it happened again," suggested 'Ao.

Wanaka did not respond to this suggestion, leaving both Mike and the child wondering whether or not it had been silly enough to cost points.

She also said no more about the forty-five-degree latitude limit. She had managed to scoop up several bits of the floating coral without destroying them, and spent hours during the next days as *Mata* was borne southward in examining them as closely and thoughtfully as possible. Sometimes she did this alone, sometimes she consulted with Keo or even Mike. 'Ao stayed at the masthead most of her waking time, since in a sense they were under way.

The ship's equipment did include a small magnifying lens. This had failed to reveal individual grains of the still unknown metal powder, but did make barely visible the separate cells in the coral that apparently held air for flotation but which shattered completely all the way through a particular specimen if given even a slight excuse. The gas might not, actually, have been air, they all realized; destroying one under fresh water—the captain decided the knowledge might be worth the use of that commodity—produced sinking dust motes and rising bubbles, but there was no way to tell what either might consist of. If the solid was at all like any coral she or Keo had seen, it was probably some form of the carbohydrate-protein copolymer that even Mike understood composed lobster shells at home. All the adults could think of ways to measure the density of the dust and become more certain about this, but sadly all the ways needed delicate weighing equipment that was not to be had. *Mata*, like her parent, was a cargo craft rather than a research vessel. The seed from which she had grown had plans for a basic ship only, with only basic equipment. The seed had not reproduced itself; it had been provided by the original ship-growers as part of the original sale, quite expensively as Wanaka had plainly remarked once or twice. Mike, after hearing the captain describe the deal, had come to regard the seed as a sort of limited warranty, which had now expired. Without actually worrying, he now did feel a little more conscious of the personal risks he had casually accepted.

Another of the huge floating mysteries was sighted in the next few days. Wanaka steered *Mata* as close as even she dared, but that was not enough to let them see any significant difference from the first one. 'Oloa, on request, reported that they were just forty-five degrees from the equator, plus or minus its—or her, as Mike was beginning to think—current accumulated three-minute uncertainty, but Wanaka said nothing more about working back to city latitudes. Keo asked no questions, and Mike of course followed—or possibly had furnished—this example. 'Ao, he had decided, really didn't care in the least where they went or how long they took, as long as she could earn an occasional few points toward adulthood. She was not exactly kept at the masthead by orders, but knew it was the most likely place to spot something useful. She would descend to eat, sleep, and salvage hailstones for the water breakers, or to sweep the deck clear of them if these were full, but that was about all. Her conversational needs seemed to be satisfied by the doll.

Kaihapa, the twin world, was now almost at the western horizon. Kainui's low haze made the other planet's equatorial cloud belt—it matched climate zones closely with its slightly larger sister—almost indistinguishable; the crew now had to look through too much of their own world's atmosphere. Its polar regions, where, as on Kainui, floe ice accumulated and raised the local albedo, were also hard but not impossible to distinguish. The apparent location of these features gave a very rough confirmation of *Mata*'s latitude, of course, but 'Oloa was much more reliable. Now that Mike had learned the doll's nature and purpose, it—she—was frequently consulted.

Days later still, and well south of latitude minus forty-five, there appeared yet another of the big mysteries. This one, however, did not rise nearly as high above the sea or appear nearly so spherical as the earlier ones, and 'Ao reported it as "something big" rather than a city. Wanaka, staring unblinkingly at it, shifted *Mata*'s heading to an almost straight-in approach. Mike was not alone in imagining a firm-set expression on the hidden mouth. None of them needed imagination to see that this thing was far lighter in color than the others and had many more of the bright, sparkling points that had proven in the others to be ice.

The general opinion, voiced by Keo, was that this was actually much like the others but had recently completed a turnover. Approaching it should be relatively safe.

No one wondered seriously why, if it had just turned over as a result of its formerly submerged ice's melting, it should now be lighter in color than the earlier ones. Mike, without the benefit of anyone else's opinion, guessed privately that since they were farther from the equator there might have been more ice in the mixture to start with.

The captain again ordered the doll to calculate as best it could how far into the deep currents this one reached. She got the same nonanswer as before, more quickly this time. The currents were only known very loosely, as calculated from their latitude and generally accepted circulation theory; the depth the object might draw was completely unguessable.

By this time even 'Ao knew about simultaneous equations. She had proved it with a navigation solution—done in her head, to Hoani's astonishment but no one else's, apparently—and now boasted several more points on her suit and displayed correspondingly higher morale. She had admitted to him once, when the others were out of hearing, that she hoped sometime to be the youngest shipmaster in history. Mike had, of course, no idea how much farther she had to go along this course, and the child herself was not very specific on the point. He couldn't help wonder just how clear she was herself about it. By his standards she was a ten-year-old, with a ten-year-old's vague ideas about adulthood; but her education had certainly followed a different course from that of his own childhood back on Earth. He couldn't guess what and how much she still had to learn.

No one was greatly worried about overturn risks as they approached the floating object, which was now looking less and less like a city and more and more like a very dirty and wave-worn iceberg. In spite of this change, Wanaka had again ordered 'Ao to keep alert for signs of people and water craft. Everyone else did the same from deck level without orders.

And without success.

There was far less flotsam this time as they approached under greatly reduced sail—Keo and Mike were kept busy trimming, following the captain's orders from her own station at the tiller. These were sometimes vocal and sometimes in Finger, as the thunder far overhead varied in volume. It was no accident that symbols in that language that had to do with ship handling could always be managed by one—either—hand. What small floating objects there were seemed to consist, to everyone's surprise, of nearly pure ice. There was coral in occasional pieces of this, but it was lighter in color, much closer to yellow than the dark red they had seen earlier, and surprisingly regular in size and shape. It was much less fragile, too; at Wanaka's order, Mike gathered several specimens and had no trouble this time with their breaking up.

Keo had been watching very carefully on his own initiative for what he had seen earlier—any signs that this big mass might be rising, however slowly; but they hove to only a few dozen meters from the huge but apparently uninhabited object with no reason other than recent memory to make them worry.

"Keo, the water is very shallow; the ice goes out a lot farther from the water line than we are. Toss two grapnels. Bow and stern." The mate complied without comment. Wanaka gestured 'Ao down to the deck, without bothering to look up herself. All remained silent for some minutes, examining every detail close enough to be seen clearly through the haze. Mike, still much more conscious of each thunderclap than any native, focused his own attention on items that looked less stable than most, wondering what effect the heavy sound waves might have on them. There were actually very few such features; he felt pretty sure that, however stable the whole mass might be, the lower parts they could now see had spent some time close enough to the water line to have experienced wave action. Most irregularities seemed rounded.

The few exceptions even he could explain. They were far up, almost too high for details to show, but they were possible pits and certainly fragments and shatter marks that might have been left by explosions.

This did not have to indicate habitation, recent or otherwise; as far as he had heard, chemical explosives were not used on Kainui. He had certainly never heard a word recognizably close to that meaning in any locally spoken language, and couldn't offhand think of any use for such material here—though that, he realized, was not a reliable guide. There would always be lots he didn't know about the Kainui people.

The explosions could be natural, though. The lowest few hundred meters of Kainui's atmosphere was much too good a conductor to allow electrical charge to build up locally; all the lightning was higher, ordinarily cloud-to-cloud. 'Ao's normal duty station was perfectly safe. The organically grown cities, however, had to be grounded to salt water; that, he knew, was one of the principal uses of copper on the planet. The grounds didn't last very long; they corroded, melted, or otherwise succumbed to electrochemical action.

This city-sized object seemed to extend quite far enough above sea level to be vulnerable to lightning, and lightning striking a surface composed largely of ice would certainly experience explosions. Mike began looking for items that might represent scattered fragments on the lower, presumably wave-smoothed areas.

He said nothing, as usual, hoping that one of the others might make a remark that would tell him how far his planetary ignorance was misguiding him.

The captain eventually spoke, but not very helpfully.

"Mike, I've heard that ice is more slippery than a wet deck, even on slopes. Do you have any experience with it?"

"Yes. Lots. You get it on Aotearoa's South Island, which has many high mountains. I'm a good—" he paused, and had to spend a minute or two getting the basics of skiing and the meaning of "mountain" and the differences between snow and ice across to his listeners. Wanaka finally nodded.

"Will it be hard or dangerous to walk or climb on this thing, then?"

"Quite likely. If there are enough small chips of the coral mixed in as there seemed to be in the others it may be safe enough, but all we've seen here are pretty big. I suggest you let me try it first. If I do slip, at least I won't be taken by surprise."

"Neither will I," interjected 'Ao. "I've slipped on deck lots of times."

"On a deck with lots of grab lines, and which is rocking so that downhill turns to uphill before you've gone very far. Do you think you'd be safe on one that kept you going downhill for thirty of forty ship lengths, interrupted here and there by a piece of coral big enough and sharp enough and hard enough, if the ones we've been picking up here are any indication, to rip off half your armor as you went by—toward the water?"

The child seemed unconvinced, but the captain wasn't.

"How safe will *you* be?" she asked Hoani. He shrugged, though his noise armor concealed the gesture pretty well.

"Not perfectly, of course. Who expects to be? At home, I'd carry a small pointed axe, or even two, to get a grip if I did start to slide, and I might have metal points strapped to my feet to forestall it. We don't have anything like that on board, though I suppose those people you mentioned who tried to build and sell icebergs probably did. But look at the shape of these bits of coral; they're fair-sized cylinders with pointed ends. Spikes, of a sort. I could use them pretty well as ice axes, though it would be nicer if they had real handles. I suggest I go ashore on the flattest place we can find, and look for some more; I want to find out why the ones we've been finding near this ice are all so uniform. I'm getting an idea about that." He paused, not for breath since he was using Finger, but to his relief Wanaka didn't ask for details. "If my suit gets a few cuts and scratches, they'll heal, after all."

The captain hesitated. Both Mike and Keo could practically read her mind, though neither could guess which tack she'd take.

"All right," she said at last rather slowly. "Hook on a safety line, though. You're not going to climb far. Keo, hold the other end, but give him plenty of slack. If you pull him off his feet you'll make at least two enemies."

"Three," said 'Ao.

"If I go off my feet, the chances are it won't be Keo's fault," Mike pointed out. "But do give me lots of slack. Even if I do slip there'll be no need to haul in until I reach the water, if I haven't stopped myself sooner, and not much then unless I've been knocked out."

"You mean you're going to keep your helmet open?" asked 'Ao in tones suggesting shock.

Mike paused. "I was. I hadn't thought of that. Thanks. The work would be a lot easier with it open, but I'd just as soon live through it, and getting it closed while I'm sliding downhill could be awkward. It would certainly get in the way of trying to stop the slide."

'Ao's own reflexes in such a situation would have been wholly concerned with her helmet, so this sentence also startled her; but she said nothing. Having caught an adult in one error was enough for a few days. The second one, after all, might have some sense behind it; she herself had never slid downhill, since Muamoku used railed stairs rather than ramps between levels, and could only guess what it might feel like. The remark about tearing armor also deserved some thinking, even if armor did eventually heal itself. *Eventually* did not mean *instantly*.

Wanaka would have been very happy to read the child's mind just then. It seemed as though the loss of points she had taken so indignantly so many weeks before had indeed been good for her.

Mike was able to give an immediate demonstration of the problems of climbing a slippery slope. He couldn't even get out of the sea until he had found, after some search and extracted after some effort from the submerged ice near the shoreline, two pieces of imbedded coral, each about twice the volume of a fist, in the ice just below the water line. Conveniently and, to everyone involved most interestingly, they were almost exactly the same shape as those picked up floating in the last few minutes and that were still on board—rods small enough in diameter to be held in a gloved hand, and sharp and hard enough to be usable as crude ice axes. With these Hoani dragged himself away from the water's edge and a short distance farther, to where the slope became almost level over a few square meters. There he succeeded without too much trouble in rising to his feet.

To the captain's unexpressed impatience, he examined his surroundings for several minutes before reporting any details. When he finally began to talk, stowing his pieces of coral in two of the tool loops in his noise armor to free his hands, he raised more questions than he answered.

"The ice I can see through, this flat part, is full of coral just like my pieces. Same size, same shape. They average half a meter to a meter apart, they're all lying horizontally and, within a few degrees, parallel to each other. My first thought is that we'd better look around for people."

"Mine is that this thing has been grown," Wanaka answered. Mike was relieved; this was the suspicion he had been hoping not to have to voice. "Are any of the rods really close beneath the surface you're standing on?"

"Yes. A dozen or more have less than a centimeter of ice over them."

"Then get down as close to one or two of them as you can. Look for details *around* them, especially threads connecting any of them to their neighbors. And look over the ones you have at your belt for anything similar. 'Ao, hook on to a safety line—I'll hold it—and swim over there. Don't try to climb out of the water, but look for more of those things where it's shallow. They should be as near to the surface of the ice as possible. I want to melt some of them out without breaking *anything*."

"How would we do that?" asked Hoani, who had kept his eyes on the captain's fingers rather than immediately following her orders. She had looked back at him as 'Ao had leaped for a length of cord, and saw the question.

"I'll show you when we do it. Do your own job now."

This was as near as the captain had yet come to addressing him as tersely and impersonally as an ordinary crew member; Mike felt more pleased than embarrassed. The embarrassment would no doubt come later, when he was shown or told about the melting technique and realized he should have guessed it for himself. The effort to guess took some of his attention from his work, but fortunately Wanaka couldn't see this. He hoped the child would not find a spicule, if that were an appropriate word for the things, too quickly; the longer she took, the better his chances of—

His safety line jerked twice. He looked toward the ship. Keo stopped pulling the line, and Wanaka shifted to Finger.

"'Ao's found one of them just starting to float. I suppose they're melting out all the time. There—she has another. You needn't spend time on the ones still under ice, at least for a while. Try climbing some more—no, come back here. Keo would have to keep an eye on you, and I want everyone to look these things over. Even you. You have no experience with anything like it, I suppose, but that could turn out to be useful."

Mike obeyed, closing his helmet again and allowing himself to slide the few meters to the water's edge. By the time he was standing on *Mata*'s deck, 'Ao was there, too, holding the objects she had picked up in each hand. The captain addressed her vocally.

"Keo and I will hold them. Take the lens and look for any trace you can find of anything even slightly like fine hair or any other fiber. Remember what Mike said and what you saw; these things are lined up with each other in the ice. I want to know whether they're *connected* with each other in any way."

"I didn't think of that," 'Ao replied. "If they were, I probably broke the fibers when I brought them over."

"Maybe, but you said they'd started to float. Don't worry about it. If you did, they're probably sticking to the sides of the pieces, since everything there is wet. Mike may have to go back over there to study the ones still in the ice, but we'll try this way first."

"May I go with him this time?"

"Maybe. If you do see anything here, I'll want you to look

for the same thing still in the ice. If you don't, maybe I'll want you to look anyway."

Mike silently admired the captain's technique, but concerned himself more with what details he could see on the spicule the child wasn't examining. He could spot nothing remarkable without the lens, other than a vague pattern that might have been scales or shingles on the main body of the cylinder. Even the lens, when his turn came to use it, showed him nothing more. There seemed little doubt that the captain was right about the objects being some form of pseudolife, but there was no sign of material connection at least between these two specimens. It was back to the main berg.

'Ao accompanied Hoani. So did Keokolo. Safety lines connected them—'Ao and Keo to Mike, the heaviest—but not to the ship, where Wanaka remained. The three reached the nearly level area that Mike had examined earlier and took turns applying the lens to the rods of coral that were close enough to the ice surface to be inside its focus. None could see anything running from any one of them to another; either the connections, if they existed at all, were too fine to be seen, or were of some more subtle type. All of them, including 'Ao, were familiar enough with pseudobiology to know the possibility of solute gradients around one "organ" controlling the growth and even the orientation of the next. They finally reported their lack of success, and even the obvious conclusions, to the captain, and without consulting either her or each other began to climb. Mike used the spicules he had collected earlier as ice axes. Keo and the child imitated him with ones they had picked up from the sea before climbing aboard the berg.

'Ao went first, again without any discussion. It was obviously safer for the far heavier men to be in a position to stop her if she slipped, though this may not have been her main reason for displaying her superior agility.

They had estimated the height of the object very roughly as four hundred meters. As they climbed, Mike felt more and more certain that it was a good deal less; the viewpoint from below had been deceptive.

Unless, of course, it was the viewpoint from above.

There was no way to determine yet the object's horizontal dimensions since they had seen it from only one direction, though all of them held a vague mental image that assumed it to be roughly circular and therefore, from the visible curvature, something like a kilometer across.

It quickly appeared that 'Ao might be hoping to settle this point by reaching the top as quickly as possible. Somehow she was managing to keep her feet and practically run. However, the length of her safety line to Mike soon restrained her.

He sympathized but continued to crawl as before, using his coral tools carefully. He glanced back at the ship from time to time, but they were already out of reach of Finger communication or, except for occasional brief moments, voice. Thunder remained as usual.

So, it suddenly occurred to Mike, did lightning. Four hundred meters up might be within that danger zone; perhaps getting to the top wouldn't be such a good idea. After waiting a short time in the hope that the other would mention it first, he finally suggested this to Keo, who agreed at once. Hoani was never sure whether the point had simply not occurred to the mate or whether he, too, had been waiting for his companion to speak.

Of course, both of them had had much of their attention on travel-and-traction problems. On Earth, something like lightning calls for thought or attention at specific *times*; on

Kainui, it's at all times when far enough above the sea. Very seldom during a voyage does one get that far above sea level, and traveling up an ice slope tends to focus the climber's attention on other matters.

Focus it too hard, apparently. When the men stopped and looked up to see how far above them 'Ao might be, the child was not in sight.

They weren't worried at first. It was not the first time; the surface was very irregular, much less rounded than Mike had thought from below, and occasional humps and hollows had repeatedly put one or another of them out of the others' line of direct vision. Even *Mata* could not always be seen. However, the safety line still led upward, and a very gentle tug on it presumably caught 'Ao's attention; it was returned at once.

Perhaps it had not been quite gentle enough, however, though the possibility was not at once evident to either man. As well as attracting her notice, it might also have overloaded the girl's already feeble friction connection with the ice. For whatever reason, she began to slip toward them.

It was two or three seconds before this became evident below, and then not as a result of sight. Mike felt the safety line slacken and took it up gently so as to maintain communication; but almost at once he realized that gently wasn't working.

"She's falling! Get ready to stop her as she goes by!" he bellowed as loudly as he could. Keo heard him, locked himself in position with one point, and held the other ready to stab into the ice and pull him in whatever direction might be needed. His own location at the moment was on a fairly level stretch at the foot of a steeper-than-usual slope; *maybe* the little one would appear directly above him, but he was as ready as possible to shift either way. Mike, on a slightly steeper area ahead and to one side, was in a poorer position for this, but did his best while also trying to get the slack out of the child's safety line. He didn't dare pull too hard; it might interfere with any efforts she might be making to stop herself. Just how fast was the poor kid coming, anyway? Would it be possible for either of the men, or both together, to stop her? Or would all three end up whirling helplessly into the sea?

Keo, Mike noticed, had already seized a moment to flip his helmet shut. Should he do the same? No. Stopping 'Ao was more important; when they all were going down together there'd be plenty of time for helmets. The sea was now several hundred meters away. He lacked Kainui reflexes, and was just as glad of it.

He felt tension on his rope and eased his pull. Then he stopped pulling altogether; the slack had disappeared. She'd stopped herself.

Or had been stopped by something.

"Keo! She's stopped coming! We'd better get up this slope and find out why!" The mate flipped his helmet back to answer vocally.

"Hoping all the time she sticks her head over the edge and tells us."

"She's been stopped for whole seconds. Don't wait for that!"

Keo nodded, and the two resumed clawing their way upward. Mike, by far the heavier, began to fall behind. Then the mate's grip failed at an especially steep point, and he slid back almost to Hoani's level before getting his coral spikes to hold again. This happened twice more before they reached the edge of the shelf or bulge or whatever it was that was blocking their upward view; even on ice, lower weight gives poorer traction when the local temperature is close to freezing.

Or does it? Should it? Mike's mind started to wander slightly in spite of the situation, though not badly enough to interfere with his climbing, and was pulled back to reality only when he could see where 'Ao's rope was leading. The men came almost at the same moment to the top of the slope, and found themselves looking slightly downward onto an almost white, nearly circular level area some ten meters across. A little beyond the center from where they were look- ing, 'Ao was getting to her feet. Her noise armor appeared intact, and the child herself unhurt.

She saw them the moment their heads appeared and spoke in Finger—the thunder was too much at the moment for even the half-dozen meters separating them.

"Sorry if I scared you. I slipped up there"—she gestured up the slope, which resumed even more steeply on the far side of the circle—"and couldn't stop 'til I hit this level. It looks funny, doesn't it? Like a lot of hailstones piled up on the deck before I could clear them off."

Mike decided that if she could ignore what had just hap- pened, he might as well do the same. He had intended to apol- ogize for pulling her off her feet with the safety line, but of course he couldn't be sure that was what had actually occurred. The coincidence of pull and fall *could* have been just that, after all; he hadn't been able to see her.

Also, her remark about the surface she was standing on seemed to deserve attention. The men pulled themselves over the low rim that surrounded the nearer half of the level area, but didn't bother to stand up; they could examine the surface better from a near-prone position.

'Ao was perfectly right. They were lying on what seemed to be packed hailstones varying from pea to golf-ball size, though only Mike made that comparison, of course. He thought rapidly, for him.

Hailstones. *Circular* area. *Level* area. Too-low-for-lightning area—that was a problem. No, it wasn't. He'd merely been wrong about the thing's rising.

Most uncharacteristically, he spoke his idea aloud. Perhaps, he thought later, it was because the captain wasn't in hearing, and of course it *was* something Kainuians might reasonably not know about.

"More water we don't need to worry about," he remarked rather illogically. "You're right, 'Ao. This is hail."

"But why so level, and just here, and in a circle?" The question came from Keo, Hoani was glad to note.

"It's collected in a lightning crater, I'd say. Explosion pits tend to be circular, and when lightning hits ice you get an explosion—"

"Then we'd better get back downhill!" exclaimed Keo. "I didn't think we were high enough for lightning! Hurry, 'Ao. You go first, and keep your safety line taut!"

"You may be right, and I suppose we should play it safe," countered Mike, "but I don't think so. It's been a pretty long time since this crater formed—"

"If it really is a crater," cut in 'Ao. "We can only see the top, and don't know how deep it is, or was." Mike was nonplussed for a moment, then started to talk again, not quite so rapidly.

"It's nearly a perfect circle, as I said," he pointed out. "Can you think of any other reason that would be? Anyway, if it is a lightning pit it was formed long enough ago to fill with hail, and I think this berg was probably higher then.

Quite a lot higher. You yourself, Keo, were pretty sure we're still below lightning-risk height. We're certainly not a hundred meters above sea level yet."

The mate thought for perhaps half a minute. Mike suspected that Keo, like himself, was wondering less about what the captain would do if she were there than what she would say later—whatever they actually did now. Mike himself was simply not constituted by habit to regard lightning as a major hazard, though his mind told him this was rather silly in the present circumstances.

'Ao, content with the fact that the decision wasn't up to her, was examining the edge of the supposed hail deposit. The ice over which the men had climbed was clear enough to see into for half a meter or more, and she was wondering whether there were coral spicules in it this high up. It took her only a few seconds to find them, and virtually no time thereafter to see something else.

"Keo! Mike! Look here! There are lots of the coral things up here, too, but they're not all lying flat. They're all jumbled around. Look!"

They looked. 'Ao had spoken after looking at perhaps a meter of the circle's circumference; her elders were silent until they had checked over half the circle, uphill as well as downhill portions. The child seemed to be right, however—perhaps unfortunately, it occurred to Mike. He decided not to report her somewhat hasty leap to a conclusion if he could help it; Wanaka might well decide that a deduction of points was in order, and 'Ao had actually been a little more guilty of unreasonable haste than had Mike himself.

To reinforce this determination by making himself guiltier, he spoke again.

"I'll bet those spicules were as flat and organized originally as the ones down below. They got knocked around by the blast that formed the crater, wouldn't you say?"

Keo shrugged, a gesture much more visible through his noise armor than through Mike's.

"Maybe. But aren't the spikes pretty regular for explosion debris, though? They're mostly pointing toward the center of the circle. But that doesn't matter right now. We're going down to report. 'Ao, I have another line. Take the end of it so we can both hold you back if we have to, and lead the way."

The child fell twice during the descent, clearly not from injudicious rope tugging by either man, which made Mike feel better about her original fall. Mike himself slipped once, fortunately on a fairly shallow slope so that Keo was able to stop him with little difficulty, and in half an hour or so the three were back aboard *Mata*.

Mike had been a little worried, but Wanaka said nothing about their having climbed out of sight. She had, after all, issued no orders on that point. She simply listened to the accounts of all three of the investigators. Mike did feel a little of his usual self-consciousness when he had to describe his own theories, but not very much; he was fairly confident in them by this time.

His old uneasiness did not return in full strength until he had finished, and the captain asked a question.

"I'm not quite sure whether all this theorizing depends on whether the berg, or whatever it is, is rising or sinking. Can you straighten me out, Mike? Someone"—Hoani was grateful that no names were mentioned—"suggested a while ago that it must be rising because a lot of the lower slopes seemed to have been smoothed by wave action. Then I hear that the top used to be up in the lightning region and is now lower."

Mike hesitated, all his old uncertainties back in full force. Certainly the berg was both rising and falling over a period of a few minutes, unless it was merely the water falling and rising; but over a long term there was no way yet to be sure. Before he could think of any sensible answer he was rescued by what he regarded as the second least likely source.

"It could have been a lot bigger before, and turned over more than once like the others," suggested 'Ao.

"Did the others show any signs of being grown by people, like this one?" asked the captain.

"Not that I saw, unless their coral counts—I know it was all irregular on the others—but does that mean they weren't?"

Mike's impression of the child's intelligence was rising with each word, though he had never regarded her as stupid. Wanaka showed no change of expression, but her next question was directed to Keo.

"You've been trying to tell whether this one is rising or sinking. I haven't seen enough change myself to mean anything, but I haven't been as careful as you. Has there been any motion you could distinguish from ordinary wave motion or float oscillation?"

"No. Not yet. We haven't been here very long, though. I don't see that it's important; the thing's certainly not going to roll over on us anytime soon."

"It's important just the same. We'll take some"—she hesitated for just a moment—"water pods, and set them just at the edge of this thing, a hundred meters or so apart, all the way around it. We can probably get them back, since they float, and if we don't, you say there's plenty of hail up in that crater. We'll learn the size and shape of this thing, too, while we do that. Mike and 'Ao, start collecting coral spikes; we can drive them into the ice at the water's edge to hold the pods. Give each one a couple of meters of mooring line; there has to be some change of height because of waves, and we don't want the floats washed away. The anchor spikes will be the real reference, of course, and the pods will make them readily visible. Get to it. Keo, to the sails, dead slow. I'll take the helm."

Mike was not quite as certain as Keo about the stability of the berg, but didn't argue. With the child, he started collecting coral spicules.

The project took more than two days. It proved quicker to let swimmers do most of the work; maneuvering the ship next to the ice was extremely tricky, neither waves nor wind nor bobbing ice, if that were actually involved, being very cooperative. The berg proved not to be quite circular, and they didn't measure the hundred-meter separation of the marks very carefully since no one thought that data important. Its circumference seemed to be about seven kilometers.

When they got back to their starting point there was no sign that the first marker had either risen or fallen significantly. The berg's water line was not, of course, perfectly definable since the sea was never smooth, but all agreed that no certain change could be seen.

"So far." 'Ao's morale was now very high, and she still hoped for points. The captain simply nodded. Mike took a chance.

"If it's melting at all rapidly, and it does seem to be shedding those spicules all the time, and they're less dense than water, the whole thing ought to sink a little, rather than rise and tip over," he remarked.

"How about if they're less dense than water but denser than ice?" countered 'Ao. Mike started to answer, hesitated, and lost his chance to answer as Wanaka spoke.

"Depending on how fast it's losing ice as well as coral below. We don't know how far down the thing goes into saltier water, only that it's deep enough to have been carried north by deep currents. Right, 'Oloa?"

"No, Captain. In the last two days its northward drift has slowed and stopped. It is now drifting back to the south at about half a meter a second." Wanaka's eyebrows rose.

"And there's no way to tell whether it's the current that's changed or the depth of the ice and coral," 'Ao added at once. "Two unknowns, one datum."

"Or both," added Mike.

"And it's certainly much too deep for us to find out by diving," Keo put in.

"So we keep sailing around it until the water line changes," Wanaka stated firmly.

"And if it doesn't, when do we try something else?" asked the mate.

Wanaka's rather grim smile could just be made out behind her mask. "Until we get a better idea," she gestured. "All hands, start thinking."

Mike's courage again rose far enough.

"Shouldn't one or two of us get back ashore and study the structure more carefully while we wait?"

"If we keep circling, those ashore won't always be in sight from the ship," returned the captain. "Still—" She thought for several seconds. Then, "Well, if two of you are roped together and you stay well away from the edge, nothing too serious should happen."

"Mike and me," cried 'Ao at once. Wanaka shook her head negatively. "If Mike falls, you won't be much good on the other end of the rope. Sorry. You've been growing up nicely and we're proud of you, but not that way. The shore party will have to be both adults, and I can't very well leave *Mata*. That pretty well narrows it down."

'Ao made one more try. "Keo's too light to handle Mike, too. It might as well be—" Wanaka shook her head again.

"You're right in a way, but Keo's a lot heavier and stronger than you are, dear. You're thinking yes or no rather than how much. I'm afraid it's still no, but no one blames you for trying. Also, it looks as though I am going to need 'Oloa here." The child shrugged and gave up. Mike was tempted to support her request; she would certainly be able to reach places neither he nor Keo could manage. However, the two of them should be able to mark such places and have the light-weight examine them later.

Armor consumables were checked, safety lines examined and attached, *Mata* stood in as close to the ice as her crew dared, and the men plunged into the sea. They had to swim a hundred meters or more to the right before being able to get ashore; being generally wave-worn didn't make the rim slope uniform. They picked up a pair of spicules each and dragged themselves out of reach of the waves, made sure of the line connecting their suits, waved to the ship, and started away from the sea. *Mata* was hove to; the captain felt no particular hurry about the next circumnavigation, both men assumed.

The climbing at this point was much more difficult. The ice slope was shallower, smoother, and generally *wet*. Waves traveled fifty meters or more up the slope from where they broke. They found it better to crawl most of the time, hitch-ing along by digging a coral spike into the ice ahead of them and pulling themselves toward it. They were over two hun-dred meters from the sea before reaching humps of any size, and were still scarcely ten meters above *Mata*'s deck.

It was easier to go around the humps than over them, however, and this quickly put the men out of sight from below. 'Ao quickly climbed to her masthead station and was in sight for a few more minutes; but finally, after a farewell wave from both parties and a loud-as-possible yell from Mike, all contact was lost. Wanaka, they knew, would not be considering them for the moment; a waterspout was bearing down on the area where the ship had last been visible, as though ordinary noises weren't interference enough. Thunder remained at standard background level; they were still far below lightning risk as far as either could judge, though the sky flickered as usual.

The general ice slope was getting steeper now, and its imbedded coral spicules regular enough in arrangement to be helpful in travel; in many areas they were projecting slightly above the ice itself. At the steepest places they would almost have formed steps if they had been closer together. It was quite possible to walk most of the time, even for Keo.

All travel was suspended for some minutes when the waterspout actually tried to climb onto the ice—both men looked uneasily for fragments of *Mata*—and died from lack of feed. The column collapsed over some hundreds of square meters of the berg's area and washed both men some distance back toward the sea. They were relieved by catching a glimpse of the still floating ship by managing to stop themselves well short of the ocean, and for Mike because the captain was not close enough to comment on a possible reason, other than rising, why the lower parts of the berg had been smoothed as though by wave action.

Distance was too great to tell whether they had been seen from aboard, and it seemed to both the climbers that the best thing to do just now was to continue their exploration. It seemed unlikely that Wanaka would have ordered them back even if they had been in touch; falls had been foreseen and the safety lines *had* worked, after all.

A little farther up the general slope they discovered a few hailstones in the occasional hollows. They wondered why these had not been visible lower down or during the earlier climb, decided that waterspouts were a plausible answer, that more extreme rise and fall of iceberg or ocean wave might be another, and that the rain that normally accompanied the hail in thunderstorms might well be a third; and Mike filed yet another possible reason for the smoothed-out lower slopes of the berg.

The only problem, he reflected aloud to Keo after making a cautious test around his mask, was the presence of liquid *salt* water in some of the hollows still holding hailstones. The mate's experience with frozen puddles on Earth was nonexistent, but even he could see that water produced by melting in the ice hollows should have been fresh, though probably carbonated. For that matter, he added, if the hail-filled hollow they had seen earlier had been exposed to rain as well, it should certainly have looked quite different.

Neither of them had any way of measuring the actual temperature, and neither knew enough to consider the effects of even slightly salty spray. Their ignorance might, just possibly, have been bliss, but made no difference in the long run.

Higher up still, another hail-filled "crater" was found. Very careful checking showed that the hailstones were not cemented together, at least near the surface of the deposit; like those in the other pit, they could easily be removed by the handful.

They ate and slept near what seemed to be the highest area of the berg. The arrangement of the coral here was just as it had been lower down. The region was fairly flat; from its center they couldn't see ocean. The whole mass was not nearly as high as they had judged from below. Their line of sight would not have reached sea level now less than three kilometers away. Even from the edge of the plateau that formed the top of the berg, where the slope was steeper than any they had faced lower down, the water itself could not be seen; too many humps and bumps intervened. *Mata* was not in sight, but could easily have been, and probably was, too close to see. The captain's suspicion that the whole structure had been artificially grown was becoming more and more plausible to Mike, from the way the spicules were arranged. Keo seemed never to have doubted it seriously.

They wandered for half a day over the plateau without finding anything more to cause deep thought. They found two more craters, both nearly full of hailstones. There seemed no particular reason to retrace their original path up, since there had been no arrangement about where to meet *Mata*, and with breathing, eating, and drinking stores running rather low the pair finally just headed downhill—with normal care, of course. If the ship were continuing to circumnavigate the berg, they'd be spotted soon enough, they assumed. If it weren't; or didn't seem to be, they'd have to decide for themselves when to start their own circumambulation. At least, there'd be no question about which way to go; the captain had assured them she'd circle to the right as she saw the ice mass, so going to *their* right was their safer alternative.

Actually, both were out of food when the catamaran hove into view. She was only a short distance from the ice, and 'Ao saw them from her masthead almost as soon as they sighted the vessel.

What the men did not see was the pods that had been left around the berg's circumference to mark the water line. Keo noticed their absence first, and wondered aloud whether they had served their purpose in the last two-plus days and been recovered, or had been lost in some way. The latter was no worry, except as a matter of policy, of course; there was even more fresh hail on the berg than they had realized before, though it would have to be carried an inconvenient distance. Keo was more concerned than Mike, of course, his upbringing being what it had been.

They were more than a hundred meters from the edge,

but the ice between was smooth. They took the easiest way to the water, still roped together of course. Neither was able to keep from a certain amount of spinning, and Mike almost failed to close his helmet in time. Their joint splash impressed 'Ao more than it did the captain, but they were aboard in moments. Mike let the mate report first. He did it tersely, and ended with a question.

"Are we still heading south?"

"Yes, more or less. About one-sixty. At more than two meters a second now, 'Oloa says."

"What happened to the markers?"

"We recovered them when they started to float. You don't have to make up your mind now, Mike; this thing is sinking. And waves aren't the only things that can round off the ice, I expect you now realize."

"Yes," he replied. "Waterspouts, rain, and probably things I haven't thought of yet. And it's sinking because a lot of ice is melting down below."

"And it's going south because?"

Mike was silent for some seconds.

"Because it's got a better grip on the deep currents!" 'Ao offered.

"If it's melting enough down below to sink, how is it reaching farther down?" asked Wanaka. The child was silent in her turn. She even glanced at Mike, who had nothing to say either.

Keo expressed a thought with no obvious connection to the problem. "Hadn't we better get away from here?"

"I—don't—think—so," the captain answered slowly and thoughtfully. "Maybe staying around will give us our best chance of finding out what our cargo is worth."

All waited for some seconds for a more detailed explanation, but the next one to speak was the child, in very excited tones.

"You think there are people here!" she exclaimed.

"Unless you or Mike or Keo can come up with a purely natural answer to what's been happening, yes. You can't disprove miracles, of course, but sane people don't count on them. If you can't find a simple natural explanation, people are the next best. Always."

"So do we tie up, or keep circling?" asked Keo practically.

"Circle. I certainly want to talk to anyone here, but I want us to have a choice, too. Besides, we don't know how much up-and-down oscillation this thing may have at max."

"When do you expect to see the people?" asked 'Ao.

"About an hour after they see us, if they haven't already. That's another reason to keep moving. I can't guess where they are, except it's probably not on this chunk of ice, and don't know which way they'll be coming from, and if we tie up it could be on just the wrong side."

"Why don't you think they're on the berg?" asked Keokolo.

"Because you and Mike and 'Ao didn't find any sign of them except the evidence that this thing was grown."

"But there's something like four square kilometers there, a lot of it too bumpy to let us see anyone else from more than a few meters, even without the haze. The fact that we didn't see any tunnel openings doesn't mean a thing."

"But if there are people here they'll maintain some sort of watch, and they'd have seen us long ago."

"Maybe they did, and are just hoping we'll go away again," suggested 'Ao. That thought stopped the captain for a moment, and probably earned the child a few more points.

"That might be," Wanaka said slowly. "The iceberg-sellers, I've heard, didn't like either guests or passengers; there were tricks to maneuvering them they didn't want others to know. Still, if there's anything this piece of ice *doesn't* resemble, it's a water-for-sale chunk. For one thing, it's far too big. If there are people here hoping we'll go away, they can change their minds when we don't." It wasn't quite an order, but was certainly a clear decision.

But even Wanaka began to wonder as the days went by, *Mata* and the berg drove ever southward, and the temperature began to drop farther and farther.

The ice continued to sink; they attempted no actual measurements, but Mike estimated that a good dozen vertical meters of ice had settled below the water level since their first trip "ashore." The best evidence was the change in the shoreline; from a relatively smooth oval, it had become indented with more than a dozen bays—they were not nearly steep-walled enough to be called fjords—reaching two or three hundred meters toward the interior.

There had also been enough thunderstorms and water-spouts to confirm the notion that these could be responsible for rounding off the berg's humps and projections; waves weren't necessary, though they might help. The berg was definitely melting; excursions by swimmers suggested that *Mata* could easily have collected a full cargo of melted-out coral spikes if anyone could have seen any value in them.

The spikes were still floating when they melted free; they were still less dense than the water, though that could simply mean that the surface layers of the ocean were now noticeably saltier. *Mata* was certainly floating a trifle higher. The berg was sinking nevertheless, so an even more impressive amount of ice must be melting. The southward speed was increasing, no longer by very much but enough to make it harder to understand why the melting berg could get a better grip on any deep current. The wind certainly wasn't helping; there was practically none of that now. The ship was reaching the mid-latitude zone of calms, and there was less and less free choice involved in Wanaka's still solid determination to stay with the shrinking, sinking growth—as she still claimed it to be. It was now by far the largest source of fresh water within reach, though of course there were still thunderstorms enough to prevent worry. Even in a zone of calms and with lower temperature, water vapor is less dense than air—especially Kainui's air—and an ocean needs very little outside heat to spawn thunderheads.

The real surprises came when they were on the west side of the ice. These were, first, the sight of four sailing craft appearing almost simultaneously through the haze in a formation that neatly cut *Mata* off from the open sea; and moments later more than a dozen sound-armored human forms walking easily toward them on the ice from the opposite direction. Mike's first, unvoiced, question was how such a maneuver could possibly have been timed, considering Kainui's long-range communication problems. What the other adults were thinking he had no idea, and it didn't occur to him to wonder about 'Ao or her doll.

The child had sighted and reported the ships; the walkers had been spotted moments later by Keokolo from the deck. Mike felt sure that 'Ao wouldn't be blamed for missing them; her job after sighting the ships was to report any details she possibly could about them.

And it was quite evident that the members of the shore party had all appeared at almost exactly the same moment from behind a single ice mound, along a surprisingly level and low ice surface that seemed to continue away from the ocean. More coordination? How?

Well, the people had probably been in sight of each other, of course; but how about the ships?

If Wanaka had had any idea of making for the open sea she must have abandoned it at once. Not only was the wind extremely weak and there was no way to tell whether they could outsail the others, but *Mata* was a trading ship; traders didn't flee from other vessels without strong evidence that they were pirates. The only such evidence to be expected at the newcomers' present distance would be the presence of very large crews on their decks, and 'Ao quickly reported that there seemed to be only three or four people on each one and that cabin size was no greater than usual. Wanaka glanced upward, not at the girl but at the pennants floating from *Mata*'s mast. These had been unchanged for many days, and Mike had been told that they signified the unknown nature of some of their present cargo.

Any behavior other than staying hove to for possible bargaining would be suspicious, even though they were being approached by a small fleet rather than a single vessel and even though the fleet happened to be spread out so as to cut *Mata* off from any reasonable escape route. That could be as purely chance as the appearance of the four vessels all at once.

Yes, thought Mike, that was a good way to put it, considering the number of other craft they had sighted since leaving Muamoto. Not much of a chance.

Keo was watching the captain intently, Mike saw, but offering no suggestions. She was the captain; he was only her husband. There was no way to guess what he might be thinking, until the situation changed abruptly. The two ships far-thest from them, the ones in the middle of the arc, changed course at almost the same moment, the one on the left of the line as seen from *Mata* to starboard, the other to port. Keo relaxed visibly as their path to freedom began to open— slowly. The wind was very low, as he had noted, but *Mata* could sail very close to it. Wanaka's reaction was less obvious, but her attention turned from the approaching ships to the people on the ice, now collected in a group partway up the smooth hummock that had concealed their approach.

Most of these, it could now be seen—the adults; there were three or four in the group of about 'Ao's size—were carrying what might have been spears, though Mike had never seen such an implement on the planet. His brief uneasiness was dispelled when several of the poles were raised vertically and waved from side to side to display signal banners that had not been obvious in the feeble wind.

Hoani was still unable to read these, but the captain ges-tured Keo to the sails and took the tiller, heading *Mata* toward the ice. The people on shore watched with little appar-ent interest as the mate swam ashore with mooring lines. He was also carrying a number of the coral spikes, which he drove into the ice a few meters from the water and used for rather frail-looking bitts.

'Ao had descended from her perch, but so far had offered neither comment nor question.

"Want me to talk to them?" asked Hoani.

"We'll wait 'til the ships arrive. I don't think there's any-thing to worry about—you were worried, weren't you, Mike? But if they all represent one city it'll be better to find who's in charge before we start bargaining, and if they don't it'll be better to have them all together bidding against each other. I wish I could even guess what this metal is. If some of them know and we don't, we could get badly taken."

Mike, for the first time since leaving Muamoku, had a little trouble with the end of this speech. She was, he suspected, using some highly specialized trader's slang.

"But don't our banners say we don't know? I thought that's what you told me when we first loaded the metal."

"Yes. I wouldn't try to fool anyone on that point. Never try to play any game from ignorance. Right, 'Ao? But I'm hoping there's more than one city in this group. If they start bidding against each other we can find out a lot, and there's no way they can help that even though they'll know we are. It would be nice to head for home, whenever we can find it, with something worthwhile aboard. We'd like to stay with our kid again for a while, but goodness knows what we'll owe the school when we do get back." Keo nodded silently.

"Keo, Mike, furl the sails," Wanaka ordered. Mike couldn't guess whether she had completely ceased to worry or was merely trying to give that impression, but the order didn't surprise him. The next one did.

"Mike, get ashore and talk to them. Find out what you can, especially about their connection with these ships. Feel free to tell them anything you want about us and our cargo and you, but don't say anything about 'Oloa beyond that she's 'Ao's doll, and not even that unless they ask. They'll see right away that there's something strange about you; no doubt they have already. They'll certainly know after the first couple of sentences that you're not a trader. They must be sure already that you're not from any city on Kainui. Let them wonder about why you can handle languages so well—and if they ask, tell them. Keep them talking until those ships get here. Don't worry about hiding any secrets except about the doll."

The catamaran's port hull was toward the ice and almost aground, so Mike simply slipped into the shallow water. There was a murmur among the masked, sound-armored figures, and even 'Ao, behind him, gave a rather shocked gasp. He did not, for some time, understand why; he did not even give the event a thought. He had been trying to decide how to open the conversation, but could think of nothing but a standard self-introduction. He chose to use unmodified Maori, and to follow the captain's implied advice toward frankness as closely as possible.

"*Kei ti pehea koutou?* I'm Mike Hoani. My captain is Wanaka from Muamotu. What's your city?" The answer came in almost identical speech, uttered by one of the group whose hands were now empty, his or her pole having been laid on the ice. Mike did his best to find some visible clue to this one's identity, since it would be discourteous not to recognize the speaker later. The main possibility seemed to be a colored pattern a little like 'Ao's on the armor, fortunately applied to both chest and back, as he could see from some of others who weren't facing him directly. Less fortunately, the pattern was extremely complex; Mike hoped he could remember enough of it.

"This is Aorangi, I am Hinemoa. We know of Muamoku, and have occasionally met crews from there. But surely you aren't of that birth?"

Mike relaxed, slightly relieved at hearing a personal name that indicated the speaker was female but not inclined to put too much trust in the clue until he learned more about the current evolutionary status of the language. He explained in detail his origin and reasons for being on Kainui.

"Why did you come to speak to us, rather than your captain?" The question's tone suggested mere curiosity rather than indignation, but Hoani felt there might be a minor breach of courtesy implied by the words themselves. He tightened up slightly, but answered with what he believed to be the truth.

"I know many of the tongues the people of the islands used when our ancestors were still on Earth. The captain has formed the habit of having me greet strangers first. The languages in the different cities of Kainui have changed through the years."

"True. But how is it you're so far south? It has been many years since we spoke to a crew from Muamoto."

"Our original ship was lost, and we drifted with an unfamiliar metal-fish while the new one's seed grew. That's why our banners say that we don't know some of what we're carrying—at least, so the captain told me; I haven't learned to read them myself. Perhaps you can tell us what we are carrying, and whether it's worth the trouble. If not, maybe the people in the approaching ships can do it for us. We also have some iron, copper, and titanium."

"If we can't I doubt that they can. The ships are of our own city, Aorangi."

"Your eyes are keen." A compliment never hurt, even Mike knew.

"Not that keen. We recognize them because we expected them now."

Mike was not as quick as some, but not entirely stupid. Something said earlier suddenly clicked into place in his mind.

"This is Aorangi where we are standing? On *Mata* we had not recognized it as a city, though we made the opposite mistake about some other coral-and-ice structures we met farther north." The listeners seemed more amused than indignant, Mike noted with some relief. "I—we had never thought of using ice for anything that big. You must have grown it much farther south than this. Might I ask why you are so far from the pole now? Isn't the sea here pretty warm for your city?"

Glances were exchanged among the others, and Hinemoa's answer was hesitant.

"The reason is somewhat embarrassing. It has to do with faulty rigging."

"I apologize, and will restrain my curiosity. I assume you are now heading south intentionally."

Actually, Hoani had been able to read a good deal into Hinemoa's words. For one thing, she was speaking the least altered Maori that he had so far heard on the planet. The term "rigging" meant a great deal more to him now than it had before *Malolo*'s session with current-riding and controllable sea anchors. Aorangi might be a good deal more maneuverable than any of the floating metropoli nearer the equator. Why? More specifically, why would the ability be useful? Was there something about the polar regions that made precise position of importance to a city and its inhabitants? Was the city's ice-based construction a cause, an effect, or a coincidence?

Also, was Hinemoa telling the whole truth? If the ships now drawing near were making a rendezvous planned in advance, how could the planning have been worked? Hinemoa had claimed, or at least implied, that the city had been out of full control long enough to get this far north—so far north that it was losing a lot of its structure to melting. Could that possibly be true?

Quite suddenly, in spite of Wanaka's permission to be frank, Mike began to feel just a little uneasy. One of her hopes, that of getting the traders of the approaching ships to bid against the people of the iceberg for her cargo, seemed gone (well, maybe not; traders were likely to be traders rather than government agents). There was still no evidence that the people of Aorangi were piratically inclined, but Mike suddenly felt uneasy. He decided to pass the conversational buck to the captain. She might know no more about this city and its people than he did, but at least she knew the planet's general customs that, considering the universal trading background, were probably fairly uniform. She should certainly have a clearer idea than did Mike of just where the boundary between ordinary trading and piracy generally lay.

He hoped.

He shifted the conversation as unobtrusively as he could back to the question of *Mata*'s cargo. Hinemoa and all her companions listened intently as Mike described the metal-fish where they had spent so much time while their replacement ship was growing. Some of the details were accepted with no visible surprise, though fairly obvious interest, including the fact that vast amounts of drinkable water were produced compared to the tiny amount of metal, the location of metal pods in the same pockets as the water, and the fact that so few of the pockets contained metal at all. It began to look as though Wanaka's cargo might have only curiosity value here; none of the listeners seemed ready to suggest what it might be.

"I'll ask the captain to bring a pod for you to see," he finally said. He turned, took a couple of steps toward the water, and called out the suggestion.

"They can't identify the metal from my description. We'd better show them a sample." Wanaka nodded and spoke to the child, who disappeared briefly into a hold and returned with one of the pods, which she proffered to the captain. The latter gestured that she should keep it, said a few words inaudible to Mike over the thunder but apparently telling the child to accompany her ashore. Both flipped their helmets closed and stepped from *Mata*'s deck. The child had to swim, of course, but her burden didn't seem to interfere.

Mike suddenly suspected what had caused the disturbance when he had come ashore himself; he had waded in open water with his helmet unclipped. The space had, it was true, been narrow enough to cross in a few steps, but he wondered how many points that would have cost him with Wanaka, and what the natives of the ice city had thought. The latter, he suspected, might have the more serious effect. He hoped his alien origin might be regarded as an excuse, but didn't dare count on it.

Kainui's people were not, as far as he had been able to tell, any more xenophobic than his own; but it might be unsafe to assume they were much less, and human beings have a tendency to be less tolerant of, or at least less empathetic toward, actions they regard as stupid than toward merely hostile ones.

'Ao, who had carried the pod ashore, now handed it to Wanaka, who held it up to give the local group its first close look. They had appeared expectant, Mike judged; now their talk stopped completely, though he was slow to realize that the cause was irrelevant to the specimen. One of the group gave a loud call, and pointed out to sea. Mike let his own gaze follow.

There were now seven of the local ships in sight, not four. More interesting, a wave two or three meters high was sweeping in just beyond the three newcomers; and as everyone watched, the eight vessels including *Mata* were lifted on it and borne toward the berg, swept past the watchers on the ice hummock, and came to rest in what had just become a shallow bay.

The wave receded. Water poured back out the channel. The bay was now a lake. No one but Mike seemed in the least surprised; Wanaka, of course, had a trader's face.

Personnel from the Aorangi ships slid overboard and waded toward the party on the hill, helmets open. Keo, the only one still aboard *Mata*, followed their example, but snapped his helmet shut before he went overside. The term "shallow water," used outdoors, was to him among the silliest of oxymorons.

Wanaka, concealing any surprise she might have felt, now handed the pod to Hinemoa, and there was silence while it was passed around among the others. Each time it was handed along, a single word was uttered by the passer. Mike had trouble making it out over the background thunder; it sounded like *waru*, but he could see no relevance in the number eight.

The pod was returned to the captain, but she was none the wiser about its identity. She was able, with practically no help from Mike, to suggest that it might nevertheless be of some trading value. Hinemoa agreed.

"None of us right here is a trader, but I'm sure there are people in Aorangi who would like to take a chance on it. If you care to entrust the pod to me, I can pass it on to the school; the chemists there might be able to tell us enough to make a better guess at its real value. But perhaps"—a smile was just visible behind her mask—"you'd rather not have that knowledge spread too far before the sale." Wanaka smiled also; she of course did not regard the suggestion as insulting, but handed the packet of dust over without comment. She also began to doubt the statement that no one there was a trader.

"You might think about whether you should place a starting bid very low or very high in iron-equivalents," Hinemoa added. "Too far either way I suppose would discourage risk-taking. Personally, I'd suggest starting low."

"It will take some thinking," Wanaka agreed, carefully not implying a preference. Her doubt was growing stronger. After some discussion, it was settled that word would be spread among the metal dealers of the city, and that these would be on hand at the next sunrise to inspect the cargo and make offers. Wanaka mentioned that she did have other metals to trade if they were wanted—iron, copper, and titanium. No one seemed greatly interested, and even Mike began to wonder whether some or all of the group might not actually be traders in spite of Hinemoa's denial.

He also, although a much better historian than salesman, could understand what lay behind Wanaka's final sentence: "Since we still don't know what this stuff is, I plan to sell no more than a third of it here. If anyone wants more, I'll need strong persuasion." Her listeners showed no surprise at this either; if none of them was a trader, they were at least not naive.

The meeting broke up. The local adults spread out to greet the crews of the newly arrived ships. Some of these spoke briefly with *Mata*'s crew as well as they could without

Mike's help, but none admitted having anything to trade. Mike wondered what they might have been doing at sea, since even his inexperienced eye could tell that the ships in the lake were indeed floating high and probably were in fact carrying little or no cargo.

Keo confirmed the latter observation when they waded back to their own ship. Mike observed proper helmet discipline carefully this time.

The mate had also been wondering about how the rendezvous between city and newcomers could have been accomplished with the former's location presumably unknown even to its inhabitants. He remarked on this at once, evidently sharing the captain's suspicions that they had not been told the whole truth. Wanaka, quite reasonably, had a different priority problem: how was *Mata* to get back to sea?

"We'll trade tomorrow if we can," she said, "and leave as soon as possible afterward, also if we can. We won't need to do any special water bargaining. Even if these people are the sort to hold someone up on water, which is hard to believe but would tell us a lot, we have plenty; and 'Oloa can get us back pretty close to where we got this load, anyway. The real question is how we get back to sea at all. It obviously can be done, since their own ships were washed up here with ours—and all of you surely realize that was *planned*. Intended. That wave didn't come when it did by chance. I can't even guess how it was done, or how they knew it was coming, but all our imaginations need to go to work on that. Even if we figure it out we'll need these folks' permission and probably their help to leave, but I'll still feel better understanding that bit, too."

"There are youngsters in the group ashore," pointed out the mate. "Maybe 'Ao should practice a little hospitality, being sure to remind her doll about the talking rules first. It'll be good to have a bunch of local kids chattering in the cabin with 'Ao and 'Oloa both listening, but remember the kids will be listening, too. Any of them could put two and two together if they heard the doll, and no matter how honest these people are we might find ourselves short one highly useful sample of concealed silicon."

Wanaka nodded. "She won't say anything that an ordinary doll wouldn't if anyone but regular crew is in hearing. She already knows that. Mike, I'm afraid I'm more worried about your possible indiscretions than about 'Oloa's. No insult intended."

"None felt. I'm worried myself. That's why I called you into the talk even though you'd said I could say anything. If I have to chat with any more of these people, except when I'm translating for you, I'll certainly be careful. Just remember, I'm a scholar before I'm a trader. Words are communication tools to me, not game pieces."

"I've noticed," was all the captain answered. Mike couldn't decide whether he had relieved her worries or added to them, but didn't feel insulted.

The four went back ashore, where even more people were now assembled. Many of these gathered around to ask questions, and Mike was kept busy translating. It was easy enough for him; the local language, not too surprisingly from the city's name, was indeed nearly unaltered Maori. Aorangi was the name of a mountain on the South Island, and probably of the ship that had brought these folks' ancestors to Kainui.

'Ao was talking to people her own age, making as little use of Mike's services as she could; and presently she and three others made their way—helmets sealed, this time, because all had to swim—back to *Mata* where, after some minutes of examining the deck and outside equipment, all crowded into the air lock.

While this was going on, Hinemoa had worked her way through the crowd back to Wanaka's neighborhood, and invited her and her crew into the city. The captain was more than willing.

"Should we leave a deck watch?" she asked. "Your own crews don't seem to be."

"The ships are safe, but no one will be insulted if you do. You are in an unfamiliar port."

"How about deploying our leaf? It's less efficient this far south, and it's the only way we can power our breathing equipment."

Hinemoa was interested, and asked for a more complete explanation of *Mata*'s photosynthetic apparatus. Wanaka, glad of the chance to improve relations, provided the explanation and supplied several clippings of the structure when it had been deployed. It would, of course, heal itself.

"We'd better all come inside together so that we will know where we sleep," the captain suggested. "I can decide about a watch later."

"Of course. Most of us are going in now, but someone will gladly wait until your apprentice has finished entertaining. One of her guests is my son; we can board your vessel and make introductions if you like. You'll want to know your 'Ao's new friends. Then we can all go to Kone's and my home and party properly."

Wanaka responded suitably. Mike was pretty sure she meant it; it would be good, he realized, if more than just 'Ao heard the talk of the children.

They waited until nearly all the Aorangi had vanished, however, before going out to *Mata*; interrupting an adult party would have been all right—they would simply have been joining in—but an all-child get-together was different. Hinemoa showed no signs of impatience, but Wanaka finally suggested, "Mike, you might visit the cabin and ask if anyone is having word troubles."

"They won't think I'm intruding?"

Hinemoa smiled behind her mask. "Eru will assume it's a hint from me. The others won't think about it except that adults are always interrupting. Go ahead."

Actually, Hoani's entrance did little to end the party; he was immediately put to work clarifying questions the visiting children had not been able to get across to 'Ao. Eventually, Hinemoa herself entered and invited everyone to her home.

This involved a trip across the ice for several hundred meters to a tunnel opening in the side of a hummock; through an air lock much more than large enough to take all the group at once; more tunnel to an area where several dozen people of both sexes and a wide spectrum of age staffed desks and tables—evidently a message and general information center, rather than a place for checking in from and out to the surface, Wanaka noted with some relief; and finally along a not-too-complex set of smaller tunnels, still walled with the ice-coral growth, to Hinemoa's home.

The party lasted there until the hostess pointed out that the newcomers should be shown their quarters and given a chance to sleep if they wished. None of the children argued.

Eru, however, promptly asked whether 'Ao could stay at their own home, and Wanaka, after a moment's thought, approved. Then she added that the child should at least come to see where her shipmates were staying and make sure she could find them if she had to. Eru came along, with the result that 'Ao got only a few words across to Keo in a moment when she was asking him to keep the doll for her. He declined on grounds that an adult male with a doll would be suspicious behavior. She didn't argue.

"*Piru*" was her important word. Then the other three were left alone, and Keo reported.

"Gold!" exclaimed Wanaka. "What use is that to anyone?"

Mike answered with a single word.

"Chemical."

Wanaka pounced. "Chemical, as in seed design?"

"Sure. All sorts of atoms can turn out to be good catalysts or coenzymes, especially heavies."

"Of course. I should have remembered that. I'm going to hold those traders up tomorrow—no, I'm not, either."

"Why not?" the two men asked simultaneously.

"These Aorangi folks may not be pirates, but if they've found a use for lots of gold, important enough to justify designing a special fish to collect it, they may want to keep it to themselves for a while. Of course you can't keep *knowledge* from spreading, but controlling the only source of a key material is something else. We could wind up here as firmly invited guests. I've already mentioned selling only part of the load here, and if they have a good reason for wanting to corner the gold supply then 'Ao might wind up having to look for a husband right here in thirty-five or forty years, and we'd be even longer seeing our own kid again, if we ever did."

"And any big economic reason is a good one," Mike interjected.

"Of course. And it would be as bad or even worse for you. I can't see anyone even from offworld spending a single pod of iron looking for a missing Earth native who most probably had gotten himself lost at sea. Especially not on *this* planet. I suppose a world only half covered by a couple of kilometers of ocean would be a different matter."

"I wouldn't count on that, especially if that ocean had sharks. That's still an awful lot of water and a lot more under water. So what do we do, Captain?"

"We get out of here, preferably long enough before they spot us and can launch a ship so we can get out of sight in the haze. There are seven other ships on that lake, or dock, or whatever we should call it. I don't see how we get out of there alone, regardless of how one does get out, and we don't know how fast any of them can sail—at least, we don't know how much faster than we any of them can. Ideas in order, gentlemen, preferably before sunrise tomorrow when I'm supposed to start auctioning something I'm not supposed to know the name or nature of. I'm as likely to make a word slip there as I was afraid Mike would a little while ago.

"Fellow brains, all of you hoist sail and set course on any bearing that seems good to you. Pardon the mixed metaphor."

"I s'pose they'll be watching us all night," Keo suggested.

"I would in their place." She smiled. "You and Mike better relieve their minds. Go outside now and look around the city; get lost if you want, it'll help our reputation. You're the ones most likely to do that, I hope they'll think. Get some idea of population, tunnel complexity, and how noticeable you seem to be. I'm afraid we can guess that already, for Mike. If either of you gets an idea, don't come in together. Separating would be a good idea anyway; you're more likely to get lost, and it'll look less as though you're doing something specific or underhanded together. Wear your armor. See if they'll fuss about your going outside, and if they don't, take a look to make sure there's really no watch on any of those ships. If there isn't, fine. If there is, we'll be even surer that our hostess was lying; go and talk to the watches. Try to make sure Keo was right about the ships themselves being empty. Especially try, if you get any sort of chance, to tell how much water they have aboard; if they have to load up on that before starting a chase, we have a much better chance."

"We'd have to check all of them for that to be useful," pointed out Mike.

"True. But do your best without looking suspicious. Whatever you've managed to think of or haven't, both of you come in again at second sunset."

"We'll have to be outside to know when that is. Don't count on perfection, Captain dear."

"I won't, one and only mate. Off you go."

Outside, where the pair eventually found their way without interference, there was a thunderstorm overhead. They had not yet separated, thinking it better to learn some geography together first. Keo automatically dashed for the lake, the ship, and the drinking breakers, then stopped when he remembered the last were already full.

Mike had followed him more slowly. Together, they spent the next quarter hour sweeping hailstones from the deck and cabin roof into the lake and noticing with interest that no one was in sight to do the same on any of the nearby craft. There might, of course, have been some asleep in the cabins, but shore watches don't sleep. Maybe they'd heard *some* truth. The two discussed this as they worked, concluding that there was no unsuspicious way to settle the question. After the storm had passed, they went ashore, without helmet discipline though Keo made a start, and walked away from the pool for a short distance rather than toward any of the ships.

"I wonder how they get in and out of this place, anyway. I

still can't imagine any way of calling up a wave when they want it."

"That might be only for getting in, anyway," pointed out Keo. "There might be some way of digging or blasting or simply opening a quick channel to let everything wash out as the lake empties. We could check the coral pattern for signs of something they could slide out of the way—some sort of channel gate."

"But some of the ships are aground now. That technique could be embarrassing."

The mate nodded silently.

"Does this city have or use any other ships?" asked Mike after a pause. "There are always lots around Muamoku, dozens of different types and sizes. This place doesn't seem to have much in the way of docking facilities, unless we missed an awful lot on our earlier walk."

"Most of our ships aren't too different from these," answered Keo. "We've never done much ship design ourselves. We seem to have brought all the varieties we've ever needed with us. Our ancestors knew Kainui was all ocean, of course. We've bought seeds from other cities sometimes, but the ships they grew weren't enough better to be worth the cost. The ice near the pole seems to call for tricky sailing, sometimes, but we very seldom need to go there."

They walked slowly back toward the city entrance, sometimes feeling a little uncertain of their way among the irregular ice hummocks. They had almost succeeded in taking the captain's advice about getting lost when they sighted two men—their gender was plain since, evidently not planning to leave shore, they were not wearing sound armor—who walked as though they knew where they were going. Trying not to be too conspicuous about it, Mike and Keo followed them, and in a few minutes recognized their surroundings once more. In another hundred meters they saw the city entrance.

The suns were still well up, and Mike suggested that they now follow Wanaka's advice, or order, to separate. Keokolo could go back to their quarters, make a preliminary report, and come out again on his own if the captain wanted; Mike would get into conversations, which they hadn't managed yet though it had not occurred to either of them that the locals might be avoiding them for some reason.

It did cross Hoani's mind that by himself he might more plausibly be asking questions in a Kainuian city than when accompanied by one who was not obviously a stranger. It did not occur to him that at least some of the natives of Aorangi might hope that Mike himself might be more willing to talk about other cities *on* the planet, such as Muamoku, than would people who lived in them. His grasp of intercity attitudes and politics of Kainui was decidedly incomplete, though he was coming to understand Wanaka's personality better every day. He also had, though in not too serious a form, the ordinary human tendency to stereotype—to assume, in this case, that he could talk to any citizen of Aorangi about any part of the city or aspect of its life and get informed and useful answers.

He had, of course, attracted the attention of the men he and Keo had been following. When he looked around alternately at the icescape and the tunnel entrance after the mate's departure, simulating indecision about his next step, both of them approached him.

Neither seemed at all suspicious of anything, as far as Mike could tell. Certainly they were talkative enough and could tell him a great deal about Aorangi. It had indeed grown from a ship of that name, which had arrived on the antarctic ice cap. Its friction-heated hull had melted its way inward far enough to trap it when the water refroze, and the colonists had had no choice but to build where they were, using what was available in ship and surroundings. The latter, of course, had been mainly liquid and solid water, and heat energy at a rather low concentration. He asked about the cap, of which he had heard no details in Muamoku though it had been visible enough from space, and was told that for some degrees of latitude around the pole itself there was a continuous floating ice sheet, its edge disturbed by storms often enough and violently enough to form temporary inlets some kilometers in length, and to send floes drifting for large distances northward. Mike could see why this might call for maneuverability of any local vessels. Less happily, he could also see that it might call for speed. Escape might be even more difficult than Wanaka hoped. Some Aorangi lived *on* the cap in experimental stations, working on projects such as designing better ice-coral structures. The speakers had a low opinion of this work, which seemed to produce mostly expensive failures. Mike suspected a possible source for the deserted ice-coral masses they had encountered earlier.

"Is either of you a sailor?"

"No. We're not much of anything; we graduate from messenger status in about half a year. There aren't enough ships to need many sailors, and neither my cousin nor I like the idea of going to sea anyway." This remark slightly jolted Mike's stereotyping of Polynesians but opened another possibly useful line of questioning.

"Were you outside when we arrived today?"

"Yes. Watching a landing is interesting, and anyway we

were both on salvage standby. Ships sometimes ground too hard when they land." Mike jumped at the chance.

"How about when they leave?"

"That's safer. The port is filling up then, so they rise instead of grounding."

Mike was uncharacteristically quick on the uptake. "My captain will want to see that. She'll probably need to be told just how to maneuver. Do you know when the next departure should be?"

"They launch at sunrise every day for the regular search." Mike decided not to ask what was regularly being sought and surrendered the conversational ball. Maybe he had learned enough along that line already. Wanaka would certainly be interested.

"You're from Muamoku, aren't you?" asked one of the others.

"The captain and the others are. You can see I'm not from Kainui at all."

"We'd noticed, yes. Does your world have oceans?"

"We call them that. They average only about four kilometers deep, and cover scarcely three-quarters of the planet. A major sailing problem there is to keep from running into land, or worse, into land that doesn't show above the surface."

This started a lengthy period of what would have been shop talk if any of the speakers had been sailors. Hoani might have learned more but decided not to ask further leading questions; he had already heard enough to demand deep and detailed thinking.

A mutual eclipse of the suns gave him a chance to change the subject, and after a brief description of the locally rare solar eclipses of Earth he bade his informants a casual farewell and entered the city. He did not quite need help finding Wanaka and Keo's assigned living space, and in a relatively few minutes was reporting to her. Keo had gone out again.

The captain was thoughtful. "Sunrise. Just when I'm supposed to start auctioning, if I really am. Maybe I'd better see Hinemoa—but maybe I'm not supposed to know about this launch business; how do I get around that, I wonder?"

"I'd expect her to come to you, if there's anything about the launch to affect the auction."

"If another wave is going to come into that lake, it will affect where I have to lay out the metal. I think we'd all better be there awhile before sunrise and start setting up, and let her hold the tiller. Presumably something would have to be done to keep *Mata* from getting washed out with the others—or maybe—" She fell silent for fully a minute. "I'll see her now and ask—no, tell her that I'll need 'Ao at the ship half an hour before sunrise to help unload, and let her take it from there. You may as well get to your own quarters. Take care of your life support, sleep if you want. Keo or I will get you when we need you. No, wait. Stay here until he gets back, tell him what you told me and what I'm doing, then you're on your own."

The mate returned first, so Mike didn't hear what might have transpired between Wanaka and Hinemoa. 'Ao wakened him, presumably the next morning although there seemed to be no clock in his quarters, by rapping on the coral door and calling his name. They were on the way to the city entrance, armored, within minutes.

The suns weren't up yet, as Wanaka had planned. There were, however, people already at the lake, or port, or whatever it should be called, and one of these approached *Mata*'s crew.

"Hinemoa advises that you bring your metal up there as

quickly as you can, and then man your ship. We will be launching in a few minutes, there are no real mooring facilities, and it will probably be washed out with the others. Would you like help moving your metal?"

If there was any hesitation in the captain's answer, Mike failed to spot it.

"No, thanks. We'll do what we can before your launch. Give us five minutes' warning and we'll get aboard. Afterward, we'll get out the rest, and see customers. Will that fit your routine?"

"Perfectly, I think. Hinemoa will arrive shortly, I expect."

Mike and Keo began carrying pods of metal ashore. The only clue to what the captain had in mind was her brief order, in Finger, not to hurry, but not to dawdle obviously. They obeyed. Perhaps a fifth of *Mata*'s gold had been off-loaded and a smaller amount of the other metals when a larger group appeared at the lake, Hinemoa among them, and the crews who had been readying the Aorangi ships stood to their posts. Someone ashore began what turned out to be a countdown, though the counts were fully half a minute apart. Wanaka was at *Mata*'s tiller, the men were ready to hoist sail, but 'Ao had not yet taken her masthead post. One of the suns was just up, though not really visible through the haze.

At the twelfth count, the sea poured into the lake. *Mata* was one of the few ships just barely afloat, and like the others was swept away from the sea by the inrush. Those still grounded followed more slowly as the water rose and floated them, too. Everyone hoisted sail, and Keo and Mike followed suit without orders. The "landward" side of the lake deepened, then the new water began to slosh back toward the sea. This seemed now to be below them. Wanaka's full attention for several seconds was focused on avoiding collisions; like the other steersmen she was not entirely successful, though nothing dangerously violent occurred; all velocities were nearly the same. Mike couldn't help thinking about infection. The water, bearing the eight vessels, poured out and downward over the path by which it had just passed in and downward.

The native craft, sails now fully up, bore away from the city, remaining in close formation, on a course some sixty degrees left of straight out—almost straight south.

Mike looked back toward Aorangi, wondering how they were to reenter the lake. To his own relief, he didn't ask the question. It answered itself; Wanaka ordered them to set sail. In what Mike judged to be about twenty minutes, Aorangi's bulk was indistinguishable. The only identifiable objects were two or three waterspouts, all of them more or less ahead, strobe-lit by the lightning flickering from every direction but down, and Kaihapa, not quite low enough to be in the heaviest haze itself. It should have been a crescent, but was merely a blurred patch of light unnoticeable except when both thunderheads and lightning were all for the moment in other directions than west.

" 'Ao!" called Wanaka to the masthead. "I know it's not really necessary, but tell 'Oloa we'll be making random course changes twice in the next two hours. When I call again, she should direct us toward where the gold-fish ought to be, as well as she can calculate." The child nodded understanding, without stopping the endless looking around that was her duty. No one could see her lips or fingers move or hear her voice, but no one doubted that she was passing the order to her doll.

She reported nothing to the deck before the second course change. Then the captain ordered her to the cabin, placing the doll on her own shoulder. She also ordered Keo off watch, and told Mike she would have relieved him as well if the sea had not been unusually rough. Both were wearing safety lines, but the captain seemed not fully to trust these just now. There was no actual storm, but waterspouts were surprisingly numerous at the moment and she wanted two pairs of eyes to keep track of them. It went without saying that she wanted someone to heave *Mata* to if she herself went overboard for any reason.

Mike's own sailing experience on Earth had nearly all been limited to calm weather, and he was getting just a little tired of one aspect of Kainui. Nowhere on his home world's oceans, as far as he had ever heard, was there anything like the microtsunami phenomenon, and even the best noise armor—and his, of necessity, was a special-order item—could not accustom its wearer to all the properties that made it wearable or, better, livable for many days at a time. Quite the reverse. Some aspects of its complex inner structure grew less and less comfortable as time passed.

Wanaka had tacked twice, with easily two hours between the maneuvers, when she ordered Mike to ring the cabin's signal bell and gave up the tiller to Keo, ordering him to heave to and attach a safety line to himself. Nothing had been seen of any other craft, not that even the captain had been looking very hard. The waterspout supply had thinned noticeably, as had the haze; Kaihapa was much clearer, though not, of course, noticeably higher in the west.

The captain gestured Mike toward the air lock; she seemed to feel that the quieter ocean justified leaving Keo alone on deck. Safetied, of course.

For the next few days, the routine Mike had come to know in the early part of the voyage was gradually resumed. It took a while for both Wanaka and Keo to get over a mild fear of pursuit from Aorangi, distant as the city now should be. The hints from Hinemoa that its motion was under control meant, of course, that no guess whatever about its position could be trusted; but as 'Ao put it when the question was being discussed, there were so *many* directions—and its inhabitants had admitted, if that were the right word, that there was too much melting going on this far north.

The word "admitted" bothered Mike slightly. Hinemoa, beyond argument, had been doing a certain amount of lying or, to use a word captain and mate seemed to prefer, selling. The launch warning she had sent had offered no hint that *Mata* would be launched with the others and that there was no way to prevent it; Wanaka had nevertheless been encouraged to unload a respectable part of her cargo. A more encouraging point seemed to be that, maneuverable or not, there was no way the iceberg city could possibly match *Mata*'s sailing speed.

That was obvious. Mike was a little uneasy about this word as well, but told himself that paranoia could lead in only one direction and that a very undesirable one. There was no point in worrying about everything. Human minds had limits, and there was nothing to be gained by stretching these limits too far. Let reality catch up occasionally with imagination.

Apparently the captain had not been wholly taken by surprise by the launch, Mike thought again. If either of the others had, they concealed it well. Of course, Wanaka might have briefed them before Mike had joined the party that morning, but he didn't ask, of course.

The doll did a good job of navigation, though not a perfect one. It eventually reported that they had reached the center of its error circle for the gold-fish, a circle now somewhat enlarged because a less-than-ideal wind had forced them to do a good deal of tacking. Since the object of their search would probably not be visible more than a few hundred meters away, the search rectangles couldn't be allowed to get much bigger each time around; and quite soon each time around was getting noticeably longer.

Everyone, even from the helm, watched eagerly for signs of their target, but the most trust was placed in 'Ao. Whenever she had to rest, day or night, *Mata* was hove to. It was the third day before the child screamed, "Port bow!"

"You're sure it's the fish?" called Wanaka.

"No, it isn't, but I think it's *Malolo*. That should still be stuck in the jelly, though. We never pulled up the sea anchor after we got there, did we?"

Keo, at the helm, had swung their bow to port without waiting for orders, and within minutes everyone could see that the child was right, both as to identification and inference. She called again.

"Keo! Heave to, or we could get stuck, too."

The captain rescinded the order.

"No, Keo. Swing to port when you can see the fish itself from where you are, and then try to follow it around its edge. I want to get an idea how big it is. 'Ao, I don't suppose any of your young friends who identified the gold at your party happened to mention how to tell which water pods have metal under them? I can't believe their miners would have to do a blind search the way we did."

The child hesitated. "Not that I remember," she admitted after a moment.

"Well, don't worry. You couldn't have asked without—"

"I know. I thought of that."

"All right. Come down. When we finish this trip around and know how big this thing is, we'll try to replace what we left on Aorangi, and then—"

"Back to Muamoku?" asked Mike, rather hopefully.

"No. Back to Aorangi. Why do you think they fooled us into getting back afloat with so much of our cargo ashore? They knew we couldn't get back to it. I don't know what they want gold for, but they want it."

Mike felt some doubt about this, but said nothing. The idea was certainly plausible, he admitted to himself. He was, however, a reasonably well-educated man, and sets of questions, all starting with "How much?" were flocking into his mind.

Soon enough all three adults were overboard. 'Ao stayed on deck, taking in the occasional metal pod that they found and trying to make some sort of record of *where* it had been found. Wanaka, Keo, and even Mike felt pretty sure there must be a system involved.

This meant, of course, that no one was on effective watch, since it was impractical for the child to climb up and down the mast between every two pod discoveries even though these were many minutes apart. So, at least, Wanaka decided after the first few hours of searching.

She rather regretted the decision near sunset, when they were going to have to stop the search anyway in spite of its disappointing results. No system of arrangement of the metal pods had made itself obvious yet.

She reached up for what she had decided would be the last one of the day when the expression behind 'Ao's breathing mask caught her attention. Although still in the water, she risked flipping her helmet back to ask, "What's the matter?"

'Ao simply gestured behind her with her head. The captain had to pull herself partway up on deck to see what she meant.

"Having any luck?" asked Hinemoa.

Mike was still out collecting, but no translation was necessary.

X

IMPEDANCE

"*Mauruuru*," was the new arrival's next word. She didn't seem to be sarcastic or ironic, though Mike, who had been a meter or two behind the captain, was a little surprised at the Tahitian word, which he didn't have to translate. Wanaka accepted the thanks, but made no pretense of knowing what it was for.

"We thought we'd lost this fish," the other went on. "It was a new type, an experiment. It should have surfaced at the latitude where it submerged. We have no idea what went wrong."

"This thing is *yours*?" Wanaka asked. Mike understood her surprise; metal-fish in general were simply released when the seed had been developed and tested, and it was generally accepted that whoever found it later could harvest it, since there was no way to plan an interception or delay its recharging and sinking again. They were no one's property. The device submerged to a preplanned depth where it had been learned, or calculated, or hoped there would be a usable concentration of whatever useful metal they were designed to reduce, and thereafter rose when they needed energy and sank again, whether harvested or not, when they got it. Maybe that idea was changing; the Aorangi people had known when, apparently, and considering the size of the planet had been only slightly wrong about where this one would come up.

Hinemoa seemed slightly embarrassed behind her mask. "Well," she said slowly, "there's no way to keep knowledge from leaking, of course." She was back to nearly unchanged Maori, and Mike had to help occasionally. "We'd have let this one circulate after we were sure it worked properly, of course."

"And had been well harvested a few times."

"Of course."

"And you knew where it had come from when I first showed you that pod." It was not a question. Hinemoa's embarrassment had vanished quickly.

"Of course. And you know what it is now."

"'Ae."

"I suppose your big guest from the Old World knew something. But why didn't he tell you sooner? Oh. Of course. He did, but you didn't know its origin, and were hoping *we* wouldn't recognize it and would be tempted to speculate."

Wanaka avoided answering; there was no point in getting 'Ao's new young friends in trouble with their elders, especially if that would make the youngsters more cautious next time. It was beginning to look as though *Mata*'s crew would be residents of Aorangi for some time to come, and the children might possibly be useful again. All seven of the ships that had, she had supposed, been left behind at the ice city were now in sight. Again, the newcomers seemed to have been remarkably close together, for no reason the captain could see. They had not been visible moments earlier.

Wanaka saw no reason for delaying the obvious question. "What happens now? Back to your city?"

Hinemoa replied promptly.

"We'd prefer it, but we aren't pirates. Especially since you left so much metal with us, though that wasn't just generosity, of course. This sort of thing has happened once or twice before in my own memory, and much oftener in history. Usually, we give the finder a full load of whatever is involved, and rights to the first trading sortie with it, in exchange for delaying the trip until we're satisfied we have the scales worked off the new fish. After all, someone has to take the risk that no one else will want the stuff. If you prefer not to take that chance, we'll give you half a load of gold and the other half in anything else you want and we can spare. But we very much hope you'll come back with us—very much. Simply stay with *Koku*."

Mike could sense no threat underlying the words, but he wasn't quite sure how Wanaka was feeling. He was a little startled himself; "koku" was not the name of any fish in any language he knew. Maybe that ship-naming custom wasn't Kainui-wide after all.

Wanaka responded at once, taking no obvious time to make the decision; she might well, Mike judged, have settled on a policy the moment she saw Hinemoa and realized that *Mata* had been caught.

"We'll come back with you. How did you follow us so quickly?"

The Aorangi people wore narrower breathing masks than the Muamoku crew, and the woman's smile was obvious. "We took some chance. Your ship's sailing qualities are obvious. We assumed you had come from here at the usual best-time-daylight sailing and tacking procedure, and your child made no secret of the time you had spent en route. Once we found that our own children had told you about the gold we had little doubt you'd head back here for more—though actually catching you wasn't the main idea. Finding the fish again was. We weren't really sure you'd come back; you might not have known enough about the metal to consider it valuable. Did your Old Worlder tell you about it? If we hadn't found you, and been unable to make our present arrangement, we'd still have loaded up our own ships rather than worry about you any further. I'm glad, however—all of us are, as will everyone on Aorangi be—that we did meet again. I hope you'll be equally pleased with the arrangement."

"Mike told us something of gold's use on other worlds, but I don't see what can be done with it here—at least, not specifically. I'm not a pseudolife engineer, of course; I suppose they might want to play with some," Wanaka replied. "If you want us to prepare the market, you'll need to supply more specific information for sales pitches. All right?" Mike, to his surprise, had to guess at the meaning of "sales pitch," which was in no language he knew. Hinemoa seemed to understand it with no trouble.

"Of course. Anything that might help establish high value."

"Is it all right if we harvest more while we're here?"

"No. You wouldn't get much in the time we have, and what you did get would slow us down—not much, but we're certainly late, and it's not at all certain when this fish will sink again."

"How long will it take to process the new load?"

"About a year, maybe more. This was a test run, and we knew when—and thought we knew where—it would surface. It wasn't really a question of how much it had gathered. The next run will involve a deeper search—really deep. We have only a vague idea of gold distribution in the sea, and made this dive to a hundred and fifty kilometers—we think; we don't have very good density-depth curves for anything below about fifty kilometers or for any latitudes below about sixty."

Mike had no way to tell how this information compared with Wanaka's; if any of it startled her she gave no obvious sign. She accepted the other's ruling about no further harvesting here—maybe, he thought, that *was* a sign of something going on in her head—and asked no more questions. Hinemoa, who seemed to be pretty high on her city's deck of authority, returned to her own vessel, *Koku*, and began to direct harvesting by her own group. The other ships had now reached the fish. None of *Mata*'s crew said anything for some minutes; everyone, including 'Ao, was thinking deeply.

It was the child who spoke—she didn't use Finger; one of the harvesting ships was close enough so that gestures might be understood, while far enough for the thunder to make vocal speech quite safe.

"Captain, I don't think she's telling the truth now, either."

Wanaka nodded slowly. "I think you're right. If it turns out that you are, you've earned some points. Everyone inside. We have some planning to do. If we don't keep a watch on deck, they'll be less likely to think we might leave without notice."

"If we did, wouldn't they just follow us again?" asked Mike.

"Not if Hinemoa was telling the whole truth," was the answer. The captain and 'Ao entered the air lock. Mike gave them the time it needed to cycle, and followed; Keo came last. Hoani was trying to find some meaning in the captain's last words, and said nothing after discarding his mask.

It was Keo who spoke, in a declarative sentence rather than a question. "We're going all the way to Aorangi."

Wanaka nodded. "Until we find out just how, and I hope just why, they're lying." Mike had spotted no evidence that Hinemoa had been untruthful, but of course didn't ask what had convinced the others. When even the child felt sure . . .

"I think I'd better go back outside," 'Ao remarked suddenly. Wanaka raised her eyebrows, but said nothing. "They all stayed pretty close to this place when they started to harvest, instead of spreading way out. I'll bet they can tell without having to feel under the water pods just which ones are covering metal. I want to watch them and see."

Wanaka smiled. "Good. Go ahead. But don't try to hide the fact that you're watching; I want them to know it. I won't say you're close to being a captain yet, but a twentieth of whatever cargo we have is yours the next time we have a chance to trade."

'Ao vanished into the air lock, glowing visibly. Keo took one of the bunks, Wanaka busied herself with the ship's log and some of the reference books, and Mike updated his own notes.

It was the best part of two hours before the captain had finished. Hoani, of course, never finished; the notes were in a constant state of revision, and were almost certainly going to need detailed statistical analysis when he got back to a place where silicon was cheap enough for electronic use.

When it became evident that the captain was going out again, leaving Keo asleep, Mike caught her eye. He didn't have to say anything. She nodded permission and gestured him into the air lock first. Neither said anything for some moments after they emerged, either, though both were startled.

'Ao was not alone on deck. There was another child with

her. It took Mike several seconds to recognize Eru, but less to see what was going on.

'Ao was teaching Finger, the supposedly Kainui-wide gesture language, to her friend. It *wasn't* worldwide, after all.

"Back to the planning table," Hoani muttered. Wanaka couldn't possibly have heard his words, or even that he was speaking aloud in the ambient noise, but she nodded. Some ideas don't have to be communicated; they grow from the same seed.

And some observations are top-class paradigm-changers. Mike was both a historian and a linguist, and this was a Michelson-Morley demonstration in both fields. He suddenly felt that he knew more about Kainuian history than anyone else on the world—temperate, antarctic, or anywhere else.

The children had noticed the adults and risen to their feet. The hostess made proper greetings. "Captain Wanaka, you know Eru. His captain saw that I was trying to understand their harvesting, and sent him over to explain to me. I've been overboard with him, but there was trouble under water. You know, these folk don't use the same Finger that everyone else does! It's not just a little different; it's so different I can't make out one sign in five! Have you ever heard of that? I know different cities have sort of different word languages, but we know that and we know why: people came from different islands back on Earth, where different languages were spoken, and like Mike says they've been trading words ever since as we traded other things with each other. But Finger was invented right here on Kainui, I thought."

"So did I." Wanaka stopped herself just in time from saying firmly, "It was." She did respond, Mike noticed, very quickly indeed not merely to the discovery that she was wrong about something, but even to the realization that she might be.

The Aorangans were different people, very different, though the captain was nowhere near Mike's theory of the reason.

"*Talofa,* Eru," she said after the briefest of hesitations. Mike translated to *haere mai,* the boy nodding acknowledgment to the translator but keeping his eyes on the captain. She went on, "Thanks for helping 'Ao. Would you like to go into the cabin? There is water, and silence. Perhaps Mike Hoani here could help; he knows your spoken language better than 'Ao or the rest of us."

The boy accepted both offers with courtesy, and the children disappeared into the air lock. Mike followed. Wanaka remained on deck, leaving him wondering what she might have in mind.

Whatever this might be, he was too busy to think of it for nearly two hours; the children were eager for spoken language as well as Finger guidance, both sets of lessons were going both ways, and both youngsters were quick enough at learning to keep his attention occupied. Keo slept through it all, until the warning bell from the deck sounded.

'Ao and Eru were first outside, Mike last. By the time he was on deck Keo was hoisting sail. One of the Aorangi vessels was only a few meters away, and Eru gestured a polite farewell, closed his helmet, and went overside, to surface in moments beside its outrigger. All of the other ships had already set sail and were disappearing in the haze to the southeast.

"'Ao, you were right," were the captain's first words when *Mata* had set course to follow the others. "Their miners went straight to certain spots, always got metal pods along with the water, and passed up nearly every spot we'd have tried, as far as I could tell."

"I know. I saw that, too, before, and Eru told me how to

tell the difference. The water pods with metal are just slightly more perfect spheres than the others."

"Good. We'll hope his elders are as helpful. If Hinemoa was actually telling the truth, they will be, at least about what can be done with gold. But . . ." Wanaka fell silent.

'Ao, morale still high, took up her sentence. "But she wasn't."

"Why are you so sure?" asked Mike, his curiosity overriding his usual reluctance to show ignorance.

'Ao looked quickly at her captain, who nodded. Her mask didn't completely hide her smile; Mike's embarrassment returned full strength.

"Hinemoa's ship was alone when she caught us there at the fish. The others showed up only after she'd been talking to us for a while. Why, if they found us the way she said they did, weren't they all traveling together—or at least in sight of each other?"

Wanaka nodded in approval. "That's part of it. Actually I thought of something else first. No, I won't tell you yet; I'd like to see if you can spot it for yourself. You might come up with a better idea, and I don't want to point you the wrong way. Keo, stay at the tiller, and see if you can catch up with the others; I want to stay right in the middle of that fleet if we can—ahead of them might be even better. If we do get ahead, have 'Oloa guide us a little to one side of what she figures is the right course to Aorangi. We don't want them to get any idea that we could lead them practically straight home; they'd start wondering how." The mate nodded understanding, and 'Ao transferred the doll to his shoulder. "'Ao," the captain went on, "I know Mike is pretty fluent in Finger by now. Is there any chance that Eru has already picked up as much? Did you teach him any while you were at his home? No? I know it doesn't seem likely after only a couple of hours, but I want to be sure."

"Nowhere near," replied the child, and "Not a chance," said Mike in the same breath.

Wanaka nodded slowly; then displaying a complete lack of Mike's fear of sounding silly, she asked another question.

"Does either of you think there's the slightest chance that he already knows our kind of Finger, and has been hiding it?"

Both Hoani and 'Ao hesitated before answering, to the captain's relief.

"I didn't think of that," the child said slowly, "but nothing happened to *make* me think of it."

"I can't remember his using any sign before 'Ao or I had given it to him," was Mike's more objective answer.

"Good. Then for now, at least, we'll assume that he's the only one of his people who can understand even a little of world Finger. That could be useful."

"Unless he's teaching it to some others right now, or more likely to his friends when he gets home. In his place I'd start doing that just to be able to talk to friends without grown-ups knowing—"

The captain's eyes widened. Then, "Come inside, not-so-little one. There's some work to be done on your badge. Just remember, I'm leaving space for possible code about swelled heads." The child subsided, just slightly, and led the way happily into the air lock.

They emerged in a few minutes, and 'Ao made her way up the mast with no words. It seemed safe to assume that she would remain in high alert mode for some time to come.

Mata was gaining slightly on the fleet, but not very steadily; Keo was making much longer tacks than the others. Wanaka looked the situation over for several minutes, but made no criticism. Unless Aorangi itself made some drastic change in course or speed, which seemed unlikely at the rate the place had seemed to be melting, it would be at least a couple of days before they got anywhere near it. *Mata* could probably draw ahead of the other ships eventually, but her captain didn't care greatly whether this actually happened. Being sure she could actually outsail the others could be useful information, of course—for both parties. Hinemoa had claimed to know *Mata*'s sailing performance, but there was the hope that this also might have been untrue or at least overly optimistic.

Mike, after the captain had been silent for over an hour, requested permission to leave the deck to update his notes. This was granted with a brief Finger gesture.

By the middle of the next day they were part of the fleet. 'Oloa, after a few tacks, claimed that it was on a course likely to pass the city somewhat to the west and almost certainly out of sight in the haze. Wanaka received this news thoughtfully, and after a moment directed Keo to remain within the fleet until further notice. Whoever was at the helm was to match the other vessels tack for tack. If any of them changed from the general pattern, *Mata* would stay with the majority. There was to be no slightest hint that she either could or wanted to get away.

"What do we do if they miss their city?" asked Keo.

"Try to decide whether it was on purpose. Guilty until proved innocent," his wife answered dryly. "We have as much water as they do, I'm sure."

But the Aorangi fleet didn't miss. Just south of the latitude that 'Oloa considered most likely to have been reached by now by the melting city the fleet turned eastward, and half a day later the somewhat shrunken ice mounds of its home port appeared through the haze.

They approached the same "beach" from which they had departed a few days earlier, but the fact was not at once clear. It was 'Ao who pointed out that the iceberg was floating a meter or two higher than when they had last seen it, producing some changes in the shape of the shoreline. Since *Mata* was now riding if anything slightly deeper, suggesting less dense sea water at the surface, this called for explanation. None of her crew spoke about it, but even the child was thinking.

All the vessels drew up as before near the ice, *Mata* near the middle of the line. No one was at hand on the shore this time to greet them. Mike felt fairly sure he knew why: no one in the city this time had known *when* to expect the fleet. Before, when it was on a planned search trip for the gold-fish, they had. He wondered when the landing wave would arrive, since there seemed no doubt about *whether* it would, and kept a sharp eye on the ice hummock overlooking the channel. Someone would show up there to look for them—or, of course, now that he thought of it, someone there might have already seen them and gone to give notice. He'd better watch for the wave, too.

He noticed incidentally that the metal they had left ashore was gone.

He missed seeing the wave's approach, but suddenly the ships were being swept into the channel. None of them grounded this time; the lake seemed smaller in area, but if anything a little deeper. If he were right about this, then it was true that Aorangi was melting fairly rapidly, and it was even harder to see why it was riding higher. The poleward retreat was pretty surely a fact. They had already been fairly certain of this; 'Oloa had informed them when the city had come in sight that it was many kilometers farther south than a few days before, about the amount she had predicted. Mike didn't actually get the idea that she was bragging, though her voice did have a much more human intonation than would have been expected by people in the early computer age.

The air temperature might have been lower, but the sound armor kept anyone from feeling that, and thermometers were not among *Mata*'s navigation instruments.

All the crews except one member from each ship disembarked; for some reason, it seemed, the fleet was leaving deck watches on board this time. *Mata*'s crew nevertheless all went ashore by the captain's order and accompanied the others toward the city air lock. The Muamokuans were, as before, having more trouble with travel than the natives; their boots lacked the traction of those worn by the latter and the thunder, doubtless with help from the sounds in the sea, was sometimes loud enough to make the ice underfoot quiver. Mike, not for the first time, wondered whether the traction spikes on the Aorangi armor forced much special deck maintenance, or whether the decks merely healed themselves.

Hinemoa said that they were still welcome in their former quarters. Mike was asked to attend a meeting of teachers if he were not too tired, to describe in as much detail as he cared and for as long as he cared his background on Earth and his purpose on Kainui. He would be provided with guidance about the city for at least an equal amount of time after he had eaten and slept. She also requested that Wanaka, Keokolo, or both check the foodstuffs carried by the fleet, and provide samples of anything that seemed different in that line from *Mata*'s farm tanks—in exchange, of course, for anything similar they might want from Aorangi ships.

All in all, it still seemed to be standard Polynesian hospitality. Mike wondered whether Wanaka's suspicions were being eased or intensified. The fact that she still didn't insist that 'Ao remain with them meant little; the captain seemed to be trusting the child with nearly adult responsibilities now, and of course it would never have occurred to her that the youngster might be in any danger. He was not sure this was a safe attitude but would not have objected even if he had had any right to. The child was not his, and Wanaka and Keo had formally accepted responsibility for her care and education. Her parents had been quite aware that they might never see her again when she left Muamoku.

And Mike realized, though he had a family of his own and couldn't bring himself to feel the same way, that this implied no lack of affection between parents and child. It was the custom. If 'Ao and her young sibling had gone to sea with their own parents the whole family might be lost, a much more serious catastrophe by Kainuian standards as it had been with their Earthly ancestors. Keo and Wanaka's child had not come with them; the idea would never have occurred to either of them.

No one worried about 'Ao, therefore, for the next twelve hours or so. Mike spent some of them answering questions from the city's teachers, and most of the rest eating and sleeping. He assumed that Wanaka and Keo had honored the request to test the food-exchange possibilities, but saw nothing of them. He had long ago, in Muamoku, gotten used to being an object of curiosity and even astonishment, especially when not wearing his noise armor, and was more amused than bothered at the renewal of this experience in Aorangi.

After sleeping he asked to be shown the city, and could hardly fault the fact that he was accompanied the whole time.

He wondered a little how that might affect Wanaka, who would probably suspect she was being steered, but she and Keo weren't with him to be asked. Not that it would have been convenient to ask, of course.

He did think of that possibility in his own case, but dismissed it quickly for the usual excellent—to him—reasons.

He and his guides met 'Ao and Eru during the day, however, and the girl greeted him enthusiastically.

"Mike! Remember how you were wondering about where they could get their energy so far south? Eru showed me! You have to come and see! And the whole city is so funny!"

There was no visible reluctance on the part of Mike's guides, two male teachers who appeared to be somewhere in the hundred-year age range. Hoani knew these could never by themselves have enforced a travel prohibition on him; but the area was fairly crowded, they could have called for unlimited help, and becoming a fugitive in an unknown pattern of tunnels seemed very poor tactics for anyone as conspicuous as he was. He put the brief thought out of his mind; Wanaka's commercial paranoia, or common sense, or whatever it was, must be getting to him, he suspected.

They walked for nearly an hour, often downward, before the tunnel maze opened into a huge chamber in the coral-reinforced ice. This contained a vaguely mushroom-shaped object near its center that to Mike's surprise proved to be a model of the city. Numerous people, mostly elderly, crowded around it adding, removing, and shifting tiny icons, while talking rapidly to each other in what sounded like Maori words but were nearly incomprehensible to him. He guessed he was hearing professional jargon, as meaningless to an outsider as the orders of a football quarterback in a huddle or a landing-orbit controller with traffic in a meteor shower.

The roughly hemispherical top of the mushroom, curved side up, presumably represented the iceberg. A change in color from white above to what Mike considered sky blue below evidently represented sea level; the volume above it was far smaller than that below. It had not been obvious, or at least Mike had not noticed, while they were still afloat that the water near the line had been as shallow as it seemed in the model. Probably wave action near the water's edge had created that shelf, he thought. Near the water line on the ice side of the boundary a set of eight tiny icons, one of them colored differently from the rest, presumably represented *Mata* and the fleet.

"Never mind up there!" 'Ao cried. "Look at this up-and-down part. Remember, the scale changes right below the berg. The cylinder's the important part. Mike, it goes down twenty kilometers, Eru says! Look at the water-sails! They use the currents to take the city where they want!"

"Only in high enough latitudes," one of Hoani's guides interjected. "If we get too low, the general current systems are too strong for the random ones to overcome. Near the ice cap the currents are mostly vertical, and spread out at the surface, of course, so we can pick and choose—or at least, good enough pilots can. Right now, we're in some trouble; we shouldn't have come so far north."

"Why did you?" Mike asked. "Something to do with the gold-fish we ran into?"

The other shrugged. "We'll get an explanation sometime, when they figure out who should, or more likely who shouldn't, be blamed. It happens every few years. There's a big file of excuses. Maybe the fish you just mentioned will figure in this one. I hadn't heard about it"—he looked at his partner, who shrugged—"but there are projects like that going on all the time. The general public doesn't usually hear about them unless and until they work, and job offers get posted." Mike nodded understanding, filed a large upward revision of his guess at Aorangi's population and a superfluous confirmation of their humanity, and turned back to 'Ao and Eru.

"But what does this have to do with the energy?" he asked. "I don't see any connection between sailing the place and powering it enough to keep the air good, and if they used any sort of leaves, especially ones big enough to be useful this far south, Keo and I should have seen them."

'Ao didn't answer at once, though her expression suggested less that she couldn't than that she was marshaling words. Eru spoke first.

"The deep water is a lot warmer, of course, and we try to keep as closely as we can to freezing temperature around the upper city. I expect that's part of the trouble now. There are five different power systems I've learned about in school so far, but they all depend on hot-water-is-down, cold-water-is-up."

'Ao started to fill in details, with some help from Mike's escorts. At some other time, Mike would have been impressed again at her learning speed, but all he could say now was, "I get it. Thanks, ki—young teachers."

The whole thing seemed straightforward enough. The heat below must be carried into the cylindrical mushroom stem, which presumably was not made of ice, through some sort of exchanger, and vaporize a working fluid that operated turbines or other mechanical devices on the way up. These in turn worked electrical generators, possibly grossly mechanical but more probably solid-state devices or, perhaps even more likely, pseudolife equipment. As long as there was a heat source and a heat sink, the engineering details mattered little.

The sink must be ocean water, Mike reflected, not only because it would be far more efficient than air, but because Keo and he could hardly have missed anything dumping a city power plant's worth of warm-air exhaust during their examination of the surface, sketchy as that had been.

And now, at least, they certainly wouldn't be using ice to cool their condensers. Not willingly, with their city melting around them.

The teachers were adding detail as he thought, but both were using professional words Mike didn't understand very well; a modest knowledge of basic physics didn't make him either a chemist or an engineer. 'Ao finally seemed to realize this and dragged the party off to see the installations she had been talking about. Mike had to concede to himself that it was all interesting, but his mind kept wandering to other matters like *when and how can we get out of here* and *how much can I find out about this "lost civilization" before we do? Did their ship get here first, or last, or about the same time as the other colonists? I can see what kept them out of touch with the others, at least at first, of course.*

Shades of Rider Haggard!

Hoani was, after all, a historian. But could he change or expand his thesis subject now? To put it mildly, his advising committee was not readily available for discussion.

Actually seeing the power devices, which were a little lower in the iceberg, was only marginally interesting, since their internal workings weren't visible and would probably not be comprehensible to him if they were. Also, Hoani's own thoughts were becoming more and more distracting. He finally, as politely as he could, pleaded fatigue, and requested guidance to his own quarters. The plea had some validity; the coral spicules they had noticed from the outside were smaller and closer together in the city, but a large fraction of any given tunnel floor was still ice. The low gravity allowed him to recover in time from each slip, but learning to walk in Aorangi was more complicated than in Muamoku. There it had been merely the gravity and the need for slow-response sea legs.

The children went their way, and Mike's guides left him at his room with his thanks.

And with his thoughts. No, he'd have to stay and finish this job. But there was nothing to keep him from coming back later with a few partners like, say, engineers who could work out when the evolutionary branching of the equipment used in Aorangi from that on the warmer parts of Kainui had occurred. He could tie this in with—

No, he couldn't. He had a family whose members deserved some of his time, and he deserved some of theirs. Suddenly, for the first time since reaching the planet, he felt a surge of homesickness that took every bit of his attention from his surroundings.

Joanie. Maui.

He didn't really notice what he was eating. He was thinking too hard. Quite suddenly, and for many reasons, he now cared *when* he could leave Kainui. The sooner the better, language project done or not. He couldn't leave from this city; Muamoku was the only settlement on Kainui with homing lights bright enough to guide a ship coming in from space. No other was willing to commit the energy needed. Mike suspected that Muamoku was quite content to keep it that way, though probably not to the extent of actively interfering with the policies of other floating cities.

So getting back to his hosts' home port was the central problem. He'd have to learn Wanaka's current feelings; it was possible that she was willing to stay here long enough to consummate the deal Hinemoa had outlined. The captain's apparent approval might or might not have been sincere. If it were, he would have to think out some more tempting long-term profits to change her mind. It seemed unlikely that anything else would.

He'd better start thinking right now, before seeking Wanaka and Keo.

His third or fourth thought suggested that something else be done first. He didn't exactly jump at it, but after some minutes of brooding decided to give it a try.

The room had a communicator for calling the office that had furnished his earlier guides. He was pretty sure he could find his way to the entrance they had used before, but didn't want anyone to think he was being secretive; he wasn't at all sure how far his hosts were prepared to go to keep *Mata* and her crew on hand. It was obvious, of course, that he couldn't make off unaided with the ship, but the locals might be suspicious on general principles. At least, the ones involved in commerce probably would.

Two guides, not the same as had accompanied him before, showed up in about a quarter of an hour, in sound armor as he had requested. Mike had already donned his own, and during the walk to the air lock rechecked the route very carefully. Once outside, he would have been perfectly happy to finish the trip on his own, but neither he nor his companions made the suggestion. His own motive was of course to avert suspicion; he wished he knew what that of the guides might be. Few words were spoken during the hike to where the ships lay, and none of those was really helpful. Mostly they had to do with the poor traction of Mike's armor shoes.

There had been at least one storm since Wanaka's crew had come inside; *Mata'italiga*'s deck and cabin roof were crusted with hailstones. Mike had given an explanation of why he had wanted to visit the craft, but this would have been a better one. He broke out 'Ao's shovel, slid the cover from the drinking breakers, and went to work. One of his guides offered to help with a shovel from a nearby ship, but Mike declined politely if absentmindedly. He had found more food for thought.

The breakers were almost empty.

This had not been the case when they had gone ashore. He filled them without comment, scraped the surplus hailstones overboard, stowed the shovel, and went to the air lock. The excuse he had given for the trip had been to get some of his own working materials. An unstated one was to check the reactions of his guides when he tried to enter the cabin alone. It was perfectly obvious that no adult could use the lock *with* him; but would they let him go in first? Or follow at once, before he could do anything? Could they feel sure there was nothing he might do to which their officials might object? Were they simply and generally suspicious of him, and presumably also of his crewmates? Or completely indifferent to anything they might do?

It was pretty obvious by now—at least to Wanaka, whose opinion tended to be contagious—that Hinemoa was a trader, whatever she might have claimed. Mike had already gathered that traders were the principal diplomats in most Kainuian cities. It had been clear almost from the beginning that she was also of high rank in whatever sort of government Aorangi had. This did not, however, have to mean that the entire population of the place either knew of or fully agreed with whatever policy she and her fellow officials might have adopted. Telephones were common enough in the city, but Mike had not yet seen anything corresponding to a newspaper or vision broadcast in the place. Technologial development here, as elsewhere on the planet, had presumably been guided by what each original colony ship had had on board and what actions had been forced on their crews by circumstances at the time of arrival.

Maybe he could fit more of this into his thesis after all.

The state of the drinking breakers had increased his own Wanaka-type suspicions; what about his present guides? Should he have admitted noticing the diminished water store? Would his failure to comment cause *them* to wonder? Or would they put it down to his presumed lack of seamanship? He had made no secret of this when describing his Earthly upbringing to the assembled teachers. Or were they completely ignorant of the whole breaker business, even that the tanks had been full when the crew had left the ship?

The guides glanced at each other as he opened the lock, but said nothing and made no effort to hold him back. That didn't necessarily mean much. It was not their ship, there were always the rules of courtesy—Mike suddenly realized that he had been remiss in failing to invite them inside; might not that make them suspicious?—and it was hard in any case to see what mischief he could possibly do.

He was back on deck with one of his record cases in a few moments, hoping that the brevity of the errand would excuse his discourtesy. Mike couldn't decide whether the guides were relieved or not. He waded ashore—he had flipped back his helmet when picking up the shovel, and now closed it again in proper routine—and started back toward the city entrance. The others followed.

He deliberately missed a turning on the way back, and was promptly corrected, but had no way of guessing whether the apparent slip relieved his guides or not. It might or might not have the effect of easing the obvious local policy of having him accompanied on all occasions, or of reinforcing it; either way he was no worse off. Once again he realized that he was picking up some of the mercantile paranoia of the captain. He didn't really like this, but just now it might be useful.

He accepted guidance back to his room, thanked his escorts, and asked when the school would need him again. They didn't know, but said he would be called in plenty of time. He nodded, remarked that he might be in the captain's and mate's nearby quarters rather than his own, waved a dismissal, and thankfully went inside to doff his armor. He had become used to wearing it for over a day at a time during the large fraction of a local year since they had left Muamoku, but it was never really comfortable. People generally accepted that no really efficient recycling wear could be, but complaining was of course discourteous and likely to be answered with a shrug and the remark "Grow your own, then."

Waiting until his escort should be well out of sight, Hoani left his room again and went to the adjoining but unconnected apartment shared by captain and mate. Keo answered his knock at once, and gestured him to enter. Wanaka, seated at a worktable with charts—columns of numbers rather than maps in the Earthly sense—in front of her, looked up. Neither seemed surprised to see him, but his report of the drained water breakers caused them to look sharply at each other for a moment, then nod slowly.

"I wondered how they'd do it," the mate remarked. "What d'you suppose they'll use for an excuse if we say anything?"

"Doesn't matter. They'll either have one, which will leave us free for a while longer, or they won't. In that case they'll either take our armor or simply lock us up."

Evidently, Hoani decided, Wanaka had not been sincere in accepting Hinemoa's trade proposal. She was intending to leave after all.

"Why should they bother with that, if they've taken our water?" he asked, and promptly wished he hadn't.

"You've refilled the breakers already. If they drain them again, we can refill them at sea easily enough. There aren't quite as many storms here in the high latitudes, but there are enough."

"Then why did they take the water at all?"

The captain smiled in a way Mike had not seen before.

"I am guessing. I'd like to make sure I'm right before we risk leaving, but don't see how I can. Have you seen 'Ao since we arrived?"

Mike reported in some detail his encounter with the children. The captain showed little interest in the city model or power information, though it became evident later that she had listened carefully. She had a higher priority.

"Did 'Ao have 'Oloa with her? I know she brought it into the city."

Mike thought a moment. "No. She must have left it at Eru's home. All her talk was with Eru and me, except for courtesy to my guides. I'd guess she didn't want to forget and talk to it."

Keo spoke up. "She wanted me to take it, earlier. I got the impression she'd been embarrassed by something Eru said about it. Maybe I wasn't as sympathetic as I should have been."

For the second time since Mike had known her, Wanaka used language that was plainly rude; this time he couldn't decipher it at all, but even her husband raised his eyebrows.

"Keo, get down to Eru's home and—can you find it?"

"Not without help."

"Then get help. Wanting to talk to her won't be suspicious. If no one answers when you get there you won't be able to go in, of course, but wait as long as necessary. If she's there alone, or comes back alone while you're waiting, make sure about the doll. If Eru or any of his family is there with her, tell her I need to see her, and while you're talking look around to see if the doll's in sight. Don't let Eru or—"

"Of course." Keokolo disappeared.

"We're leaving?" Mike's words weren't entirely a question.

"If we can. It depends on two things I don't know yet: just how the breakers were emptied, and whether we still have the doll. We could do without it—maybe—but I'd rather not. If the breakers were emptied through the regular drains, then these folks will probably take our armor or restrain us by force if they catch us trying to leave. If, as I'm hoping, they punched holes, we may have a better chance."

Mike raised an eyebrow himself, but didn't ask for more details. He was startled when the captain supplied them.

"I *hope* they just punched holes in the breakers. It would mean they didn't expect them to heal. Did you know those seven ships we've seen are all the city has?"

"Do you know that, or did they tell you?"

The captain gave him an approving glance, which rather

worried Mike. If he were getting cynical enough to please Wanaka, maybe he was in trouble. He shouldn't be taking for granted that anything he was told was probably a lie. These traders . . .

"There are no others around the city; the place they are lying seems to be the only port. The city is moving. How could the others, if there are any, find it?"

"We asked about that before."

"And got an answer. Did you believe it?"

"It seemed plausible to me," Mike evaded.

Wanaka merely looked at him. He changed the subject.

"How do you expect to find Muamoku?"

"Circle the world westward at its latitude, of course."

"And why couldn't these folks do just the same thing?"

"You didn't notice, either?" The captain looked rather smug. "*This city doesn't try to maintain latitude!* They're quite casual about north and south drift. They worry about melting if they get much too far north, of course, since the town is made mostly of ice, but they certainly don't care about keeping their latitude range narrow enough to be useful for searching ships; remember the mists at this far south are even heavier than closer to the equator.

"Besides, they've been too far north too recently; they've lost a lot of city to melting—"

"You've seen this, or just been told?"

"*We've* seen it! We've seen the change in water line."

"All right, they have only a few ships. How does that connect with empty drinking breakers?"

But Wanaka simply smiled again. It seemed that Mike was not yet on full crew status.

Keokolo was more than an hour returning from his errand, and Wanaka seemed to be worrying slightly about how close they were to sunset. When he returned, 'Ao was with him, but the doll was not.

When the captain, clearly restraining her temper with an effort, asked where it was, the child replied that she didn't think she'd need it on watch and had not wanted to bring it for fear of rousing suspicion, and she didn't want to carry it on the tour of the city because someone might wonder why anyone as old as she was would be carrying a doll around. Wanaka cooled down at once. Mike could guess the captain's thoughts; the child was using her head. He wondered in passing whether games theory was a formal science on Kainui. With trading a major industry . . .

"All right. Very good, in fact. Can you get back to Eru's by yourself?"

"*Mau.*"

"Do it. Get 'Oloa and your armor, and tell them you're on watch tonight if you haven't already. Can you get back to the ship on your own, too?" 'Ao merely nodded this time.

"It doesn't look as though anyone gets stopped at the air lock, but if they worry about someone your age going out alone this close to sunset tell them you're on watch, and if they're still bothered ask for someone to guide you so you can obey orders. You don't like admitting that you're too young to do without a guide, of course. Be insulted if you like, but not so much they bring you back here instead of to the ships."

"*'Ioe.*" 'Ao looked appropriately indignant.

"We'll be with you somewhere around sunset, no later if we can help it. I wish I knew when that was; we're farther south than I've ever been, the tables don't give sunrise and sunset for latitudes greater either way than fifty. At least we're close to the solstice, though.

"Check the water supply when you get there. If it's

down—Mike refilled it a little while ago—don't worry and *don't* try to refill it unless there's actually a storm going on."

The girl looked indignant once more, but the remark about obeying orders had sunk in and she only nodded. Wanaka decided against having her repeat her commands and gestured toward the door. 'Ao disappeared.

"Now, Mike. Can *you* find the air lock and the ship by yourself?"

"Yes, Captain. No trouble."

"Good, because I think you'll have to go last. Keo and I probably won't be noticed in armor, especially if we don't go together, but people will see and remember you. You have one of your note cases ashore? Good. Keo will go first, I'll follow in about ten minutes, you wait at least twenty more, then head back to the ship with your case—I hope there's just one? Or at least not more than you can carry? Good. We'll hope no one wonders; maybe the fact that you took cases with you on other trips will keep them from wondering—"

"They're not all traders, I noticed," Hoani couldn't help remarking. "I get the impression that most of them wouldn't know what I was doing. They just wouldn't care, except for congenital loafers, and there don't seem to be many of those on this world." Wanaka may not have interpreted the remark as a slur; at least, she let it pass. She put just one more question set.

"Did you notice whether the watch on the other ships were clearing hail while you were?"

"They weren't."

"Had they done it before you came? Were their decks clear?"

Mike strained his memory. "Yes. They were. Maybe that's why the watch was there this time."

"And why not before? What's changed since then?"

"We're farther south. I don't know what else."

"There are fewer storms farther south, and a bigger change in buoyancy after a storm, because the basic surface salinity is greater the farther one gets from the tropical rain belt. It increases away from the equator, at least until we get to the neighborhood of the ice cap, where I suppose melting dilutes it again." She paused, eyed the man thoughtfully, then seemed to make a decision.

"Mike, you didn't think these folks were *making* a *wave* come in at just the right time, did you?"

"I—oh. Of course. No. They must change the city's buoyancy. They can raise and lower it. Not very far either way, I'd guess, but two or three meters anyway. I must be twins; I couldn't be that stupid all by myself. You know, whoever is handling the buoyancy tanks right now must be very, very uptight."

To Mike's relief, he had gotten slightly ahead of Wanaka. "Why?"

"Because the tanks must be big enough to lower or raise the city far enough to be useful even when all its normal floating ice is present. Right now, letting them fill too full could submerge everything—and if the sea gets to the air lock there'll be more than buoyancy tanks getting filled. I'm sure they must have some emergency way to forestall that, but they won't like to use it, any more than you'd like to see all of Muamoku's floats submerged."

Wanaka nodded slowly. Mike had an alarming thought.

"Captain, you wouldn't try to—"

"Of course I wouldn't. In the first place, I wouldn't kill anyone, let alone a whole city. In the second, whatever happens to get *Mata* back to sea will have to happen with all four of us aboard. I'm simply assuming that Hinemoa won't let us go, which is pretty obvious, you must admit."

Mike was somewhat relieved that she had put the first and second items in that order, but said nothing. He had little chance, actually; there was a knock at the coral door. Mike was closest to it, and opened it at Wanaka's nod. As they had expected, it was 'Ao. As they had not, it was also Hinemoa and Eru.

Wanaka as usual controlled her expression perfectly. Mike hoped that his own was less readable to the native. The latter spoke at once.

"Captain, how many children can you carry?"

"Why—well, for how long?"

"With good luck, about two days. With bad, indefinitely."

"*Mata* can feed and breathe about four more of 'Ao's mass without overloading oxygen and food equipment, I'd say. I'm guessing, because this far south our leaf doesn't get as much power. Why?"

"We're launching in just under two hours, carrying as many childen as we can."

"Why? Or would you rather not say?"

"I'd rather not, but I will. We're making an emergency drop of the bottom kilometer of the city shaft, so as to float higher. We're getting close to the ice cap. We have to reach it to get more ice, but from here on south the ocean gets less salty because of the melting cap, so we'll be settling. There's no saying just how far. We can't lift any higher without the drop because of melting loss—Mike must have noticed when they showed him the city chart that there was a lot less than a tenth of the volume above water."

Mike made no comment since he had in fact failed to notice this, but Hinemoa wasn't asking for confirmation and anyway he was busy translating. She went on, "We can't risk settling far, so some weight has to go, and we've already dropped all our regular ballast. What's come in on the last few loads hasn't been processed into slugs we can handle rapidly, and even if we added yours, which I hope you realize is still yours, there wouldn't be enough to make a difference. Once we've made the drop there'll be no way to get the ships off, assuming it does lift us as far as it should. We're launching as many people as we can, and if we don't lose the city, hoping to take them back in a couple of days when we've started to gather cap ice. The times this happened before we came through all right, but we're not taking chances."

"Of course," agreed the captain.

"So get your people aboard pronto. Eru wants to go with you if you're willing. Other children are being selected and siblings separated, and will come along. You can take three besides Eru, you say."

Mike was not a hero by instinct, but there are some things a civilized adult can't, and some things he or she simply must, do. He answered without translating for or consulting with the captain.

"Add three more to *Mata*'s load. They won't use more food or air than I do, and I'm not important in handling *Mata*."

Hinemoa showed no expression. "Good. We can use your muscle here. Since Eru is going, my husband and I will stay, of course. Captain, you and your crew get to your ship and prepare for launch. Your other passengers will be brought to the harbor." Mike translated the order and reported his offer. Wanaka showed no surprise, either. Keo gripped his hand briefly but said nothing.

"The tricky part will be submerging just enough for

launch," was Hinemoa's parting remark. "If we don't over-shoot on that, there shouldn't be any trouble later. We'll get ready for the drop, then sink just enough—we hope—to let the fleet off, and immediately let go of the shaft segment. Don't wait for orders or warning; go out with the spill. In a minute or two after that you'll know whether a standby or a hunt for another city is in order." She gestured to Mike to follow her, and left.

Fortunately there was no need to descend nineteen kilometers, or even to the bottom of the ice part of the city. In another large cavern a few hundred meters below the city model dozens of washers, presumably of some variety of coral, obviously not ice for several reasons, nearly covered the ice floor. Each was about five meters across. The floor was more than usually reinforced with coral also, to what depth Mike could only guess; he had no way of telling how much of the twenty-kilometer shaft's weight was counteracted by buoyancy, though obviously it couldn't all be. The ice part—mushroom cap of the model—clearly had to be at the top.

Each washer supported a half-meter-thick rod, apparently of the same material. The top of each of these was threaded, with a huge capstan shaped like a wing nut keeping it in place.

Four of the "nuts" were pointed out to the crew of men standing by. One of these said loudly, "Those are the ones to unwind. We have to get them off all the way; the actual release is remotely controlled and is down at the separation point. These are simply safety backups." Mike wondered for a moment why he was explaining this to natives as well as to him, then realized these were probably a group selected for muscle rather than a permanent emergency crew. The work started, with six men at each side of each wing nut.

Hoani had supposed he could do the work of two or maybe three, but had forgotten his traction problems; the others wore studded boots. The foreman saw the difficulty, but a glance convinced him that looking for anything to fit the visitor's feet would be a waste of time.

Fortunately the threads were well lubricated, and the capstans were free in less than a quarter hour. Nothing visible now supported the projecting rods. Everyone backed away from them and watched tensely.

The people at the main release controls, whoever and wherever they were and however the controls themselves worked, were holding the buck. Until the rods vanished . . .

After a reasonable time of suspense, they did vanish. There was no way for Mike to tell whether they were encased in pipes or wider shafts or anything at all, and the sounds that accompanied their departure weren't informative, but he thought he could feel a slight and brief upward acceleration.

The end of the tense silence suggested that others had felt it, too. There was no shouting or cheering, though most of the danger was presumably over; but conversation resumed. At the foreman's order, all started up the ramps.

Mike assumed—no, hoped—that he had merely not felt the much smaller acceleration when the city had settled to allow the launch. If for some reason that had not occurred, and the ships were still in the harbor, of course, it still *might* not be a catastrophe; the launching had been merely a worst-scenario precaution, after all. It would bother Wanaka, though. There would be no way for *anyone* to get to sea, as far as Mike knew, until tons upon tons of replacement ballast had been collected and processed. Of course, water for the control tanks might now be enough; there was no telling without a supply of numbers he didn't have.

And preparing the other ballast would take a very long time, considering how much would obviously be needed and how slowly it would be collected.

He felt quite sure, now, what the ballast was.

He wondered what Wanaka would do if the launch had indeed taken place. If she decided to get away, leaving Mike behind—this somehow seemed improbable—it was unlikely that anyone would follow, unless someone badly wanted to recover the children. He knew the basic planet-wide customs pretty well now, and Aorangi seemed to be following them fairly closely as far as family matters were concerned, but couldn't feel quite what the reaction would be this time. The people could be sure the kids were safe enough, except for the normal risks of the sea, but they didn't seem enthusiastic about contact with the temperate-zone cities.

Don't worry, idiot. There's nothing you can do about it now. It would be nice to get home again sometime, though.

The group paused in the cavern of the city model; apparently everyone regardless of profession could read its various symbols. He was encouraged to see that the icons he had interpreted as ships were no longer visible—encouraged, since it seemed likely that if this implied anything worse than a successful launch there would be a lot more general excitement.

Quite sure that he could now find his way from here to the entrance, he unobtrusively left the crowd and made his way into the tunnel maze. He managed not to get lost.

As he approached the air lock he found a large crowd of people, mostly men and unarmored like himself, going in the same direction. He began once more to wonder, since about half of them seemed to be carrying hail shovels.

It couldn't be an emergency; while noise armor was not really needed in air—the thunder was a nuisance above water, but not the deadly menace the overpressure waves from the core-ocean interface represented to a swimmer. Something must be expected, though. He saw no sign of Hinemoa anywhere, and of course didn't want to look foolish to anyone ignorant of his background, so he simply went with the crowd. It could be that they just wanted to make sure the ships with their children were all right, but there seemed far too many people here to be only the parents, or even uncles, aunts, and adult cousins, of the youngsters who could possibly have fit in eight vessels, even if only one child from each family had been launched. Besides, that didn't explain the shovels.

Outside, the crowd didn't even head toward the lake. It divided, with very little conversation, into five streams, each fanning out in a different direction. Mike joined one of these, and shortly found himself in a crowd of somewhat over a hundred people assembled around one of the hail-filled craters he, Keo, and 'Ao had found on their first walk and blamed on lightning.

It was not, however, filled with hail now; it was a gaping hole of indeterminate depth.

There was plenty of hail on the ground; there had, after all, been at least two storms since *Mata*'s original arrival, and very probably more. The shovels went to work at once, and loose hail began to vanish into the pit. Mike could only watch and wonder.

In a few minutes it became evident why there were fewer shovels than men; the latter tired fairly quickly—once again, it was plain that only a small fraction of the citizens could be sailors—and the tools changed hands often. Hoani, seeing nothing complicated about whatever was going on, began to take turns himself. This seemed to be appreciated, but after he had slipped and fallen two or three times someone suggested that he work a little farther from the pit. It was not, after all, necessary to hurl each shovelful all the way every time, and if he went in himself it would delay matters seriously, they pointed out.

Most of the hail by now was too far from the edge for anyone, even Mike, to toss it all the way. Throwing *toward* the hole was enough; someone else could make the next toss.

The basic ice had been cleared of hail for a radius of fully two hundred meters when Hinemoa found him.

"Thanks," she said. "I didn't know where you'd gone, but you're being about as useful as you could have been anywhere."

"What's going on here, anyway? You don't need all this water for the city."

"Not as water, but we need the ice. The shafts take it down about a kilometer. It gets drained, packed, and shoved outside. The lump floats up and catches on the bottom of the ice section. Any meltwater, plus any that gets in through the lock while the ice is going out, drains to a lower tank and vines take it back to the top and dump it into the sea at the edge."

"Vines? Oh, I see. Sap rising. I should have guessed. I wonder why we didn't see them when we were sailing around the city. Plants—trees most impressively—do it on Earth. Osmosis or capillary?"

"Osmosis, usually, but we're always trying to design better vines. Better hand that shovel to someone else; even you must get tired sometime."

Rather gratefully Mike obeyed.

"I take it the launch went all right."

"Oh, yes. And we've found a good current and are mov-

ing faster toward the edge of the cap. The hailstones are helpful, but wait until you see how we do it with the floe ice. The
big chunks are hard to get up to this height; it's lucky ice is
slippery. They lose a lot less to melting than the hail does,
though. Within a year or so we'll have the bottom of the city
cap replenished, and be on our way to replacing the emergency ballast. What do you think we could offer your captain
for her supply?"

Mike was speechless for some seconds. He had been
almost sure before, as several pieces of formerly disconnected
information had joined up, but had not expected confirmation from Hinemoa, of all people. He'd have to start ridding
himself of the Wanaka Conviction.

"The gold? You do use gold for ballast."

"What else would tonnes of it be good for? A couple of
kilograms would keep the pseudolife designers happy for a
year. I know the stuff is pretty, but how much could the people of one city use up in jewelry? Why do you think we grow
gold-fish at all, and try to keep improving them?"

"I really must be twins," Hoani muttered again, more
softly this time. Hinemoa looked slightly puzzled, but did not
ask for an explanation. Courtesy again; the man had obviously not been speaking to her. He recovered himself after a
moment.

"Then you have other gold-fish. Why were you so concerned about this one?"

"The others are moored to the city, can't get as deep as
we'd like or wander as far as we'd like, so they collect very
slowly. This one had a modification that was supposed to
guide it back to the edge of the ice cap. It didn't work as well
as we'd hoped. That's another reason we're grateful to your
captain; we'd actually given up hope of getting it back. We

recovered the guiding equipment from the fish the first time you helped us find it."

Mike felt he might be getting cured of the trader's paranoia he had been acquiring from Wanaka. Hinemoa couldn't be lying; everything fitted so perfectly and made so much sense. This place should certainly be trading with the temperate-zone cities, though it was a little hard to see just now what either had that the others might want very badly. Cities riding on normally grown floats certainly didn't need gold or much of anything else for ballast; Aorangi, with its thermal-gradient power source, didn't need other metals for battery electrodes even if its latitude made pseudolife photosynthesizers relatively ineffective. But at least, neither could really have anything it needed to keep secret from the others. The city rulers would realize that even if the traders didn't—if they were different people.

"How is any guide method supposed to work on *this* world?" he asked. "There is no long-distance communication, and nothing is going to do celestial navigation from kilometers under the sea, certainly. A smeller like the one we thought *Malolo* had picked up wouldn't work at any great depth in your thermal and salinity turbulence. How?"

Hinemoa smiled, perhaps regretfully.

"Sorry. 'Fraid I can't tell you," she answered.

And Hinemoa really *must* be a city official, not just a trader. So much for reason. Mike changed the subject, but not because he wanted to.

"When do the ships dock again?" he asked.

"Not until we have a good supply of ice away from the cap and down where it's useful. Half a year, maybe."

"But—"

"You said the ships. We'll have the children back inside the lock in a few days. They have their noise armor, and can swim from the ships. The crews will have to stay aboard, of course; we can't afford to lose any vessels. It takes a long time to grow new ones, and some parts can't be replaced at all. The ship seeds are incomplete, though I'm afraid I can't tell you in just what way."

"How—oh, all right. How about *why*? Just plain bad design?"

Hinemoa looked thoughtful for a moment. Then, "Well, you're not a sailor any more than I am and I won't give details, but I don't think it's possible to design a seed which will grow every single bit of a ship or any other complicated machine. Weren't you and your crew lucky to have salvaged a good deal of your original ship's equipment? Didn't you need to use more than one seed, anyway? Could you have replaced *everything*—in life support, for example?"

"I don't know. I got the impression that Wanaka and Keo weren't too worried, but maybe that was because we *did* have all the stuff we couldn't grow."

"I'd almost guarantee it was. I won't be any more specific, but we can grow all the new hulls and sails and paint we want. They just wouldn't be very useful at sea."

"Maybe Wanaka can supply the seeds you need. If she can't from our present stock, surely she could get them from Muamoku or any other of the temperate-zone cities. I don't suppose they'd charge any *more* than the traffic will bear."

"I doubt very much that they could, but I'm not going to tell you why."

"Because you don't want anyone to know just what you're lacking? I suppose because they *would* charge the ocean for it?"

Hinemoa shook her head negatively.

"They couldn't supply it. And now, no more discussion. I may have said too much already. I know you're not a sailor but I don't know all your background, and I have mixed feelings about how worried I should be. Why don't you go back to your quarters and get some food and sleep? We're going to ask you to help move ice later on, if whatever loyalty you feel to your captain allows it, and it will be hard work even for you."

"You said we were approaching the ice cap. I'd like to have a look at that first, if there's no objection."

"That's all right. I'll be busy; you can find your quarters by yourself, I gather."

"Sure. No problem."

Hinemoa nodded, gestured a farewell, and took a shovel from a nearby laborer. Mike glanced at the suns, estimated their height above the invisible horizon, and made his way south. This happened to be the current direction of the lake-cum-harbor, which was nearly enough empty so that swimming and wading across seemed easier than going around. The iceberg's treacherous footing emphasized the preference. Whenever possible he worked his way uphill, and eventually found himself able to see the water's edge in every direction.

This had not been the case earlier; much of the edge of the berg had been hidden behind closer ice hummocks even from its highest points. Now, he realized, the city was riding considerably higher than before and much that had been under water was now exposed. The sea was farther away.

Just coming into view through the haze was the ice cap. He had assumed it would be about at water level, since what had frozen at the ocean surface could hardly be sunk very far by hail landing on it and would presumably be melted from below by warmer and saltier water about as fast as the hail piled up above.

This was true enough, but the equilibrium did bring the ice sheet's surface half a meter or so—a little more in places—above the water. This meant, he realized, extremely large and heavy fragments to haul aboard the berg and slide to the collection pits. With, it seemed, nothing but muscle power.

Hinemoa was right; he'd better get food and sleep. He had no trouble in finding either the air lock or, once inside that, his former quarters, and never knew just how long he slept. He was awakened by 'Ao's shaking his shoulder. He sat up in some surprise.

"You're back already? Hinemoa said you youngsters would have to swim."

"Most of us did. A few stayed on the ships. I'm going back pretty soon, but the captain wanted me to talk with you."

"Important, I expect."

"She says so. At least, she wants you to tell me anything you think is important that's happened since the launch."

"I don't know for certain what's important. She's right about there being only seven ships in their fleet. Hinemoa admitted they couldn't make more, but wouldn't say why. They use their gold mainly for ballast, to keep the low end of the city pointing down. You can see how much they'd need for that. Tonnes and tonnes. No other city could use even a tiny part of what they have to collect, and Aorangi needs that badly so I don't see yet what they'd trade any of it for. If Muamoku or any other city were collecting gold itself, then *maybe* something could be worked out, but these people have a lot of gold-fish tethered to the city and except for times like right now they always have plenty for themselves."

"All right. I'll tell her all that. Anything else? And do you think you'd have a chance to swim back to *Mata*? Or would they try to keep you? Or can't you guess because they haven't said anything about it to you?"

Mike thought for a moment, and answered very slowly, still thinking between words.

"I don't know whether they'll care if I get away. Hinemoa told me a lot, and may have been assuming I'd never be able to pass it on. Perhaps we'll find out when she doesn't let *you* go back.

"There's another point, though. If I stay, I might be able to find out some of whatever Hinemoa wouldn't tell me. If whatever holds them down to such a small fleet turns out to be something Muamoku can provide, there *would* be a good trading base. I think I'd better stay at least until the ships can dock again, and find out all I can in the meantime. Tell Wanaka that, anyway. If you're back here soon because they won't let you off the iceberg, we'll think of something else. *Pono?*"

"*Pono, Kahuna.* If they won't let me go back to the ship I'll come right back here to tell you, and we can think some more. If you're not here I'll leave a note and then go looking for you." The child left before Mike could think of a good way to thank her for the compliment. He rather feared she might be praising his skill at mercantile intrigue.

He was awake now anyway, decided he'd probably slept long enough, and ate again slowly and thoughtfully. It seemed likely that his muscles would be wanted by now, and while he might possibly come up with something useful just sitting here thinking, it seemed a safer bet that he'd pick up worthwhile information from company. Also, it might be a good idea to do some more heavy labor; there was no telling what this gravity might have done to his muscles by now.

He donned his armor and opened the door, to be met by another child who had apparently been waiting patiently for him.

"You can pull better with these, Hinemoa thinks," the youngster said as he handed the man a pair of well-spiked soles evidently designed to strap to his armor boots.

"Thanks, I probably can. Should I wear them inside, or not until I'm out of the city?"

"Now is all right. The floors will heal. Shall I show you the way?"

"Thank you, I know it. But stay with me if you like. Is the ice being brought in? Do they need me?"

"Yes. Your strength will help a lot more than mine, but I'll go and help, too."

Aorangi was only a couple of hundred meters from the ice pack by now—actually much less, Mike realized as he remembered the very shallow slope of the submerged ice. Several large chunks showing above the water between city and ice sheet were clearly being supported by something underneath, and were being towed and pushed by waders rather than swimmers. Everyone he could see, even his young guide, he now noticed, was equipped with the same extra-traction equipment the youngster had brought him; it was evidently not a special-order job after all.

He learned very little during the next several hours, since very little was being said by anyone. He kept an eye out for 'Ao, but didn't see her. No ships were visible, but the water was probably too shallow for them between city and pack ice, he guessed. 'Ao might, of course, have been confined in some way to keep her out of his sight, but he managed to keep from worrying about the possibility. There were many children helping with the transportation, especially close to the cap where the loads were deeper in the water and closer to floating, but most of them seemed older than 'Ao.

He'd listen and think, since the muscle work didn't interfere with either, until someone relieved him. This determination resulted in his putting in a very full day's work. He was beginning to wonder if they might let him work until dropped when someone—not Hinemoa—who had been near him for several hours told him that it was up to him to decide when he needed food or rest; the job was organized only in the sense that everyone knew what had to be done. He thanked his informant and returned to his quarters.

There was a brief note there, in something less than perfect spelling: "No trouble. I'm going back to *Mata* again. We're to the west. Get to us even if you have to sneak away, the captain says. No people on the shore there, but some of the other ships are around. If you think you can swim far enough, get in the water out of their sight. Don't wait for night if you can help it. You'll be hard to recognize swimming anyway."

Mike wondered how long ago the message had been left, how long the captain might be willing to wait for him, what she was planning, and whether he should take a chance on swimming in his present state of fatigue. The thought of nearly three thousand kilometers of water below influenced his decision, for no good reason since his armor would keep him afloat anyway and he could drown just as readily in two meters. He ate lightly, rested for an hour, and then sought the outdoors again.

Sneaking was not really necessary. There were, as he already knew, several pits being served by the ice carriers. People were traveling in many directions between the holes and the source to the south, and no one showed any suspicion of him even when he passed the westernmost pit and kept on going. The Aorangi people evidently knew that what they were doing was important and didn't believe in letting themselves be distracted from it.

It was a long walk; Aorangi had risen some distance in the water, and the "shore" was averaging at least half a kilometer farther than before from the center. Once past the hummocky central area that Mike was now sure had never been submerged he could see a wide stretch of ocean and, fairly soon, four of the ships, drifting with sails down or possibly, he realized, at anchor. They were spread far enough apart to make the invisibility of the others reasonable.

The northernmost of the four he could see was easily recognizable as *Mata*, leaving the suspicion that the other three were all still farther north. Heading in that direction until the nearby ones were out of sight would be pointless if that were the case; he'd merely come in sight of the others. He might as well start swimming from here. After a little thought he removed his traction soles, and after a little more ran their straps through his tool belt; they might be needed again if he had to come back ashore.

After his first step toward the sea, he thought the time might already have come; he slipped and fell at once. He snatched the coral spikes that were also still in the belt, but by the time he had them properly in his grip, the grip was inadequate. Even with the shallow slope of the ice and Kainui's feeble gravity, he had picked up enough speed to tear them from his hands as he jabbed them into the ice, and just barely had time to close his helmet before reaching the water.

He wondered what Wanaka would say about that. She, or at least someone aboard *Mata*, had certainly seen him; the larger sail was already rising and the bows turning toward him. In less than five minutes, he judged, he was climbing aboard. If anyone on the nearest Aorangi vessel had noticed him, the fact was not yet evident.

Greetings were brief. Both sails were now up, and the bows pointing almost northwest. Even this seemed unnoticed from the other ships. Didn't they care, or did they merely lack relevant orders? There was no point in asking Wanaka or Keo, presumably, but perhaps 'Ao might have heard something to explain it while she was ashore. He'd ask later, if the little one when she came down from her station didn't bring the matter up herself.

Their course puzzled Mike, who now knew enough to

recognize that this was not the top-speed heading. He did ask about this, since it seemed a perfectly reasonable question.

"I'm hoping the gold-fish is still afloat, and we'll have time to pick up more," was the answer.

"I thought we had a pretty good load now."

"No. We were asked to put the rest of it ashore before the last launch, and nearly all our other metal as well."

"And we're getting them some more? Didn't 'Ao tell you they had a lot of tethered fish?"

"Yes. It's not for them. I'm hoping to get *us* some more."

Mike, reverting to type, didn't ask why, but did have another question. "Since we don't know it's still there, how long will we look for it?"

"One day. Then close enough to pure north to reach Muamoku latitude as soon as possible."

Mike's relieved feelings must have showed on his face, but the captain didn't seem to notice. He asked permission to sleep and went to the cabin without thinking to ask about the water supply. The trivial thought did slip across his consciousness that the captain obviously would never say "up" north. Kainuian charts weren't pictorial.

He learned, after waking up many hours later, that the breakers had been essentially full this time; there seemed to have been no effort to drain them again and, he was told, no evidence that the previous emptying had been done by violence. The drain taps must have been used, and since Mike himself had found them closed, shut again by whoever had done the job. That left another minor question or two: why had it been done at all in the first place, and why not again?

It did not occur, and never would have occurred, to Mike that Wanaka and Keo had only his own report as evidence that the tanks had ever been emptied at all, or that the captain would ever have allowed mere courtesy to interfere with getting the answer to an obviously important question, or even that she would have regarded the term "mere courtesy" as an oxymoron like "only theory."

Aorangi had made a great deal of progress south while they were there. They had sailed for several days longer than on the fish-to-city trip when 'Oloa told them that they were in the neighborhood of the gold source. To Wanaka's unconcealed delight, this was still afloat and took less than four hours to find.

'Ao was left at the masthead this time, with Mike on deck and only the other two mining. Now that they knew the system, however, things went much faster. The fish still showed no signs of imminent submersion when they had taken aboard all they dared; Mike wondered whether another design flaw was showing up or merely that its leaves were slower picking up energy this far south. He raised the question, but no one could either choose between the possibilities or suggest a better one.

Then at last at *Mata* headed north. Not exactly north, but a compromise between best sailing speed and shortest distance to the desired parallel, as directed by the doll. 'Ao's time on the masthead had been wasted; there had been no sign of another ship.

Mike hinted once or twice, but Wanaka offered no explanation why she had collected a cargo with no obvious use. He did not resent the time spent at the fish, however, even though he was having increasingly frequent spells of homesickness. For one reason, he had now been fully and formally accepted into the crew, would receive an appropriate if rather small share of the trip's profits, and there were plenty of worlds where gold, for various historical and technological reasons, still had significant exchange value. The expense of interstellar travel came mostly from paying off ship construction mortgages; time of flight meant more to freight charges than mass of cargo.

There was one world he knew of less than a hundred parsecs from Kainui where most of the value of any art form stemmed from its permanence. Maybe Wanaka knew about this, too, but Mike as usual chose not to ask. It was not, he told himself, merely that it was embarrassing to have something explained to him when he should have figured it out for himself; there was the triumph of actually figuring it out for himself.

Even he was beginning to feel bored when 'Oloa reported that they were at Muamoku's latitude, and *Mata* pointed her bows westward. For all they could know eastward might have been better, but there was no way to tell. The city might have been just out of sight in the haze in either direction, or halfway around the planet. As the doll would have said and even 'Ao now understood too well to ask, "One equation, at least three unknowns." West was the standard way to go in that stage of a navigation problem, because cities in general had an eastward drift and the odds were slightly in favor of a shorter trip if ships went to meet them.

Mata's crew settled down to an almost unvarying, though busy, routine. The tacks were short, since the wind came generally from the northwest, and they did not want to be carried farther than city-spotting distance from the parallel they were following. 'Ao spent most of her waking time at the masthead, though it seemed very unlikely that she would sight anything for which Wanaka would want to dump any of the gold—though maybe, Hoani thought, she hoped to trade some of it for something of more certain value. That would presumably be to ships of other cities. If she had told even her husband about what was in her mind, which Mike considered most probable, the mate had been equally secretive.

It was unlikely that they would meet any homeward bound Muamoku craft, of course, since these would be traveling in the same direction and at comparable speed. Mike had no way of guessing the chances of encountering representatives of any other city. The two they had seen prior to the Aorangi event had both been met in the first few days of their now nearly year-long trip, which would discourage even the most inexperienced and optimistic statistician from risking a public opinion.

They had been tracing the parallel for over four weeks of Kainui days when 'Ao did sight a ship, however. Wanaka and Keo eyed it carefully, since 'Ao had not reported its course along with its presence; maybe it was actually bound for Muamoku as well.

But it wasn't. 'Ao had not reported the course because it was hove to, and she hadn't been able to believe her eyes.

"What sort of fish?" the captain finally called.

The child still hesitated, but finally, "I can't see any," came back.

"That's silly. Why else would anyone be hove to in the daytime?"

"I don't know, but I can't see anything but the ship itself."

The adults fell silent. Mike had an idea, but details were still coming together and he didn't dare announce it yet. *Mata*'s crew simply stared, all but Hoani with minds as open as their eyes.

"No signal flags," the child finally reported.

Mike almost spoke. Wanaka did. "Not pirates, I hope. How many on deck, can you see?"

"Just one. It looks—well, I'd say young. Maybe my size. I can't be sure, because I don't know how big the ship is."

There were a number of clicks that he felt must be audible as drifting items connected in Mike's brain. He forced himself to speak.

"There'll be someone else out to take the tiller in a few moments," he said. "Wait and see. They'll turn on an intercept heading after that happens."

"You're sure? You *know* they're pirates?" asked Keo.

"I'm about ninety percent sure of what I said, but I'm equally sure they're not pirates."

"Why? Who or what are they? What do you think they want of us?" Wanaka asked.

"Put your trading hat on. You wanted gold, when we first met them."

"You think these are—but I wanted to *sell* gold. Then I found out no other city would want to buy it; it's good for nothing but ballast, and regular cities can use sea water if they need that."

"But you've thought of another use for it, or you wouldn't have collected another load. I don't know what you have in mind, but you wouldn't have mined that fish again just for jewelry."

"But these folks wouldn't know what I have, and if they don't know and come for us anyway, they don't care. How do you know they aren't pirates?"

"You haven't recognized that ship yet?"

"Recognized it? How—?" The captain's eyes turned back to the other craft. Two more people—adults this time—had appeared on its deck, and one had taken the tiller from the child. The other was working sails, and it was already moving toward *Mata*. Mike allowed himself to smile, and went on.

"I don't know very much about Kainui ships, so I can't guess what the chances are of two looking so much alike, but this one is a single-outrigger just like the Aorangi ones. It has its leaf deployed, you can see; why would that leaf be so much smaller than ours?"

"Why would they have a leaf at all? Aorangi, if that's what you're trying to tell us this is, uses a different power system!"

"Which they can't use on their ships; it takes up a lot of their city and would act as a sea anchor. Their gold-fish *did* have leaves, remember. Why do they have so few ships? Why do those ships stay so close to their city except in emergencies? Having a spread of boats around the city to help slightly off course homing ships doesn't apply to them. They even gave up early in their search for the very important wandering fish we found."

"Where did this one get the leaf it has?"

"From you; remember? You gave them a clipping of ours, and told them how to feed it. It's still growing. That's if they weren't able to modify one of their own leaves on short notice."

"I didn't think a ship's leaf would be much use to them that far south. I was just impressing them with what we could do."

"It *wasn't* much use to them—that far south. They were taking chances now on breathing equipment, though not on food; you can see the plant trays. I'm guessing those three people—one of them a child—are all that there are on board.

Look again, Captain. That *is* the ship Hinemoa was using, paint pattern and all. It's *Koku*. Ask 'Ao."

The captain didn't. "But why? And *how* under Kaihapa?"

"Why? Because they're either still having an emergency or have spotted an opportunity. How? How did they get so precisely to Muamoku's latitude? How did they dare this time to come so far from Aorangi? And, as part of the same question, why do they have so few ships? Want a good, solid guess?"

"Yes! Of course! They're getting close."

"They have their own version of 'Oloa. I don't know what it's built into, but they have inertial systems and computers at least good enough to handle navigation problems."

"Then why aren't they traveling all over Kainui?"

"Because they have only a few of them, and can't make more. They've never had more—at least not many more; they may have lost some ships down through the years, I suppose. I expect what they have was on their original colony ship. Just like your people, they used what was available. They had pseudolife skills, an ocean, and a lot of ice, and all the carbon, hydrogen, oxygen, and other light elements anyone could ask. They needed a power source, and circumstances steered them in the temperature-difference direction, so eventually they had to hug the ice cap. Sort of like Earth; we headed in a direction that let us develop and get addicted to heat-engine technology. That set us to finding better and better ways to make and use heat engines—powered by nonrenewable fuels. I wonder if they had a period when they used mercury instead of gold for ballast? I'd like to study that part of their history. Gold's more plentiful than mercury in the universe, but maybe not this near the surface of the ocean here—"

"You're wandering, Hoani."

"Sorry. Back to why you should get into trading mode. They'd like to have more ships. To them, that means more inertial systems. They'd never be patient enough to circumnavigate the planet every time they lost track of home, just as an Earth native now would never, except in really unusual circumstances, have the patience to spend weeks crossing a continent—I hope you know what that is."

"I've had some history."

"They can't get silicon on this world; its compounds aren't soluble enough in your acid ocean. Maybe you should devise traveling fish; you could give them real guidance systems now—though I suppose they still wouldn't know where to go to find their cities. Aorangi wants to trade for silicon, I'd bet all I have but my family, and so far at least Muamoku is the only place they can do their trading. Nowhere else has physical offworld contact. They probably do know that gold has trade value on other worlds, even if it's only to provide a value scale. Whether they'll pay more for raw silicon or finished navigation units I wouldn't guess; you're the expert in that field. Either way I can see Muamoku and one Captain Wanaka doing rather well for themselves and quite a few other people. So, Captain, I suggest again—get into trading mode. They can see your ship is carrying cargo. I doubt that they know or care what it is, but they're not stupid and must realize that their gold-fish is the most likely place for you to have found it. They should see no reason for you to distrust them; was a single one of your suspicions about what they were trying to do ever really confirmed? Think it over— quickly. They're almost here. What are you going to say to Hinemoa?"

"Nothing," cut in 'Ao placidly. "Hinemoa isn't there."

Three faces quizzed the child silently, and a triumphant expression appeared around her mask.

"That's Eru," was her completely adequate explanation.

"Heave to, Keo dear," was Wanaka's response. "Maybe they're not even traders. It's surprising they even have any; I wonder where Hinemoa got her skill. Aorangi shouldn't know what trading is."

She was wrong, of course. Mike had little time to think independently for the next few hours of translation, but it did occur to him that in a city that must contain several thousand people there should be plenty of opportunity to acquire sales competence without developing a foreign trade.

The seeming fact that nobody had been trying to sell his labor to the community during the recent emergency, but had simply done what obviously needed doing, did suggest something interesting about the city's culture. It might be the most civilized on the planet; he should go back to add a few more footnotes to his observations, obviously.

But that would be later, he decided as a storm swept over the linked ships and 'Ao and Eru went to work with their shovels.

The adults aboard *Koku* were one sailor, named Rua, and one of the teachers who had guided Mike around his city earlier, called Wherepapa. The latter, amazingly to Wanaka and Keo, was in command, at least in the sense that he gave orders about destination and any activities like mining or not if the chance arose; Rua was captain in maritime emergencies. Eru was his apprentice, though Wherepapa could give him instruction when there was time available from ship's duties. Mike was impressed by the fact that neither adult seemed bothered by any aspect of the arrangement.

He was even more impressed by the discussions between

the captain and the teacher. Wherepapa might regard trading as an exercise in logic, but he had picked up enough background facts—Mike wondered how long that had taken him—to make his logic work.

He admitted that Aorangi badly wanted silicon, but pointed out that the materials for gallium arsenide, or boron and nitrogen for doping diamond, could probably be obtained from Kainu's own oceans. Wanaka questioned the possibility of making or working with diamond at pseudolife temperatures. He suggested that Aorangi could sell gold for electrical wiring; the captain pointed out that copper was a somewhat better and silver a much better conductor. Wherepapa countered that gold was far more corrosion resistant than either and wouldn't need replacement so often, if ever. Wanaka was not sure this was desirable.

Wanaka pointed out that since silicon could be processed so much more easily on worlds with better developed high-temperature technology, Aorangi would be better advised to trade for finished semiconductor equipment for which the captain could make arrangements. Wherepapa conceded the point.

Since personnel often visited between ships for a night or more at a time, the children listened in with increasing frequency, only partly to profit from Mike's translations. What interested Eru was unclear to Hoani; the youngster was a city offical's child and might reasonably be fascinated by anything at all, whether or not visibly connected with administration. 'Ao seemed to be most impressed with how useful it was to know things, though Mike tried to impress her with the existence of trivia. She was still young enough to have an extremely capacious memory, and found it hard to believe that this would ever fail her.

As a student himself, Mike considered the ability to think more important; facts could always be looked up. He began to feel a little worried about the responsibility he might have incurred; after all, he had been collecting facts, obviously and carefully, for this whole trip. Had that been a bad example? His language skills, essentially memory, had been of almost continuous use to 'Ao's captain. Did Kainui's schools teach people to think? Wanaka was a skilled sailor, which was a matter of knowing what to do at a given time to produce given results, with most appropriate actions necessarily reflexive; Keo had the same training and qualities. Of course, the captain's trading skills represented something else—Mike couldn't quite decide what, but it was something else. But 'Ao?

Well, what did she get points for? That was a comforting thought. Having skills, certainly—he remembered the points she had earned from setting up the division of the iron-fish. But there was judgment, too; she had lost some for risking her armor to infection.

Maybe he shouldn't worry; she wasn't his responsibility, except as any adult shared some responsibility for any child.

He was talking to her, still with this question in mind, just before she climbed to her station after the wake-up meal.

"You recognized that iron-fish just at the start of our trip," he remarked. "Was that just because it wasn't anything else you knew?" He had been confronted with that trick question, he remembered, during his own school days.

'Ao looked indignant. "Of course not. It might have been something I'd never seen before. It just *looked* like iron."

"Aren't there any other fish that look like iron?"

"Some. A little."

"What would you have said if you couldn't tell any differences?"

The child was beginning to show a why-are-adults-so-silly expression. "I wouldn't have said anything until I was sure, unless the captain asked me. Then I'd have said I didn't know, of course."

"Suppose you'd been wrong, and missed something that should have told you it wasn't iron?"

"I'd have lost some points, unless the captain missed it, too."

"So if you've eliminated all the wrong answers, you have the right one?"

"Didn't you go to school? Sorry, that was rude. Maybe it's your school's fault. They used to tell us a lot of stories with morals in them. Pretty often they were stories from the Old World, I expect just to make them interesting. I know what a wolf was, because they gave us the one about the boy who cried 'wolf.' They gave us that Sherlock Holmes one you're trying on me, too—you know, the fellow who said that when you've eliminated all the impossibles, whatever was left must be right. He never said anything about making mistakes in eliminating. He didn't say a word about the things you hadn't thought of, either. Isn't Wherepapa just wonderful; with the things he can think of to say why the captain's wrong? I wouldn't say that to her, of course; you won't tell, will you?"

He felt relieved, a little.

Half an hour later, he felt slightly embarrassed, since captain and mate were both on deck at the time.

'Ao shrilled from her masthead, "City, two hands port." Then just as loudly, "It's Muamoko, Mike. I'm certain of it."

RAIRAI